Running on Dreams

Running on Dreams

Herb Heiman

Autism Asperger Publishing Co.
P.O. Box 23173
Shawnee Mission, Kansas 66283-0173
www.asperger.net

© 2007 Autism Asperger Publishing Co.
P.O. Box 23173
Shawnee Mission, Kansas 66283-0173
www.asperger.net

Publisher's Cataloging-in-Publication

Heiman, Herb.
    Running on dreams / Herb Heiman. -- 1st ed. -- Shawnee Mission,
    KS : Autism Asperger Pub. Co., 2007.

        p. ; cm.

        ISBN-13: 978-1-931282-28-4
        ISBN-10: 1-931282-28-5
        LCCN: 2006932486
        Audience: young adult.

        1. Asperger's syndrome--Fiction. 2. Autistic youth--Fiction.
    3. Friendship--Fiction. 4. Trust--Fiction. 5. Young adult fiction.
    I. Title. PZ7.H456 R86 2006   [Fic]--dc22 0611

This book is printed in Palatino and Myriad.

Printed in the United States of America.

*Dedicated to my
brother, Kenny.
I will miss you.*

Without several people, all of them women,
this novel would not have been written.
I bow and kiss the hand of each one of them.

For motivation: Stephanie Bartlett –
famed author and friend

For creation: Lisa Lieberman –
famed author, friend and Jordan's mother

For perspiration: Kirsten McBride –
my accurate and persistent editor

For devotion: My dear wife, Elaine –
understanding, loving and dearest of the dear

Chapter 1

Through a fuzz of sleep I hear Mom's voice, "Justin, time to get up." My head feels like a balloon on a string ready to float right up to the ceiling. I didn't sleep well last night. I was too excited to sleep, but I can't remember why. I open one eye, then the other, like I do every morning and look around my room. That's also what I do every morning. The window is open just right; my shoes are lined up perfectly, everything on my desk is in order just the way it needs to be. Then I catch my breath 'cause I remember why I couldn't sleep. I zoom out from under my blanket. Today is my birthday. It's a cool deal!

I hear a soft knock as Mom pokes her head through the door. The picture of her actually putting her head through a door makes me smile to myself. I learned that saying someone "puts his head through the door" doesn't mean that. I know what that expression means 'cause it's printed in my mind. It really means putting your head through the opening of the doorway.

Mom smiles, which makes her face all crinkly, and sits down next to me on my bed. Smelling her sweet flowery perfume is a good way to start the day. "Good morning, sleepyhead," she greets me.

She's right; my head does feel sleepy. "Mom you don't have to tre - treat me like a kid anymore." I sit up and put out my jaw and show her the start of a beard; well, kind of one. I feel older than I ever did before. My voice just jumps out loud from my mouth and bounces around my room. "I'm fifteen years old now."

"I know, sweetheart; I know." And then she holds my hand and sings in her low voice the Beatle's oldie but goodie, "You Say It's Your Birthday …" And like always on my birthday, she has a gift hidden behind her back.

"Good morning, Mom." Thank - thanks for the gift you have behind your back."

"Hey smart aleck, bet you can't guess what we got you this year," she says, putting a medium-sized box on my bed wrapped in splotchy-colored paper. "Go on, Justin, try to guess."

"My name's not aleck," I say with a grin on my face. I mostly know when she's joking and wants me to joke back, so I say to her, "A Boeing 747?"

"Nope, but close." She plays her fingers on the box like on a piano.

I try to whisper so I won't wake my dad. He works nights and goes to sleep when I get up. "A vacation to Disneyland?" I know that would make her remember the trip we took last summer. She laughs out loud, then covers her mouth with her hand.

"Woops, I forgot about your dad trying to sleep. Did you get the hint?" she asks while her fingers play on the box again. But I don't get it. Finally, she whispers to me, "Just go ahead and open it."

I take a scissors out of my upper-right desk drawer, slit the tape and then slowly work the wrapping off the box. I fold the paper into a square and put it in my lower left-hand drawer with the other wrapping paper I have been saving. The box is filled with little styrofoam pellets, they're called peanuts, but I don't know why.

"Mom, why do they call these peanuts?" She rolls her eyes up at the ceiling. That's one of her cues to me that the question I asked was one of the questions she had never thought of, or didn't have time to answer. "Justin, not right now. I've got breakfast on the stove and … and, besides, I don't know why." Then she smiles and helps me pour the peanuts in my trashcan.

The gift's a double CD boxed set of hit singles of the 1960s. "It's a cool deal, Mom!" I hug her and run into their bedroom to hug my dad too. I think I woke him, but I don't care. And neither does he. "Thanks, Dad. Just what I wanted! Look, there's 'Working in the Coal Mine' and 'Hello, Mary Lou' by Ricky Nelson, and …"

Dad rubs my head with one hand and raises his other arm, stretching out. "It's a cool deal, Justin. I'm glad you like it." Then he hugs me with both arms. I can tell he had just brushed his teeth with Colgate extra-strength toothpaste before he went to sleep. A cool deal!

In the excitement over my birthday, I had totally spaced out the other reason why I couldn't sleep. Today is also the day I had been scared of for weeks. I squeeze closer in Dad's arms and repeat his words, "Yeah, a cool deal." But my heart is pounding like the bass beat on one of my CDs.

With squinty eyes, Brad spied minute germ-beasts floating around his room. Since dawn he had examined the little squiggly monsters, the strangely shaped dust particles glittering in the sunlight. The window drapes billowed in the cool breeze, casting oddly shaped shadows across the far wall. His thoughts and his body were both comfortably snuggled into the blankets on this chilly morning. *I wish it was Saturday.*

Mom's voice pierced his privacy. "Bradley. Hey, sleepyhead, it's almost seven. Time to get up."

The aroma of coffee brewing glided up the stairs and slipped noiselessly under his bedroom door, teasing his nostrils. *How could anything that smells so good taste so bad?* He yawned deeply and stretched, his long legs flinging the blankets from the bed. "Oh, man. It'd be great if school started a half hour later," he mumbled to himself. He stopped and blinked at least a dozen times as his feet touched the cold hardwood floor. Then he remembered. *Today is my birthday, my fifteenth birthday!*

As Brad quickly washed and dressed, he thought about last year's birthday and all his birthdays stretching back as far as he could remember. The kids' chant still rang in his head. "Brad, Brad, you're so bad, you're the trick played on your parents. Sad Brad." And that wasn't the worst one either.

Why, oh why did his mom have him on April Fool's Day? Ucchh. Most of the birthday presents he ever got were gag gifts, except from his folks, of course. They always gave him sweaters and clothes. Amy, his older sister, sometimes she could be cool. Like last year she got him a gift certificate for The Emporium. She had let him hug her and say thanks, but he couldn't remember any time since when Amy had let him hug her.

The fresh mint taste of toothpaste swished around in his mouth, and as he spat it out, he made a face at himself and shaped his initials in the splattered mirror over his sink. What do other kids do who are born on April 1? Lie, he thought. They probably shrug and say, "Oh, my birthday's on April 2. Always has been, always will be." Yeah, right!

Breakfast at the Lockwoods: Mom insisted that everyone eat a wholesome and nutritious meal but, as usual, she put three boxes of cold cereal on the table, a carton of two-percent milk and a pile of unbuttered whole wheat toast. She was so busy running – the hospital, school, whatever. And anyway, his Mom wasn't the best cook in the world. Today was a little different; there was a birthday card in his bowl that Amy had put there before she went to work and a little candle placed in the dry toast. The card was a flowered, girly type that said, "Happy Birthday to a Sweet Brother" and was signed, "Love, Amy."

Mom had a soft smile on her face. "Isn't that a sweet card, Brad?"

"It's really nice, Mom." *I'll bet a hundred dollars you put Amy up to buying it.*

Dad lifted his chin and looked over the top of the sports page. "Lydia, isn't it possible to have a bagel or a sweet roll around the house for breakfast?" He smiled. "Hey birthday boy, new quarter starts today, right? And track season is just one week off. Not too excited are you?"

"Naw." Brad couldn't keep the biggest grin in the world off his face. *It's only been like the major topic around here since the end of last track season.* "Well, maybe a little."

"Atta boy, way to go, big Brad." Dad beamed like he did at last year's assembly when Brad got the award for breaking the two hundred meter track record. "I'll make it a point to be at a few extra practices – and don't forget, the Booster's Club is awarding *real* trophies this season."

As if Brad could forget. There was a shoebox full of ribbons up in his closet, mostly for first- and second-place finishes in sprints. But now, ninth grade, senior year at middle school, this was the time to start collecting the actual keep-'em-for-a-lifetime trophies. And there won't just be a box in a closet. No way. There will be a glass case, as big as the living room wall, filled with plaques and stuff, each one with a gold inscription like: *First Place Two-Hundred-Meter Run, Southern Oregon AA District Finals, Brad Lockwood.* And in a year or two the calls from U-of-O and Oregon State will swamp the family, and he'll have to fight off the scholarship offers. By mail, on the phone, the requests will pour in, all begging, "Please, come to our school, Brad."

"Bradley. Bradley!" Mom's voice replaced the athletic director's voice, and the telephone he had been holding was once again his spoon dipping into a bowl of half-eaten Grape Nut Flakes. "Will you remember to ask your math teacher when I can meet with her? We need to work on bringing up your algebra grades." Dad sighed, but he didn't say squat.

Somehow Brad just couldn't picture Lance Armstrong's mom nagging him about his algebra grade. No way.

Chapter 2

The big yellow bus was filled with about fifty kids: seventh-, eighth- and, ninth-graders kidnapped from their homes and dragged kicking and screaming to the bus stop to start another day at Pearblossom Middle School. At least that was the way a lot of these dudes acted. Brad was probably the only one in the world ever to imagine parents actually tying up their kids, putting them in a trash hauler and carting them to the bus stop every morning. Where did these weird pictures in his head come from? Probably from Mars.

Paper airplanes sailed across the aisles, skimming and buzzing baseball caps. "Hey, Travis is throwing stuff!" yelled a kid, swiping at his runny nose with his sleeve.

For the tenth time that morning, the bus driver shouted over her shoulder, "Travis! Hey, Travis! One more time and I am going to write you up. Got that?"

Brad scrunched down in his seat, pretending to sleep so the kids wouldn't get on him about his April Fool's birthday. The boy next to him was cracking his gum, releasing the strong smell of artificial watermelon flavor. Sick! The bus was not exactly a screaming, shouting, rap concert, but it was close. Brad opened his eyes and focused on a small tail of blond hair bouncing to the rhythm of the moving bus. One row up and across the aisle sat Crystal.

How many classes this new term would he have with her, he wondered.

"So, what are your folks gonna get ya?" Pat's voice was a foghorn, a one-of-a-kind that destroyed eardrums at fifty paces. Even after hanging together for years, Brad had never gotten used to Pat's voice. He shrugged as they started the customary parade through the halls for the fifteen minutes before the first bell. School was like a teeming anthill, pairs or small groups going in different directions crashing into other ants. Bump, bang, dozens of mini-collisions taking place while everybody rapped with their friends trying to find out who called who last night. It was cool to watch.

Pat's glasses flopped down on his nose, and he slid them back without thought. "Seems like ya got all the clothes you'll need to get you clean through college," he said with a sidelong grin. He was a little pudgy, and shorter than Brad. They had been pals since first grade when they had lived near each other, and their folks were still close.

Although Brad usually hung around with his jock buddies, he managed to find time to pal up with Pat. Pat was not much of an athlete, not at all in fact. And he hit the books pretty hard, so the two of them didn't really seem to be running on the same track.

"So happy birthday, Godzilla. I'll give ya your gift right after school. I can't say what it is, but I can give you a hint. You'd better eat it before it eats you."

Bong, bong! The warning for first period sounded through the noisy halls. Brad smiled, "I wonder why they call it a bell? It really doesn't ring; it just kinda chirps like a chicken with a lung problem." Mostly when he did stuff like that, kids just looked at him funny and walked away, but Pat laughed.

"See ya," Pat called and was swept away by the swarm of ants.

Brad headed for his first-period class where everybody would get new schedules. He'd still have his three-hour social science block with Mr. Laipply but the rest was uncertain. For his elective he had signed up to be an aide in the computer lab right after he heard from one of Crystal's friends that she was taking computers. As he fought his way through the crowd of kids he thought, *I'm really qualified for computers, but you never know for sure where they'll put you.*

Brad tried to slide unnoticed into his first period art design class, but a freckled-faced boy spotted him. His voice sang out through thin lips, "Hey Brad, Janine really likes you. She's gonna give you a big smackeroo right on the lips for your birthday. Aren't you, Janine?" The painfully shy girl built like a vaulting pole stood trembling next to the art table. She turned crimson and studied the floor as if she was checking out a weird bug or something.

"Funny. Like, real funny, man," Brad said, promising himself that next year in high school nobody would know when his birthday was.

"Special ed?" he said aloud as his jaw almost hit the desk. *Special education, that's where I'm going? Oh man!* Brad looked at his new schedule and rubbed his eyes. *What jerk figured that's where I should be an aide?*

At least the rest of his schedule was cool: P. E., choir and, ugh, algebra 2. While walking down the hall to the special ed class, he planned what to say. "Gee, Mrs. Gargus, I really want to be in your class, but you know, my Mom is super anxious for me to get, eh, competent; that's it, competent at computers. Would you mind changing my class? It's for her, really." Brad figured on brown-nosing it with his best "please help me" smile. Making a plea that came from your mom always worked. Well, almost always.

Brad scoped out room thirty-two; it was like most other classrooms at Pearblossom only somehow lighter, airier. Bright mid-morning light came streaming through a row of windows on the far wall. Some big scenic posters were pinned up on the walls, tables and chairs were gathered in small clusters, and a couple of computers stood in a corner. The room smelled like microwave popcorn. About half a dozen kids were joking with Mrs. Gargus. Although she had never been one of his teachers, he knew who she was. She laughed and teased a girl who was leaning against a cluttered desk. Brad couldn't help thinking what his friends would say and what they'd call him when they saw him coming into this room every day.

"No way, Mrs. Gargus. You're so weird," the girl giggled and shrieked like seventh-grade girls did.

"Oh, you must be Brad," the teacher smiled over at him. "I'll be right with you."

Off in a corner at a computer sat a stocky boy pecking at the keys, making some art on the screen. He was really good. Must be another aide. With another aide it should be a cinch to get out of working as an aide here. He was dressed in khakis and a t-shirt, and his dark hair was plastered down except for an unruly bunch standing up in back. "Oh man, it's a cool deal," the kid said in a loud, flat voice. His speech sounded like a talking mechanical robot, a loud one. *Wait a minute*, Brad thought. *This kid's not an aide. Maybe it won't be so easy for me to get out of here after all.*

Mrs. Gargus turned toward the new kid. "Hang on a few minutes, Justin. We'll get you situated as soon as I talk to Brad here." Justin seemed not to hear. He looked past Brad to a boy who zoomed into the room, leaving a tidal wave of papers flying off the surrounding desks. "Sorry I'm late for class Mrs. Gargus, I … I guess I kinda got lost."

Mrs. Gargus threw him a look that could have melted a hard drive. "Just take a seat, Kenny, and we'll deal with tardy number one hundred twelve in a little while.

Kenny flopped down in a back-row seat. "Ahh, it's not anywhere close to that." Brad had seen this kid around school and always wondered if he was in special ed. Now he knew for sure.

"Mrs. Gargus ... " Brad began.

"I'm so glad to have you as an aide, Brad. Of all the applications I got, yours was the most impressive." She picked up the form he had filled out a few weeks ago. "Sports, computers, excellent communication skills, choir; besides, you seem very mature. How old are you?"

"Fifteen. Today. I mean, that is, my birthday's not really until tomorrow. That's it, tomorrow."

"Brad, just when is your birthday?"

"Eh, I guess it's today." This was not going the way he had planned. Little drops of sweat started to trickle down his armpits.

Suddenly Justin spun in his chair, his eyes widened, "That is so co - cool. Today is my birthday, too. Hey, do you know who else was born on our birth date? Nobody famous, that's who." He laughed like it was rehearsed. "Ha, ha, ha. My name is Justin and I'm fifteen today too. What's your name?"

Before Brad could even get a grip on all the questions and stuttering this kid had fired at him, Mrs. Gargus motioned to steer Justin back to the computer. "I'm so glad to hear about your birthday, Justin. We'll talk about it soon. Now how about going back to work on the computer while I speak to Brad, okay?"

As she came back toward Brad, he started his speech again. "I need to talk to you about, well … It's my Mom. She wants me to be in computers." Mrs. Gargus wasn't listening.

"Justin is just starting at Pearblossom today." Without lowering her voice she continued, "Justin's going to need some help around school, you know, getting to classes, learning his way around."

Justin turned on the swivel chair and shouted, "It's nine forty-seven, and first period ends in eight minutes at nine fifty-five. I've got choir, and social science later this morning, and in the afternoon …"

Mrs. Gargus interrupted him, "I'm just going over your schedule with Brad; thanks, Justin."

"That's a cool deal." He said this like he'd said it a lot of times before. Justin was really from another planet. Brad's thoughts raced as a ball of discomfort grew in the pit of his stomach.

Mrs. Gargus pulled Brad aside. She had a round face and eyes that sort of landed on you like a big kiss. "Of all the kids who applied to be aides, you were my first choice."

He didn't even want to ask why. Sweat began to itch his skin under his shirt.

"And in case you're wondering why …"

No, no, I'm not wondering why. Don't tell me. Please!

"It's because of all the things you do so well like, computers, track, choir."

A choked, high voice Brad hardly recognized as his own floated toward Mrs. Gargus. "My Mom, she, it's her who really wants me to …" The sound of a printer clacking away swallowed his wasted words.

"You'll be perfect as a peer aide for Justin."

Ohhhhh, I'm a sunk skunk.

Justin moved by Mrs. Gargus and put his chin up, singing to Brad in a full-voiced monotone, "'You Say It's Your Birthday.' That's the Beatles song re-recorded August 18, 1968. Lead singer, Paul. Time, two minutes and forty seconds. Hey, maybe they'll sing that for us today in choir. What did you say your name is?"

"My name is Brad, and I'm …" Brad exhaled a long sigh. The vision of bouncing blonde hair next to him in the computer lab painfully drifted into nothingness. This had to be another April Fool's gag.

"… I'm here to work with you for the next twelve weeks, Justin."

"You … to … birthday … happy …"

Brad scooted down, raised his shoulders high, and tried to disappear into his chair while eighty kids in choir sang Happy Birthday to him and Justin. It was being sung backwards. Brad was sure his face glowed like a ripe tomato.

The risers shook as one hundred and sixty hands clapped

and feet stomped. When the singing and shouting ended, Brad smiled and waved, glad the celebration was over. Yet, in a way, he felt pretty good about being in the spotlight. Not as cool as when he won a race, but maybe okay. It was like Dad always said, "Sometimes it's hard to know exactly what your feelings are."

Justin laughed, a big grin painted across his face, and pointed at Brad. Together they shared this very special day. But Brad didn't want to share this, or any other day, with Justin. Wasn't it enough that he had to help take care of his sister? And now here's Justin with whatever was wrong with him barreling into his life. Geezo! Mrs. Gargus had asked Brad to meet with her later during homeroom so she could tell him about his responsibilities. Meantime he had to escort Justin from class to class to make sure he got to the right place and was introduced to his teachers. Man, everyone in school, including Crystal, will see him in the halls, with his shadow, Justin. What a lot of fun that will be. Yeah right.

I guess it's okay. At least nobody in choir laughs at me, but nobody sits next to me either, not even my new friend, Brad. Well, he's not really a friend. Dad says a friend will go out of his way to do nice things for you, and Brad, he sits with his buddies over across the room. I should be used to that.

The teacher hands all the new kids a music sheet with the words to a song I don't know. I can read the words okay, but the black dots, the notes, look like little bugs crawling across the page. I never tell anyone, but if I look at the paper too long, it makes me sick. Anyway, the teacher says we have to sing in front of class while she plays the piano. That's so she can tell what our voice range is. I like to sing, but even Mom sometimes puts her hands over her ears and says, "Enough, Justin, that's enough, honey." I hear the right notes in my head, but they seem to come out of my mouth different. Maybe in choir I'll learn to sing better.

This school is really big. I'll never find my way from one class to the next. It's so different from the school I'm used to: only about twenty kids; some like me, but some in wheelchairs and one kid who can't see so good. I wanted to stay there but my folks said, "It's time to move on to a mainstream situation." Then they explained that means regular school with some regular classes, but mostly I'll be learning in the resource class with Mrs. Gargus. They tried to make it sound so cool, but to me it means being stared at, pointed at, and made fun of. Mainstream sucks. Oops, I'm not supposed to say that.

Chapter 3

Brad had decided with Pat in science class that morning that they would walk home together after school. Now he hung out in the commons waiting for Pat, giving hi-fives, tugging hat brims and laughing at stupid jokes. Through the windows, Brad watched the flood of kids dash out the double-wide front doors, then mill about noisily in the parking lot waiting to get onto the buses.

"Hey, dude," Pat's voice boomed above the sound of lockers banging down the hall. "What do ya say, let's go by my house. I got a surprise for ya', remember?" Pat grinned like he had this big secret. As they left school, taking a shortcut across the pasture, Brad raised his face to catch the warm afternoon sun. The sweet smells of spring wildflowers leapt from the gold and purple blossoms. It had been a long winter.

And it could be a long spring what with Justin hanging on his back like moss on one of the oak trees lining the orchard. What had Mrs. Gargus told him? Justin needs to have things "just so;" like he needs to sit in the same seat every day, and let him pick which seat he wanted. Brad had to meet him at the same time and place at the end of each period, and all of Justin's teachers knew about not pulling any surprise quizzes and having prepared notes for him and stuff like that. She said it was all written down in his I.E.P. But she didn't say what that was. And she said that Justin was smart, but in a different way than most kids. He could remember some stuff perfectly, but maybe not remember what class he had next.

Then Brad thought about his party this weekend, and the image of Justin's flat notes in front of choir class, and the strange looks on the kids' faces – all that faded. The party is going to really be super, except ... except he hadn't yet gotten up the nerve to invite Crystal. *I'm being stupid, really stupid. All I've got to do is come up to her and say, "Hi, there's a way cool party this weekend. Want to come?"*

"Hey dummy, look out for the cow pies!"

Brad jerked his foot up and planted it about two inches from a fresh pile. He laughed and punched Pat playfully on the arm. "Hey, I'm glad we're not taking the bus."

"What do ya say we cut school tomorrow and go to the mall, okay?"

Pat never cut school in his life. And the only time he went to the mall was with his Mom to buy clothes. About every week he came up with his "to heck with school" idea. But they never cut school, never split to the mall to hang out.

Brad shrugged as they walked together without words. The swish, swish of their steps in the lengthening spring grass was all that cut through the silence.

As they neared Pat's house, Brad smelled the full, white blossoms on the trees in the orchard. The two boys shared smiles and memories of the many late-summer evenings when they had slipped into the orchard with empty packs and left with full ones. It was their personal secret – sneaking, creeping over fences, darting into the shadows like two thieves in the night. Good thing it was one of the orchards his dad oversaw.

Brad looked at Pat trying to scramble up a pear tree. "I'm stakin' out this one for October."

Who needed to skip school and go to the mall anyway?

While Pat went to get the birthday gift, Brad looked down at a large slice of the Rogue Valley through the floor-to-ceiling picture windows. The James' house sat high on a bluff in the middle of about thirty acres; it had a private drive that wound up a hill. The walk every day just about wiped Pat out. His folks both worked at the college nearby and must collect some pretty big bucks, Brad figured. He glanced around and took his feet off what probably was a zillion-dollar stuffed chair.

"Pat. Hey, Pat. Shake it up will ya? I got homework to do and some more calls to make for my party." Pat would probably give him something weird. Like last year it was a huge box filled with bananas and a gift certificate for a year's subscription to *MAD* magazine. Actually, the subscription wasn't half bad.

Soon Pat returned with a medium-sized box and a funny grin on his face. "Hey!" he said and plopped down on the sofa next to Brad. "This is, well, shoot, it's embarrassing. Go 'head, open it."

Brad mimicked him, "'Go 'head, open it.' You can be such a dork sometimes." He shook the box. Boop, boop. After tugging at the string, he tore the wrapping paper off and opened the flaps. "Well, no bananas this year."

"It's better than bananas. I hope you ..." Pat's voice trailed off.

Brad removed the crumpled newspapers and pulled out Nike Blazer track shoes! With sprint spikes! "Geeeeezo!"

Pat studied the sofa, stroking its puffy, cream-colored arm. "I knew you'd need 'em for the season."

Brad's eyes opened wide.

"Hey, it's no big thing. I saved up from allowances," Pat said, grinning over the top of his glasses.

Brad's heart pounded in his chest and the little hairs on his arms stood up. After what seemed like a year of silence, he swallowed hard. "With these on, if anybody tries to get in front of me in a race, I'll run right up his backside and over his head. And when I win, it will be a win for both of us."

Pat looked up. "I thought you'd like 'em."

"Hey, quit your shovin'."

"Creep, I was here first."

"I'm gonna tell coach you're messin' with my locker."

Noise, tension and stale sweat filled the boys' locker room as about four dozen boys came tromping in at the close of seventh period. Brad's locker was in a corner grouped with the lockers of other ninth-graders, all pretty much his friends. But being friends with a guy didn't mean you had to take it when he crowded you with his sweaty body. No way.

"Whoooeee! Glen, you smell bad." A kid with a long po-nytail yelled at another while holding his nose. "I'd rather be at a skunk convention than be here with you. Man!"

Glen spun and wrapped his meaty arm tightly around the other boy's neck, twisting him to the floor. A circle of kids formed around them just as Mr. Hunnicutt came in with Justin. "Hey, hey! Break it up before I ship you both off to Mr. Fischer's." Hunnicutt was strong. He was like a bear, a big bear! He grabbed both kids by their arms and twisted them up behind their backs until they yelled in pain. "Now, do you two bozos want to settle this quietly here, or do we visit Fischer with a guaranteed suspension for about three days?"

The boys snarled, continuing to bad-mouth each other, but finally they backed off. Mr. Hunnicutt was now a part-time aide in special ed … budget cuts had changed his job. He would be keeping an eye on Justin part of the day, including P. E. "Okay, Justin, here's your locker and lock. Let me show you how …" Justin drilled him with a fierce look. "I can do it myself. What do you think I am, anyhow?" He snatched the lock from Hunnicutt, read the combination and tore the paper to shreds. Then he spun the knob and opened the lock on the first try. "I'm sorry Mr. Hunnicutt, I was mean to you, wasn't I?"

Hunnicutt just shrugged and went to the coach's office.

"Hey, my name's Alex." A short, red-haired kid introduced himself to Justin.

Justin waved hi and introduced himself in a formal, clipped voice. "How do you do? My name is Justin and I'm new to Pearblossom School. It's good to meet you." Then he rambled on, sucking in breath between phrases. "Today is my fifteenth birth-birthday. Most kids think I'm older because …"

Alex stared at him for a quick moment and stole a glance at Brad. "That's cool, man. Catch you later." He moved off with a bunch of guys and Brad overheard some words trailing after him. "A cue ball … weirdo …"

Just then a few of Brad's track buddies straggled by on the way out to the field.

"You coming, Brad, or what?"

"Shake your butt, Lockwood."

Brad's eyes hit the locker room floor with a thud so loud you could almost hear it. "Ah, I got a rock or something in my shoe. Be with you in a minute." Then he fumbled with his laces as the guys punched one another scrambling out of the locker room.

Brad sat on the bench, the damp odor of sweat hanging in the air. He had one shoe on, the other in his hand. He pretended to dump a pebble from the shoe. Special ed class, then P. E. and choir seventh period too? Geeez, it looked like this kid, Justin, would be like a real pebble in his shoe. Maybe for the rest of his life.

It felt good even running this lap alone. It was super smooth gliding along the track with the crinch, crinch, crinch of the new Nikes kicking up little dirt clods behind him. Brad coasted into a new gear, accelerating around the curve of the track, something he'd never been able to do before with plain tennis shoes. The bite of the cleats held him firmly to the ground for a split second just before he lifted each foot. It wasn't running. It was flying. Two hundred meters. Flying!

When he crossed the finish line of his final heat for the day, the other sprinters cheered, "Way to go, Brad!" Sarah, Coach Goodwin's daughter, held the stopwatch high and pointed to it. "Best early-season time yet," she yelled over the noise. She was just an eighth-grader but was like an assistant coach for her dad. Sarah never missed a meet or a practice.

On the sidelines a special smile caught his eye. Crystal. Her teeth were evenly spaced, and pink gums were showing at the top of her smile; it made her whole face glow. When he thought of her, that was what he saw in his mind: a wide smile and pink gums, her eyes kind of closed shut, scrunching when she laughed. Brad wondered if she could see when she did that. Maybe one day he would ask her. When open, her deep blue eyes seemed to dig right into him, and he couldn't keep his eyes from drifting up and down her body. Geezo! The fluff of her bouncy blonde curls waved in the late-afternoon breeze.

Still puffing from his sprint, he said, "Hi, Crystal."

"You were awesome," she responded.

Brad knew she was talking to him, but all he heard was her sweet, quiet voice in his ear saying, "You were awesome. You were awesome!" And all he saw was her wide grin.

"… and happy birthday too."

Her last line brought him back to reality and his Saturday party. *Is she busy? Does she have a date? Will she want to come to my party?* "Yeah, thanks." Brad inspected the top of one of the hurdles. "You know, I been kind of wondering. I mean, ya see I'm having this party at my house on Saturday. And …" He was out of breath again, but this time not from running. The words tumbled from his mouth in a rush, "Would you come to my party? "

When he looked up, he noticed Crystal had a serious, thinking-it-over look on her face. It seemed like he had run the two hundred meters in less time than it took for her to answer. *It's going to be no. I just know it.*

"Yeah, that would be cool. I gotta go shower now, but call me later, okay? See ya." She turned and caught up with a group of girls heading for the gym.

In a daze, Brad plopped down on the top of the high hurdle. Crystal's words echoed in his mind. "Yeah, that would be cool." He smiled to himself. That would be way cool!

Perched on the hard wood, with no one near him, he closed his eyes and experienced that familiar, tingling sensation he got after he had had a strong finishing kick and won the race. Yes! He was sure he was going to win a lot of races.

Chapter 4

The lights flickered for an instant. Then the far-off rumble of thunder in the Cascade mountain range reverberated around room thirty-two. Three heads snapped up: Justin's, Mrs. Gargus' and Brad's.

"That's thunder," Justin nodded, commenting, "It usually means that some cumuli nimbus clouds have formed. They build up when …"

Brad stopped Justin from running off at the mouth by interrupting. "Right; you're right on the button." They were sitting at the worktable across from one another as Brad scored Justin's algebra test.

Justin pointed to a button on his shirtfront and cocked his head to one side. "You mean like on this kind of button?"

Brad started to answer the joke with a joke of his own but he saw Justin wasn't joking. The dude was serious. Mrs. Gargus was busy at her cluttered desk but overheard the conversation and chimed in. "'On the button' means you got it exactly right, Justin."

"Yeah … right on the button," Justin added. "I get it," he said and laughed his strange cackling sound.

"That's enough math for today boys. How about starting to clean up, okay?"

As they put the calculators and markers away, the room darkened – a foreshadowing of the coming storm. Justin sang just loud enough to be heard. "'I've Got Sunshine on a Cloudy Day … da da da, my girl, talkin' 'bout my girl.' Temptations gold record, 1965."

Brad looked out the window past Mrs. Gargus's shoulder at the overcast day. The electric storm was on its way, rolling in from northern California. Typical for spring, it threatened rain, but hardly ever got up enough of whatever it took to actually do it. But this storm looked like the real thing. Brad sighed. There went today's track practice. His thigh muscles flexed, pressing against the inside of his pant's legs.

A low rolling drum beat interrupted Justin's solo. Then he sang louder as though to drown out the thunder. *What the heck is going on with Justin?* "Is it the thunder that's bothering you? 'Cause you know it's just some big clouds filled with electric-charged ions that are crashing together."

"And they cause a large spark … spark that's called lightning," Justin finished the thought.

Brad couldn't quite get a fix on how smart Justin was, at least as far as remembering information. Funny how different his sister, Amy, was from Justin. They were both smart in their own ways, but a lot of stuff Justin just didn't get; like everything had to be spelled out for him in simple terms or it sailed right over his head – he wouldn't have a clue of what "sailed over his head" meant. But Amy, even though she was a little slow remembering things and stuff like that, she seemed like she could read every thought Brad had in his head.

Brad noticed that Justin was starting to tremble and the color was draining from his face. "Are you okay?" Maybe he could get Justin's mind off his fear. "What do you suppose the caf's got for lunch today?"

Justin didn't even have to look at today's bulletin for the information. He blurted out between short bursts of breath. "It's Wednesday … Chicken … nug … nuggets with coleslaw, corn bread, and fruit cocktail for dessert."

Mrs. Gargus came over close to Justin. "You're awesome, Justin. I'll bet that's one of your favorite lunches."

Suddenly Justin sat up straight as a board, then he pulled way back in his chair, screaming, "No, don't touch me."

Then it happened! The storm that had been building crashed with a clap of thunder and an almost immediate flash of lightening. The room shook, and so did Justin. Brad hardly blamed the guy; Justin went white as his fingernails scratched the surface of the worktable, leaving marks that trailed behind his fingers. Then he stiffened as though touched by a cattle prod. "Hunnnng." His chair crashed to the floor behind him and he collapsed under the table. His intake of air was loud like the hiss of one of those big, antique steam engines. Everything froze in time; it was like somebody had hit the pause button on a video. Not a movement, not a breath stirred in room thirty-two. Mrs. Gargus and Brad crouched down next to Justin's curled-up body and looked at him. One of his eyes opened a crack, and Mrs. Gargus spoke to him in a low, calm voice.

"It's okay, Justin; we're right here. You're doing fine. That-a-boy, just sit back and relax."

Her voice also calmed Brad, who swallowed hard and leaned in closer to Justin. His labored breathing was loud and Brad could smell this morning's chocolate milk floating on his breath.

"Is he … is he all right?"

"He'll be fine. Remember I told you that loud noises like lots of people talking, thunder, whatever, can really set him off? For Justin many sensations are amplified beyond what we can imagine." The rain pounded on the closed windows, but the thunder finally quit.

"Are you doing better, Justin?"

"Today is Wednesday … and … and the caf has my favorite, chicken nuggets."

Brad closed his eyes, willing his breath to slow down, but his heart pounded and his mouth was dry like after a race.

"Are you all right?" asked Mrs. Gargus.

Brad opened his eyes, licked his lips and managed a small nod. Mrs. Gargus turned from Justin and took Brad's hand. "You'll understand Justin in time, really."

Brad tried to listen to her and at the same time, tried not to. *My party Saturday night will be so neat. And Crystal will be there. And I wish I were there right now.*

"… so take a few minutes break. Take the hall pass and go for a walk."

Brad stood up and forced his numb legs to move to the window. He let the air out of his lungs, fogging up the cold glass. It was dark as night outside as the rain poured down, making huge puddles in the parking lot. He leaned his forehead up against the window; its coolness was like a wet washcloth. Being an aide in the computer lab would have been so much easier.

I just finished my algebra problems with Brad when the lights in Mrs. Gargus' room flickered and I heard sounds of distant thunder. I don't like that sound, and I put my hands in my pockets so I wouldn't put them over my ears. Sometimes when I am at the mall and pass a video arcade that makes a jumble of crazy sounds, I put my hands over my ears to keep the noise from getting in my head and people stare at me. I don't like to be stared at!

My stomach knotted up and my body began to twitch. That's an involuntary reaction to something that makes you nervous. Brad looked at me, and his eyebrows joined in the middle of his forehead. He asked me if I was okay, but I didn't say anything. Then he asked, "What do you suppose the caf's got for lunch today?"

I had read the weekly bulletin a few days earlier so I could answer his question right back at him without thinking," It's

Wednesday … Chicken … nug … nuggets with coleslaw, corn bread, and fruit cocktail for dessert." I started to shake a little more and Mrs. Gargus came over close to me.

"You're awesome, Justin. I'll bet that's one of your …"

She reached out to me. "No, don't touch me," I screamed at her. Only my Mom and Dad can touch me. Everyone else makes me feel like they're touching right inside me and I can feel their fingers on my lungs and bones. I pulled back, and my chair crashed to the floor behind me. That's when I couldn't help myself. I clamped my hands tightly over my ears. Then it happened. The room exploded with a bolt of lightning that flashed in my closed eyes. The sound erupted, coming through my hands as they covered my ears. It sucked all the air out of me.

The next thing I remember is that I'm under the table and I hear Mrs. Gargus's voice, "It's okay, Justin, we're right here. You're doing fine. That-a-boy just stay there and rest." Her velvety voice sounded just like my Mom's when I'm feeling sick or sad. I opened my eyes a crack. She and Justin were bent over me looking at me with eyes as big as marbles. But neither one touched me.

Chapter 5

"Well, excuse me!" a heavy-set man wearing bright-yellow suspenders snarled as he shoved his way down the aisle, pinning Brad against a shelf of gigantic, three-pound popcorn containers.

"Cashier on number eleven, please," the muffled voice on the P.A. system shouted. Brad rolled his eyes up to the high warehouse ceiling – Costco on a Saturday morning. Man, oh man! Amy pushed the shopping cart along, her body swaying to the music that was blasting from the electronics department. She wore her favorites: the denim cut-offs she wore almost everywhere. Her sandy, shoulder-length hair was tied back with a colorful ribbon. She looked cute – for a sister. Amy loved shopping, especially today for his birthday party. But in spite of her happy mood, you never knew what would set her off. Brad had to keep a watchful eye out for her. She got confused easily, and she'd just sit down and rub the material on her coat over and over for a long time. Today she would be okay. He was sure of it.

Suddenly she slowed down and turned to him, her pencil and shopping list on top of the brimming cart. "How many kids are coming to the party?" This was the zillionth time she'd asked him. Brad smiled, hoping she wouldn't catch the impatient edge in his voice. "About twenty. Here's the plan. I think we should pick up the soft drinks and then pick up the cake last."

He could see her thinking over the sequence. "Cool," she said, finally. Having a nineteen-year-old sister – especially one like Amy – was a royal pain in the butt, but Amy had her good side too. Like she knew how to help him treat pimples that wanted to explode in the middle of his forehead right before school picture day or a party.

The sweet smell of cake icing reached across the counter. Brad imagined that the row of layer cakes could hardly wait to be eaten at a hundred parties all over the valley. The pretty girl behind the counter smiled at him and said, "Sorry, yours will be about fifteen more minutes. Can you do the rest of your shopping and come back? Just ask for me, I'm Carole." *She smiled at me. Right at me. This is so cool being fifteen.*

Amy nudged him with her elbow. "How about getting a Coke at the snack bar while we wait? My treat." They sat at a tiny table crushed between the soft pretzel stand and the ice cream machine. "So tell me about … about what's her name, again?" Amy started.

"Crystal. Her name is Crystal and she's in the ninth grade, but very mature for her age."

Amy's voice got her big-sister tone. "So tell me, what's she like?" Looking just like Mom, she pushed her lips out like a small kiss was just forming. She rubbed a hand over a high cheekbone and her dark eyes looked directly at him across the table.

"Did I tell you she's on the track team? She watched me run the other day and told me she thought I was an amazing athlete." *Well, she didn't exactly say that, but she implied it.*

"And you're sure she's coming tonight?"

He looked away for a moment. "Yeah, I guess. I mean, well, sure." Was he blushing?

She pushed her drink aside. "Lemme ask you, do you kinda of, well, rehearse what you're going to say to her. You know, like work it all out in your mind?"

Brad could tell his eyebrows arched. How'd she know that he memorized lines before he talked to Crystal? Before he could answer, Amy spoke again. She seemed agitated ... no ... unsure of herself. "When I'm around this guy that works with me at the store, I never know what to say. I usually end up trying to say something about the shoe inventory being low or that I finished stocking the racks. But then I stutter, and everything comes out sounding stupid. Sometimes I try to figure out all the stuff in my head before he comes on the floor ... you know, trying to plan ahead." She sighed, then a small tear formed in her eye. "I guess I really am just plain stupid."

This was the longest serious conversation he'd had with her since Dad's illness more than a year ago. It wasn't all that serious, like a mild gall bladder attack, but Amy had freaked out.

He took her hand, still cool and damp from the waxed cup she was holding, and took in a deep breath. "Amy, you are not stupid, you hear me? Listen to me. When I talk to Crystal I feel just like that too. I get all jittery inside, and I'm sure she can hear my heart pounding in my chest."

Amy's squeezed his hand tightly. "You feel that way too?" She brightened and forced a little smile. "You … you're just saying that to make me feel better."

"No way. Come on, get real." This was one of the few times he didn't have to say stuff just to make Amy feel good about herself.

It didn't matter that it was Saturday afternoon, the day of his party. Doing wind sprints and a 5-K jog was a must for Brad. Just up ahead was his house on the rise of a small hill. He pushed hard, even though his breath shot jagged little agonies down into his lungs. How come when he walked or even biked up this incline it was hardly noticeable? But at the end of a tough workout, it was like climbing Mount Ashland. Pump! Got to do it! Pump! Coach always said, "What you earn during the week, you lose on the weekend if you flake off." So every Saturday, pump, dude, pump!

Usually his Dad joined him, but today he had to work so Brad put out some extra juice, finishing with a determined sprint. Not something he did when Dad was along. Brad didn't want to make him feel like he was old. He struggled up the driveway, hands on hips, sucking in large gulps of air through his mouth. The sun baked the sweat on his arms and shoulders, but his San Francisco Giant baseball cap shielded his head. What a change from the heavy rains just a few days ago.

"Hi, Mom, I'm home," he called slamming the back door. He pulled off his smelly shoes and socks, leaving them on the service porch, then he headed for the fridge and downed a whole pint of juice. Mom came into the kitchen wearing her "get down and scrub" clothes.

"Hi, honey, how was your run? Hot enough for you out there?" She gave him a hug, took a whiff and backed away. "After your shower, the living room needs a good vacuuming, and not like you usually do."

"Yeah, yeah. I know"

He started for the door, then turned quickly and gave her a bear hug; he could almost see over her head. Didn't seem like he could do that a few days ago. Fifteen was so neat! "And who says I'm even gonna take a shower?"

"Hey! Hey! Now cut that out before I call off the party. You're impossible. Go! Oh, yes, before your father left this morning, he told me he wants you to remember to call Sarah and make sure she's coming tonight."

Geezo, he *couldn't* remind her to come. He hadn't even invited her. But Dad, he figured, was trying to kiss up to Coach, as if having his daughter at the party was going to get Brad a scholarship or something. Dad could be a real doofus. Anyway, who needed an eighth-grader there tonight? He started out of the kitchen, calling back over his shoulder, "Yeah, yeah sure, Mom. I'll remember to call."

Dad would have a stroke when he found out he hadn't even invited her. In the living room, he stripped off his sweaty t-shirt, leapt up and fired a hook shot right into the big antique bowl sitting in the corner. "Swish!"

The sounds of the vacuum, the dishwasher and Amy's hair dyer were finally silent. The house was ready. But not Brad. He stood in his underwear looking into the mirror, wondering if he'd had too much cut off his sideburns. It was too late to worry about that. If only his hair were a lighter color or maybe darker like Dad's. The color was so-in-between-nothing. At least the zit he had on his chin last week was gone. Thanks, Amy. He posed, admiring his well-defined chest outlined through his t-shirt. He shot another last glance at his pecs. Not bad. "Got to do some pushups before I get dressed."

The big clock downstairs chimed seven. An hour to go. He wondered what time she would come. Then a moment of panic. He said to his reflection, "What if she can't make it? Naw, naw. She'll be here. She even said something about bringing a friend." He pulled shirts from the closet to try on, tossing the "outs" in a pile on the bed. Maybe she would bring somebody for Pat. Sure, they could double date. Really cool. He hit the floor counting pushups: "One, two, three …"

"So if you need us, hon, we'll be upstairs watching that new movie with what's his name. Keep an eye on Amy, you understand? Mom told him that for the third time that evening.

"Mom, I know, I know. I gave Pat a head's-up, and most of the kids are cool with her. It's all under control, okay?"

She squeezed his arm and gave him a kiss. "I know, sweetie. Have a great time, and happy birthday again." "Fred," she then called upstairs, "did you remember to pick up the DVD?" She looked at Brad and winked. This was a repeat of an often-played scene.

"I got it, I got it," returned Dad's voice.

Looking into the dining room mirror, she ran her hand through her hair and lightly climbed the steps. "Give us a yell if you need me," she called over her shoulder.

Just as Brad thought he'd escaped the clutches of the protective parents, Dad's voice bellowed from upstairs. "Did you remember to call Sarah Goodwin?" Why he used her last name Brad couldn't figure. There was only one Sarah he could be talking about.

"Yeah, Dad, no problem." Yep, a stroke. His Dad would have one for sure if he only knew.

Eight fifteen. The house was empty. Not a person had shown up. Balloons hung motionless from the walls and ceiling, nobody popped them, no scrounging them under armpits to make obscene noises. In fact, no noise at all.

Did everyone forget? Had he told them the wrong night? No way, people just don't show up at parties on time. No one wants to be the first one through the door. The smell of fresh-baked croissants billowed from the open oven. Great idea Mom had to put them in before she went upstairs. He cracked his knuckles, a habit he had quit months ago.

Amy and his mom had teased Brad all week about the surprise birthday gift they had for him. He had guessed at least a dozen things – all gag gifts – like an electric sock warmer or a prune de-pitter.

Amy came in wearing a pair of new cut-offs in his honor. "Have you figured out what we got you yet, little baby brother?" It bugged him that she called him that, but, of course, that didn't stop her from doing it. "Mom told me I could show you after they left. Close your eyes and count to ten." He heard sounds of scraping furniture and then noises he couldn't identify. "Okay. Ta-da!" Their gift: His Mom had rented an entire DJ audio console for the party and there, crowded into the room, were two big speakers, an amplifier and dozens of CDs.

"Oh, wow! I can't believe it. Thanks Amy … and thank you, Mom. "He threw a kiss upstairs, then hugged Amy, lifting her off the floor and twirling her in a three-sixty. This night was guaranteed to be super. Talk about a surprise gift; it blew Brad away. The doorbell chimed. Eight thirty; his first guests had finally arrived.

My folks have decorated the house like you wouldn't believe – balloons hanging down from the ceiling … yellow, my favorite color … And the furniture is all changed around in the front rooms. I don't usually like it when they move stuff, but for my party. I guess it's okay. The dining room table takes up most of the living room and is covered with food. There are little cheese crackers, potato chips that I'm not allowed to eat, baked fish sticks, and lots more … everything is placed just like the chart Dad and I made on the computer. It's a cool deal! And right in the middle of all the food are thirty-one chocolate cupcakes Mom made without preservatives or real chocolate. My doctor says those things can ex … ex-a-ber-ate my condition. The small table by the door has our Parcheesi game board all set up ready to play. I can't wait till everybody gets here.

Some of the kids from my old school are coming. Sometimes when Mom wakes me in the mornings I forget that now I go to Pearblossom, not Evergreen Special School, and I start planning the day for my old schedule. I sure miss my friends and Mrs. Thayer, my teacher.

While I'm looking at the clock that says 8:06, Dad says, "Come on, Justin, let's sing along with your favorites." Then he hits the play button on the CD player and my birthday album starts.

We look at each other and laugh out loud, then we sing together, "Help me Rhonda, help, help me Rhonda, yeah, get her out of my heart." As soon as the music starts, I say to Dad, "Beachboys, spring 1965. 'Help Me Rhonda' is the group's second number-one record in the country."

The music fills the room. I close my eyes and feel the beat on my skin. The song sort of wraps itself around me, and I forget all about my party, and my friends – even the cupcakes. I hear each of the four harmony parts, and the instruments are like another voice holding the voices together. Then they kind of join like the strands of thread on Mom's necklace – it all becomes one, but I can see the different parts in my mind. Sometimes I feel like I can even taste the music. I like classical music too, but not as much as the Beachboys.

"Pat. It has to be Pat, I'll bet." It was – and he had a girl with him. He never said a thing about bringing a girl. And he had thought maybe Crystal would bring some-body for Pat. Go figure. As they came into the living room, Brad noticed the girl was, well, not really very pretty. Her weird, green plastic-rimmed glasses seemed to take up most of her small, pale face. Pat introduced Linda.

Brad remembered from his Spanish class that her name meant beautiful. Oh man, what a mistake that was. Linda sent a half-hearted smile at Brad revealing her shimmering row of braces.

"Nice to meet you, Linda."

Her voice was just above a whisper. "Eh, hello. It's nice to … eh, meet you too, Brad."

Half an hour later, Brad could hardly hear himself think, the house was so filled with kids talking and carrying on.

"So Jennifer said, 'out of my face you witch …'"

"Jamison took one look at my test and …"

"Little miss innocent came to my house at nine in the morning in a dress and I swear to God, nothing on underneath …"

"*Help me Rhonda, help, help me Rhonda. Get her outta' my heart*" blared the music from the huge speakers.

The music, popping can tops and screams from thirty voices all made for one great party. Brad smiled, he laughed, he cracked jokes, but each time the front door opened, his breath caught in his throat. It wasn't a great party for him. Not yet, anyway.

He and Pat made their way to the kitchen to get some more soft drinks and from behind the half-open door, he heard a couple of their buddies talking.

"Man, is Pat ever lame. What a dog he brought."

"That chick's braces could tear open a can of tuna fish."

Brad and Pat froze in the doorway. Brad felt the blood rise up his neck and redden his face. Pat's hand fell from the doorknob and he slowly backed into the living room unwilling to look at Brad.

"'Scuse me," he muttered.

"Pat, hold up." Brad's jaw ached from clenching so tightly. He thought, *I should throw those butt-heads the hell out of here.* But instead, his hand froze on the handle and slowly slipped from the knob. He was not being a very good friend.

A few minutes later, hiding from the situation, Brad was aimlessly cleaning up a spilled Coke from the kitchen floor with a paper towel. Alone, maybe he could sort out a solution to the problem. What if he asked Linda to dance with him to try to get to know her better? Then Pat would see him and … Suddenly he heard a slight whoosh as the kitchen door opened and a sweet, familiar rose fragrance surrounded him. From on his hands and knees, he looked up; Crystal was here.

She crouched down opposite him, her eyes slits, as she smiled that broad, sexy grin of hers. "Happy birthday, Brad." Her voice hummed low and mellow like a tenor saxophone, and it reached across the inches between them to touch his face. Freckles on her cheeks made her look like a little girl, but her blue eyes, her scent; they were not a little girl's. Just the thought of leaning across that small space between them and kissing her lips sent a tingle through his body.

Before he could stop himself from saying it, he blurted, "Someone, someone spilled a drink." *Now that's really a clever thing to say. She could see someone spilled a drink. Stuff really does come out dumb.* They both stood. "Thanks for coming. It, it was getting late and I thought maybe you couldn't make it." His voice was up an octave like the time when he sang his first solo in choir. "I'm glad you're here."

Crystal wore a short pink dress with frills attached to the sleeves and around the hem. On her feet she wore white slippers with little heels. Her earrings hung down, shiny pink and blue teardrop shapes. She didn't look at all like she did on the track.

She picked up an empty glass, inspecting it as she ran her finger around the lip. "And I'm glad you invited me. You've got a really neat house." Crystal looked straight at him making him feel like she really meant he was neat, not his house. "You know this is the first time we've met outside of school; well, except for track practice." They stared at each other as the high voice of Roy Orbison could be heard from the other room. "Pretty woman, oh, pretty woman …"

"Do you want to dance?" he asked.

At that moment an older boy, one Brad didn't recognize, pushed open the door and popped his head in. The guy had long, dark, slicked-down hair, and unlike the rest of the kids at the party, he wore a Western jacket, cowboy boots and a red bandanna around his neck. He looked about seventeen or eighteen. "Oh, there you are, Crystal. Hey, baby, I been lookin' all over for you."

Brad stood straight up, but he was still not as tall as this dude.

Crystal looked toward the boy, then glanced furtively back at Brad. "Oh, Brad, I hope you don't mind that I invited my friend, Jerry." She moved a short step away, took his hand and guided him out the door. Over her shoulder she said, "Later, Brad. I promise to save you a dance for later."

"It's my party and I'll cry if I want to cry if I want to ..."

The party dragged out till midnight, but for Brad, it had ended in his kitchen at nine fifteen.

Chapter 6

The pukie stink of spoiled eggs filled every corner of the science lab and even clung to the students' clothes. There at the front of the classroom stood Mrs. Schofield in her stained lab coat stirring up a concoction of chemicals. Peering over her granny glasses, her pudgy, owl face wore a mad-scientist smile. "See, you guys, this is the smell from hell. Anyone know how I did it?"

Most of the kids clamped their fingers over their nostrils or made gagging sounds. Juan, Brad's lab partner, fell on the floor shouting, "Mrs. Schofield, okay, you got us." He crawled, then staggered to the lab bench, sucked in a deep breath and collapsed. He was dead. Only thing was he laughed so hard that Brad was afraid Juan might wet his pants.

"Juan, party time's over, kid. You're lucky I don't bust your chops for that award-winning dying act. Okay, you and Brad need to finish your project before the bell rings, got it?"

Mrs. Schofield was smiling all the while she chewed on them. She meant business, but no way would she give them detention. Mrs. Schofield was, well she was odd. She wore hippie clothes from the sixties: baggy, bright, multicolored pants, a huge, tie-dyed blouse from Goodwill and a vest that hung down almost to her knees. She said things like, "my threads are far out, dude." One day Justin had seen Brad talking to her in the hall and his eyes had gone wide, then a big grin spread across his face. Later he asked, "Who was that?" He didn't believe she was really a teacher here. What a character she was. Yet, Brad admitted, he liked the way she taught.

She picked on another couple of kids once Juan and Brad finally got down to work. "Hey man, you got those chemicals wrong." Juan pushed a different bottle across the table. Schofield kept threatening to break him and Brad up as lab partners because the two of them did some wild and crazy things together. They made a cool comedy team. When they got together, everything seemed to turn into routines from a Chevy Chase movie.

"Hey, I hear from my cousin in Medford that a kid from Stockton may be transferring in and he's really somethin'. You know, speedy like a train." Juan's dark hand flashed in front of his face. His eyes, which had a sort of electric charge to them, really glowed now.

Brad looked up from his test tubes; he didn't have a clue who Juan was talking about.

"Name's Carlos, and I hear he says he gonna wipe you."

Brad nodded. "Yeah, yeah, yeah. I heard that trash last

year and I got beat only twice." Brad put on his most honest expression. "Look, Juan, I just do my best and try not to worry about all that talk." Well, the part about *trying* not to worry was true. "I suppose your friends are all coming out to root for this dude, huh?" As soon as Brad said that, he knew it was one big mistake. It sort of slipped out before he thought.

Juan pushed his long, dark hair back out of his eyes and parted the bottles on the table; his hands trembled. "What the hell you talking about, man?" His voice, sharp as a dagger, was ripping into Brad. "You think that 'cause some dude's got brown skin, I just dump my friends? You think everybody in that class . . ." He nodded his head toward the ESL room, which stood for "English as a Second Language," "... you think we sit around talking in Spanish about how we gonna get them Anglos?"

Brad leaned back in his chair feeling the force of Juan's anger hitting him like a test tube explosion. That was not how he felt about Juan or the other Hispanics at school. So why did he even think or say that stupid remark? "You think we *want* to stay off by ourselves in the bus or in the halls, that we don't want to sit with everybody else in the cafeteria? But who asks us to come on over and join them? Nobody, that's who!"

"Juan, listen. That's not what I think. You're my friend and you're welcome to come join me anywhere. I swear."

Juan stood up, knocking over some bottles. He did not care if anybody heard him. "I didn't see no engraved invitation to your birthday party last week. Why was that?"

Brad tried to speak but couldn't find any words to defend himself.

"You think I'm not good enough to come to the fancy party at your house just because my father works for your father?" The pulse in Juan's neck stood out throbbing.

"Juan, listen, man. I'm sorry. I just didn't think."

"You got it! You and a lot of kids …" His arm swept the room. Even Schofield watched, eyes wide, mouth open. "… amigo, you just don't think. Well, I got news for you. Maybe me and my *Beaner* friends just might come out to cheer at next week's track meet. And maybe it won't be for you."

I take a special van to and from school. It's so my mom doesn't have take me, but I don't like being here in this mini-van with five other kids from my special ed. class. I told Mrs. Gargus that I want to ride the regular bus, but she said I needed to ride the van until she was sure I was safe.

The first day I got off the van at school a boy made a bad gesture at us; he put his finger up to his ear and twirled it beside his head … and then he crossed his eyes. I didn't know what that meant, but I didn't like it. The other kids pretended not to see him, but I walked up to him and asked him as politely as I could, "Hey kid, why are you making that ugly face and laughing at us?"

He grinned and said back to me, "You wouldn't understand, geek." But I understood. He is making ass-ump-ions about us and underestimating our abilities like we're more challenged than other people. But I've figured out that you can't always compare who has more life challenges just by looking at someone. There are people who make ass-ump-ions about others because of their religion, their race, economic status, or their size. Just about every human at certain times needs extra support, just like some students at school need an assistant.

I always sit on this side of the van and close my eyes so I can feel the sun on my face when we go to school in the morning. It makes me dreamy. I think about last night's discussion with my folks. It made me want to leave the room, but that's rude. Not the whole talk, the part with my Dad was cool. Since he works nights he will be able to take me to see Brad run at the school track meet tomorrow. I heard some kids talking yesterday, and they said Brad is really fast but that this new kid might beat him. I liked the part when we sat in the living room eating popcorn with two tablespoons of soy butter and one quarter cup of brewer's yeast sprinkled on top. Mom asked me, "Have you made any friends at school, hon?" She tried to act like it was just a casual question like how was my dinner, but I can tell that the answer was very important to her.

"Brad is my friend. He hangs out with me a lot, and we talk about really interesting stuff like the orbit of the moon or Elvis Presley."

She nods her head. "Uh-huh. Does he ever have lunch with you or spend time after school with you?"

I fidget with the corners of the pillow on the couch. "He's very busy; it's tr … track season and he practices a lot … and … n … no, I don't see him except in the resource room and music class. He doesn't sit with me, but he is my … my friend."

Dad puts down his newspaper and takes my hand. I don't look at him or Mom. The room is awfully quiet and we just sit. This is when I want to excuse myself.

I know what it is to be a friend … friends go out of their way to be with someone, and ask them questions – more than just, "Hi, how are you?" A friend is someone who really cares how you feel and what you think. I guess I don't have any of those.

Long shadows of early morning alternated with splashes of sunlight as Brad peddled his bike along the tree-lined street to Pat's house. There hadn't been any good vibes between them since the party. An occasional "How ya' doin', dude?" was about the longest conversation they'd had. Just as he had only told Pat bits and pieces of the Crystal birthday party flameout, Brad hadn't been able to bring himself to say, "Shoot, I feel really bad about those dorks that trashed you and Linda. I should have told them to stuff a sock in it." Something was definitely frozen between them, and it looked like Pat wouldn't be the one to say anything about it.

As he biked along, Brad looked up at the dark, green leaves of the madrone trees skimming over his head; at least it was Saturday – no school, no Justin and no Crystal. Well, *maybe* it would be okay if he ran into her. Maybe.

Hot smoke used to warm the blossoms and save them from late frosts hung densely over the valley. Its biting smell, so familiar to Brad, still managed to make his nose crinkle in disgust. Dad really ought to come up with an answer to the pollution. But that topic was for another day. Right now, Brad's immediate problem was: *No matter what, I'm going to see Pat and start a thaw. No matter what! So right now, pollution's no big deal.*

Pumping up Pat's outrageously steep driveway was a bear. It deserved to be called the "b" word, 'cause it was. Until this year, Brad had walked his bike up the hill, but now it was a test, a point of honor, to ride all the way up. It was kind of like when he knew he had won a race without really being pushed hard, but there was always that guy with a stopwatch standing at the finish line fifty meters away counting off the seconds. He just had to go for it. Had to try to bust his best time.

At the top, he dropped the bike on the drive, and with wobbly legs, eased his body down onto the cool lawn. Man, running a race would be a lot easier than doing this. Maybe he would skip his afternoon run.

While he was still sitting there panting, Pat plopped down on the grass beside him, gave him a nod and muttered, "Hey."

"Hey, yourself." Brad's breathing slowly returned to normal, and he gulped from his water bottle. "Nice driveway you got here. Any chance you could level it out for me?"

Pat sent a steady stare at Brad. Then a small smile started at the corners of his mouth. Soon he broke into a wide grin. It was like he was saying, "Welcome back to the world of the living, dude." Pat's smile and poke to Brad's arm seemed to say it all; Pat wasn't holding a grudge.

They talked some about how lame those creeps at the party acted.

"You gonna see Linda again?"

"No way, man. You see those huge, green specks of hers? This thick." He made a wide space with his two fingers. "Besides, she's only in the eighth grade and who wants to go out with a dorkus like her?" His head was down as he made a project of cleaning his glasses. They looked clean already. At first Brad didn't get it. Pat said she was a dork, but he must have liked her. After all, he had invited her to the party.

"Ya know, Pat, she didn't seem that off-the-wall to me. And she's a cool dancer." That part was true, anyway.

Pat looked up with a small smile on his lips. "You think so? Yeah, I really dug dancing with her."

Pat put his glasses on, jammed them back high on his nose and twisted his mouth the way he always did. "Hey, Brad?" He shifted positions, now sitting cross-legged. Finished fiddling with his glasses, he tore blades of grass from the perfect lawn. "You, you kinda got aced by Crystal, huh?"

Brad drew in a long breath. If he only knew how he stood with her, if he could just understand why she had brought that cowboy to the party, or why suddenly now she seemed to want to be with him. He wiped the sweat from his forehead. "Ya know, man, basically, it sucks! My head's messed up and I feel like crap."

There! He actually said how he felt. This was the first time he had really told anybody what was going on in his mind. Somebody besides Mom, and she didn't count. Telling Pat wasn't too bad. Actually not bad at all.

"You kids want some breakfast? It's ready." Pat's Mom, Mrs. James, stuck her head out of the kitchen window. The smell of sizzling bacon spilled out, teasing Brad's appetite.

"Yeah, thanks Mrs. James, that sounds great."

As they stood to go, Pat playfully slugged Brad's arm. It was his way of saying, "hang in, guy."

What an appetite Brad had worked up. The food was good, and so was the hot chocolate with whipped cream topping. Mrs. James was super. If only his mom would take some cooking lessons from her instead of trying see how many ways she could serve shredded wheat. And then there was Amy; how could she live on yogurt and tofu anyway? Now she wouldn't even look at a burger.

Pat pointed at Brad with his fork, trying to get words out of his mouth, but all that came out was ummmmph, ummmph and a spray of little yellow pieces of egg. Finally, he swallowed and gulped some milk to wash it down. "Listen to this flash. Coach Goodwin told me in P.E. yesterday that it's confirmed … this new kid from Fresno or Stockton, some place in California, has transferred to Medford Middle." Pat stuffed another slice of bacon into his mouth. "This dude is in ninth, and he is supposed to be fast. Coach said the guy's maybe gonna have some of the best times in the state in the sprints." Pat reached for some more toast. With his arm out, he paused and looked right at Brad. "And he's running this Thursday against you."

"Some more eggs, Bradley?" Mrs. James didn't wait for an answer. She just scraped a pile onto his plate. Pat had dumped this new concern on Brad as easily has his mom had dumped the eggs onto his plate.

Chapter 7

Two days to go. Brad couldn't remember if he had ever had this much trouble sleeping before a track meet. At night he tossed in bed from side to side. Cover on, too warm. Off, too cold. The pillow felt like it was stuffed with raw lima beans. He peeked out of one eye at the illuminated clock on his bed stand. Eleven forty. Not that late, but for a school night, late enough. Laughter from the TV downstairs didn't help. Mom had Letterman on the tube, and Dad was probably already in the sack. He toyed with the idea of going downstairs to sit with her for a while.

If I can't fall asleep by midnight, I'll go down. About every thirty seconds he cracked open an eye to see the time. "This is stupid," he finally said as he got out of bed and grabbed his robe from the closet.

Mom sat curled up on her big stuffed chair, a cup of tea steaming on the table next to her. Flickering lights from the TV played across her face, but she was only half watching. She was engrossed in a book of crossword puzzles, deciding which word fit. Her lips shaped that little kissy expression of hers. Brad stood at the door to the den for a moment watching without a sound.

"Ummm, no," she muttered to herself. "Oh, it's Philadelphia, not Pennsylvania." She erased and wrote new letters.

"Hi, Mom."

She looked up startled. Then a warm smile appeared, a smile that invited him to come sit next to her and talk. Brad plopped down on the little footstool next to her.

"Couldn't sleep." He took a sip of her tea; the strong orange taste made his lips pucker. "Needs honey."

She tousled his hair, her warm hand comforting him. "Looks like you've got a lot on your mind. Want to talk?"

"I guess." There was so much stuff scrambling around in his brain all yelling for attention that he could hardly focus on one problem for a minute when another trampled the first one shouting, "out of my way, think about me!" There was the track meet, actually the whole track season with a possible scholarship riding on it; there was that kid, Carlos; then there was Justin; Crystal and, of course, today's blowup with Juan. Why was he so teed off? It was too much. Too much.

Brad put his head on his mom's lap.

"You know, hon, you hardly ever talk about that boy you're helping. Justin, is that his name?" Her voice vibrated through her body like the deep purr of a cat. "What's he like?"

Brad thought about it, then without lifting his head he said, "He's, well he's hard to describe."

"Why don't you try?"

"First of all, it's really difficult to understand him because he stutters and his voice, well, it's like having somebody talk to you from out of a science fiction movie. And he just rambles on and on about the most trivial things. Oh, and he says things that some people just think, but he stuff just pops out of his mouth."

"Like what?"

Brad thought for a moment. "Like the other day, we were waiting for the door to the music room to open, and some dumb boy said something rude about this girl who is, well, she's pretty heavy. So Justin walks right up to him and says, 'Why don't you like fat people? Do they say bad things about you?' See what I mean?"

"And you thought Justin was out of line for speaking up to defend that girl?"

"Well, Mom. It's just that ... that, oh you know what I mean."

"I'm afraid I do, Brad. I'm afraid I do."

From the way his mom looked at him, Brad figured he'd better change the subject. "And everything has to be 'just so' like we've got to have the same schedule and the same routine every day. If we have an assembly schedule, Justin gets so upset he has a hard time functioning."

"Brad, come on, I know he's not all that hard to deal with. You've spoken about him in much more positive terms than this."

Brad raised his head, smiled sheepishly. "Actually, he can be cool to be around. He knows stuff about a lot of things, and he can tell you details about every artist and record from … from way back when you were in high school."

She laughed, "You mean from back in the stone age? Does he have any friends besides you?"

"I … I don't really know." He thought about it while he absently played with the teacup. "I do know that behind his back some of kids call him lame or a retard."

"Do you ever tell them that's not acceptable?"

"I … eh … I guess I just pretend I don't hear that stuff. It's hard, I mean they're my friends and all and I …"

"And that gives them the right to make fun of him? Bradley, you know better than that. What would you do if your so-called friends said that about Amy?"

Brad bit his lip and clenched his fist. *I'd punch them out, is what I'd do.* "Ahh, it's not the same."

"But it is! You know the word "retard" comes from the clinical term, mental or physical retardation, but when people just use the shortened expression, it's a catch-all that can mean stupid, dense, crazy … all those generalizations that are put-downs and not true. Maybe it's time you let those guys know how you feel about Justin. If you take a stand they may not like it, but they will respect you for telling them. And I bet you'll feel a lot better about yourself."

Mom sure was dishing out medicine in hard-to-swallow doses. She sipped from her cup as Brad let their conversation sink in. How did he really feel about Justin? Then the image from that afternoon came to mind; there was the picture of Juan, red-faced and out of control. How had Brad treated him and the other Hispanic kids? Angry, hurt, left out of things like the party. How long had Juan felt this way about Anglos, about Brad? *I must be pretty dense not to have seen this.* But whose fault was that anyway? That's something to think about.

He laid his head back down on his mom's lap as troubles swirled through his mind like a fog covering the nearby Siskiyou mountain range. Her fingers soothed, gently touching his scalp, his neck. His eyes closed, and his head swam in a murky sea of darkness. The sounds of crickets and chirping frogs drifted in through the open windows. He felt her fingers threading through his hair. The cricket sounds drifted in and out of his consciousness and his mind let go a little at a time until …

Peppermint is one of the best smells in the whole world, and our room smells just like the herb garden we have out back of our house. It's because Mrs. Gargus just took her cup of mint tea out of the microwave oven. I can recognize peppermint anywhere, like when it's in candy or ice cream, and especially when it grows in our garden. The smell makes me feel floaty and like summertime is here. Too bad candy and ice cream are on Mom's list of foods I can't eat, but I sure can chew on mint leaves. When I do, even my mom turns her face away and says, "Whoooeee, Justin, you smell like a big candy cane." That's pretty funny since I can't eat candy canes either.

"I've got to catch up on filing these forms," Mrs. Gargus says to Brad and me, "How about you boys working on that Civil War assignment?" She raises her cup and looks over the top before taking a sip.

Brad pulls out my social studies book and I tell him, "page 235, Brad. We just read the part where in 1862 the Battle of Shiloh took place in Tennessee. General Ulysses S. Grant of the Union lost over thirteen thousand men, and the boys in Grey lost almost eleven thousand. It was one of the bloodiest battles of the war and the hills were covered in blo … blood from the loss of life. Grant was …"

"Okay, okay, that's great information, Justin, but what were they fighting about?"

I sit across the desk from Brad, look at the ceiling and think about his question. I get all the dates and names of the battles right, but sometimes teachers ask me questions that I don't understand. "Do I n … n … need to know that?"

Brad twists his mouth funny-like.

"Did I say something to make you upset, Brad? If I did, I'm … I'm sorry I did that."

"No, no, it's okay, really. It's just that's one of the questions sure to be on the next quiz. I'm pretty sure we covered this a few days ago. Don't you remember?"

Brad is not a good liar. I can tell from his face and the way he is wringing his hands that he's upset. I don't think he wants to lie to me, but just the same, he should tell the truth. I always tell the truth, but Dad says that can get me in trouble and that I should just learn to say nothing when telling what I think is the truth might hurt someone's feelings. How do I know what I say will hurt someone's feelings? I should put that on my list of things to ask my folks.

Brad turns the book toward me, pointing to a paragraph of tiny print, "Try to remember, the North and the South are enemies. That means they don't like each other at all. And that's because they think differently about slavery, land use and economic issues. Got it?"

"Slavery, land use and economic issues. Yeah, I got it." I don't get it, but I think I just learned how to lie.

The days went by at a snail's pace, like trying to get through one of Mrs. Compton's algebra tests; each class was endless. The track meet was marked on his calendar in red. But there was no way he would forget *that* date.

The sweet smell of new-cut grass on the infield drifted across the track at after-school practice. In past years that scent had been a strong reminder to Brad that the season was powering on. It was a good feeling. But today there was no excitement when he took in a deep whiff. Brad tried to focus on his starting strides out of the blocks and on the change in style caused by his new spiked Nikes. After a few half-hearted tries, he stood, hands on hips, glancing up at the soft, dark clouds that drifted aimlessly overhead. They mirrored his mood. He should have been practicing, but instead, he kept an eye out for Crystal even though meeting her was sure to bring memories and pain. He had successfully avoided her even though the workout track was small. But now … now he really wanted to see her. Where was she? Last time he looked she was next to the old bleachers with her hang-out friends. Then she was over at the water fountain giggling with some freaks. *Now where is she?*

"Hi, Brad. I've missed you this past week. Where you been hiding?"

A knot formed in the pit of his stomach, but he quickly painted a smile on his face and turned. "Working on my starts. How are you, Crystal?" She stood there smiling at him as though nothing had gone down between them. He tried to act casual, but his fingers kneaded his palms, feeling the moist sweat.

"I had a great time at your party. I'm sorry I couldn't find you for our dance. Where'd you disappear to anyway?" She ran a finger along the back of his hand and tilted her head. Then, her warm voice, sweet as a song said, "I looked for you; I really did."

Brad knew in his heart that this was a lame excuse. But he really wanted to believe her, so he didn't push the issue. He stumbled through their conversation right up to the time for sprint practice. Crystal said something about how she loved watching him run. In a few minutes he wouldn't remember a single word she had said, but he would remember her touch, her smile and her voice. *Maybe, just maybe, she really did look for me.* He felt great!

No. He felt totally bummed out!

"See ya soon?" she asked, kind of like inviting him to ask her out. She walked toward the gym, her ponytail flopping and her hips swaying.

He stripped off his sweats and headed for the starting marker, willing himself to forget Crystal, forget Pat, forget Juan and forget Justin, who now seemed to be waiting for him everywhere he turned. The first track meet was in little over a week and he really had to get down to business. Just before he had left for school that morning, Dad slapped him hard on the butt reminding him, "This is track time, Brad. Not too early to think about …" he lifted his chin and nodded, "… to think about the future." When Dad said future, he meant college scholarship. "No second-place finishes, hear?" He heard – and knew he owed winning races to his Dad. Forget all this mental junk mail? Yeah, right.

As he rounded the bend at the far end of the track, his foot gave way, turning his ankle a bit. No harm, not this time, but that was the second time he had found this mushy spot on the inside lane of the dirt track. Pearblossom's home meets were usually held at the high school, but the surface was undergoing some repairs so the first meet would be here. Brad mentally stored the information about the soft spot and kicked hard for the finish line.

Chapter 8

Thunk, thunk, thunk.

Brad's spikes sang a high, metallic song as they scraped across the cement runway leading to the track. A warm breeze slapped him in the face as he ran out with the team onto the Pearblossom Middle School track.

Thunk, thunk, thunk.

Brad recalled from previous years Coach Goodwin's speech before every meet, "You boys and girls will run onto the track, and win or lose, you will run off with your heads high. Show 'em you have determination and pride." Brad jogged out with that determination and the pride he had been working on for years. Those were the ingredients every college coach looked for, maybe as much as talent. Even though scouts from the colleges didn't come to middle school meets, they would have the results and times of every athlete with potential for a scholarship on their desks by each Monday morning.

Out on the field, the Medford boys looked like a precision drill team performing their stretching exercises as a unit. Dressed in bright royal-blue sweats with gold trim, they were impressive. Too buff to lose? Brad snorted. "No way!" *That's just what they want us to think with their fancy warm-ups. We'll show them a warm up. Wait till they see us run!*

Even though the boys and girls competed at the same time, the events were run separately, so there wouldn't be much chance of seeing Crystal. Nope, he wouldn't even consider looking around for her. But yesterday she sure looked cool in her shorts and running top.

"Brad. Brad, over here." Pat's unmistakable voice bellowed from down the track. He was an assistant trainer for the team, a fancy way of saying water boy or go-fer. His jobs were doing things like searching for missing pieces of equipment and keeping track of events so kids didn't forget where and when they were supposed to compete. Brad was glad to see him.

He waved back, and they walked toward each other. "Hey, sorry I didn't call you back last night. Really whacked out."

Pat shrugged.

Brad lifted a foot, wiggling his ankle. "The Nikes are in-cred-ible. It's like being out in space." He did a slo-mo imitation of an astronaut's bouncing walk on the moon.

A big smile, a push of his glasses. "Cool."

"Thanks again, bro." Pat liked to be called that. Brad brushed his hair back and glanced over at the bleachers. "Hey, any chance that you've seen Juan around?"

Looking like an owl, Pat swiveled his head from left to right checking out the stands. "Naw, why?"

"Oh, no reason. I thought he just might be here." *Yeah, and rooting for the other dude.*

Pat checked the clipboard in his hand. "Looks like you and this Carlos guy will be cruisin' the hundred meters pretty soon."

Usually the sprinters ran in the hundred, two hundred meters, and a relay, but last year Brad substituted in the four hundred meters and even the long jump once or twice. Coach said getting experience in other events was a good thing, but Dad was not really tuned to that idea. The relays came at the end of the meet, and whether Brad ran or not would be decided by how close the meet was. Coach called the shots, and Brad wouldn't know until the last minute what event he would be in.

Rickety bleachers stood on opposite sides of the field, each in need of sanding and paint. Mostly just Moms and Dads came to see their kids compete, but today lots of students from both schools were filling the bleachers and standing along the edges of the track. Still no Juan. Were there so many people here because this would be a dynamite meet or because Carlos and he were going to tangle? He took off his sweats as sticky beads of perspiration formed in his armpits. He would be ready.

Over on the far side of the bleachers, Brad's Dad was talking to a group of athletes who would soon compete in the field events. They were huddled around him as he gave last-minute instructions; mostly he tried to build confidence, especially among the kids competing for the first time. In a few minutes, they would peel off, one or two at a time, and head for the bathrooms. It got really crowded there just before a meet.

Dad spotted Brad and joined him. They stood silently kicking at the dirt on the track. "Too bad Mom couldn't get out of work this afternoon. Lots of flu going around at the hospital. She sends her love and, well, you know, good luck." Brad nodded. Anyway, his mom had been at most of the meets last year.

Cheers rose from the other side of the field as the Medford visitors broke from their team huddle. They looked big even from this distance. Brad turned away, not allowing himself to get psyched out. He stared up at the low clouds hanging over the field; the breeze wasn't crisp enough to scramble them. *Wouldn't it be freaky to be laid out on one of those big puffy clouds up there and watch all this action down here? And I'd be so mellow, eating sunflower seeds and spitting the shells on the kids in the bleachers.*

"Hey, Brad, are you listening to me?" Dad's voice jerked him back to the ground.

"Oh, sorry, I was just trying to focus on the meet." He rotated his hips and continued to loosen up parts of his body even though they were already loose.

His dad cleared his throat and put his arm around him.

"You know, this isn't going to be the only meet of the year. We got six times, a whole season, to prove what you can do, so don't start thinking you've got to do it all today. And listen, you want to come out of this healthy; no pulled muscles or torn ligaments, you hear? Smooth out of the blocks … don't accelerate too quick. You know when to coast and when to pump. No big hero thing, understand?"

Oh man, Dad was really hassled. He had never put out this psychology junk before a race before. It was always, "burn their butts" and a big slap on Brad's behind. Geezo, this was only a middle school track meet. Then why were the bleachers filled? And why did he feel a thousand butterfly wings fluttering in his gut all about to take off at once?

I told Brad this morning in class that I was coming to watch him run, but I have never been to a track meet before so I asked him, "Where do I sit?" His eyes opened a little wide and he thought a minute before touching my shoulder, "You just find Coach Goodwin's daughter, Sarah, and tell her I want you to sit on the team bench. Just ask anyone on the field for Sarah right after school. Got that?"

"I was listening to you Brad. I got it." It irritates me when people talk to me slow and repeat themselves. I should be used to it, but I'm not.

I watch the runners warm up and run short sprints. I think our team looks good, but theirs looks better. Brad told me all week, "There's no way we're going to lose to those guys." I want to believe him, but I think he's doing what Mom calls "wishful think-ing." I like when she explains new words and phrases to me, and I especially like the idea of "wishful thinking." I do that a lot but I didn't know other people did that too.

I see Brad talking to his father. Maybe I'm not supposed to, but I want to go over and wish him luck on his running today. I might not have thought I should do this, but he touched my shoulder this morning ... and it didn't get me all upset. I wait till his dad walks away before I talk to him.

"Hi Justin, I'm really glad you made it. How are you doin'?"

This makes me feel real good because Brad is not looking over my shoulder to see anybody else. He looks right into my eyes, and I think really wants to know how I'm doin'. This is one cool deal.

After Justin has said in his sharp monotone, "Good luck in your races today, Brad," Brad joined the team gathered around Coach Goodwin. Soon he was caught up in the crush and the spirit. Everyone started a chant, first in a low voice, "Go, go, Bulldogs," then louder, and louder, and finally they shouted in a wild scream, "Go, Bulldogs!" Dozens of arms lifted high over their heads, waving frantically. Brad laughed to himself, they were just like a bunch of movie Indians doing a war dance before a battle.

When the huddle broke, Brad and Jesus Macias, another Pearblossom sprinter, went to the start of the hundred-meter race. Directly across from them were the Medford

Tiger sprinters. Standing out from the group was a tall, brown, muscular kid with a black ponytail. He strutted in front of the Medford bleachers like a rooster, waving to the kids in the stands, who stamped their feet in a rhythmic response.

"Go, Carlos, go!"

Suddenly he turned to face Jesus and Brad. A crooked grin appeared on Carlos's face as if he was looking at two bugs ready to squash them. He put his hands on his hips like some gunslinger dude in a Western, then he drew an imaginary pistol, took aim and shot Brad and Jesus with his finger.

"Kashoo, kashoo!" he yelled. "Got both of you butt-mouths." Then he turned and bowed to his laughing fans while making an obscene gesture to the Pearblossom runners. "Losers," he chided.

Jesus shook his head in disgust. "This guy's bad; I mean an A-number-one jerk."

Brad couldn't believe how Carlos was playing to the crowd like some kind of bad-taste circus performer. This guy needed to be straightened out. He started toward the arrogant runner, but Jesus stepped between them. "Come on, man, let him do his garbage-mouth routine where it doesn't mean anything." He pushed Brad away from the scene. "We'll settle Carlos. We'll wipe him clean off the track."

There were six runners shaking it out behind the starting blocks. The starter had given his instructions about staying in lanes and waiting for the sound of the pistol.

This was the time most runners got the jitters. Not Brad. To him there was a hole in space, narrow like a track lane and totally silent. The world closed in around him. He saw only the long stretch of track out in front of him, and there at the far end, was a group of raised stopwatches, poised and ready. And so was Brad.

"Runners to your blocks."

A steady thump, thump, thump beat in his chest as he placed his feet into position. In the next lane was Carlos who, since the gun-fighting scene, hadn't said a word to Brad or Jesus.

"On your marks."

Brad exhaled, then took in a long, slow breath.

"Get set." The starter's voice was in Brad's ear speaking only to him.

Then the sound of the shot echoed over the crowd's cheers. The one-hundred-meter race was on.

Low at the start, he threw his arms out in front of him, driving his legs in short, choppy steps for the first fifteen meters or so. He saw no one ahead of him, no one beside him, only the raised stopwatches at the finish line.

Now longer strides, stretching out, upper body leaning forward. His breath was in tempo with his pace. He was now halfway and had only a vague awareness of the runner to his right. But there was no one to chase. The hands holding the stopwatches lifted as he drew closer, closer. Brad raised his head, arching his chest to breast the tape.

Suddenly, a blur of blue and yellow was at his shoulder inching forward. Carlos! They both moved as though in slow motion. Slowly, so slowly, Carlos glided forward. Brad was unable to call on his reserve to fight off the challenge. A long leg crossed the finish line a split second in front of Brad. Carlos had won the race.

The other runners pulled up, hands at their waists, panting for breath. Brad sucked mightily for air.

"You were asleep man. Dead asleep." Carlos's mocking laughter drifted off as he made his way toward the stands.

An arm crossed Brad's shoulder. Jesus, who had come in third, draped his arm around him as they walked away – away from the finish line, away from Carlos, and away from the fans in the bleachers chanting, "Carlos, Carlos."

The winner glided like a Roman victor in front of his fans, combing his long hair and nodding to the students of Medford Middle School.

His dad stormed over to Brad on the sidelines far from where the team hung out. His face was flushed and he was chewing on his lip as Brad looked for a rock to slide under. "You let up. You had him and you let up!"

Brad heard the sermon in his head, the same message his dad had repeated for the past three years, "Remember when we were fishing and you played that salmon, reeled him in, reeled him in, and then you plain didn't land him? You didn't close him out. Don't ever, ever, let a runner blind-side you. Close him out! Bring the win home. Got it?" This salmon named Carlos got clean away. A few years ago, Brad might have cried, burying his face in his dad's chest, but today he couldn't do that. He had let his dad down and it hurt. It hurt. Bad.

"For what it's worth, you ran your best time ever." His voice had no forgiveness in it. He started to walk away, then turned back, putting his hand under Brad's sagging chin. Softer, he added, "All right, this is just the first meet. There will be other races and lots of wins."

Brad forced a smile. "I know, I know." But there was no conviction in his words.

At that moment, Pat charged up to them. "Sorry to interrupt, but there's a change in assignments you need to know about. It's sort of a lame piece of info." He handed Brad the clipboard, then, fidgeting with his cap, he backed up. Brad's name was crossed off the two-hundred-meter race and penciled into the four-hundred-meter race. No way!

Carlos would be in the two-hundred, not the four-hundred race. What the hell was Coach Goodwin doing pulling him from the chance to wipe that garbage-mouth piece of crap? "No way!" He threw down the clipboard and as he left to find coach, he heard his dad's voice, "What's going on, Pat?"

Brad charged Goodwin, getting right in his face, smelling the sweet odor of Dentyne gum. "Why the hell are you yanking me from the two-hundred? You don't think I can take this jerk, do you?"

"Brad …"

Brad's breath came in short gasps. His fingers clenched in his palms like they wanted to punch somebody out. But he wouldn't take on Coach, and they both knew it.

He heard himself yelling louder than he intended to. "You think 'cause he beats me in one race, that I can't take him? You're supposed to back up your team. Well damn it, back me up. Let me race him!"

"You watch your language, young man." Red-faced, Coach pulled himself to his full height and leaned over Brad, facing him down. "Just remember who you're talking to and check that mouth and attitude in the bathroom where they belong." His voice was sharp and brittle.

Brad swallowed hard and backed up a half step, unable to speak.

Coach let out a long sigh. He chewed hard on his gum, teeth grinding like he was struggling to spit out just the right words. Then he put a firm hand on Brad's arm. "Listen to me. I know you're really upset and you want to rub that jerk's nose in it more than anything. I'd love for you to do it. I know you can do it, but we're not here to play get even. This is a team sport and we're here to win the meet. Look, Greg pulled up lame in the long jump so he's scratched from the four-hundred. Without him there, we got ziltch. Jesus takes at least a second in the two-hundred. You take the long run and we don't lose points. We can still be in the meet against these guys coming up to the relay. Are you hearing me?"

Brad closed his eyes trying to sort it all out. If only Pearblossom could pull out a win that would mean something. It was not all that he wanted, but it would have to be enough, wouldn't it?

"Brad?"

"Sorry, coach. Yeah, I hear you."

Brad jogged back in front of the bleachers filled with Pearblossom students. He forced himself to keep his chest up and his chin held high.

Chapter 9

A yucky, sour smell filled the boys' bathroom; Brad was not the only kid who had to chew his cookies between races. He lifted his head from the toilet and sucked in a deep breath in spite of the stench. His rib cage ached. God, he hated this, but it was the price some runners had to pay: First you spilled your guts on the track, then in the john. Ugh.

Grateful for being alone, he got a package of gum that was stashed in his gym locker and sat down on the hard, wooden bench chewing in silence. Okay, so he won the four-hundred-meter race. Big deal! He should have coasted against weak competition and saved his legs for the relay. Stupid! Why did he have to be a hot dog sprinting the last one hundred meters? Left his wind and legs on the track, that's what he did. Geezo!

So what now? In just about fifteen minutes, the four-by-four-hundred relay was coming up, and if Coach's calculations were right, that last race would decide the winner of the meet.

"Brad, you're a horse's butt." His words echoed off the tiled walls shouting back at him, "You're a horse's butt!"

I know, I know," he answered his own hollow voice. If only he hadn't sprinted that last one hundred meters, but his legs and lungs reminded him that he had.

Earlier, just after the race and before Brad's belly decided to turn into a horrible mixture of slime and last night's pasta, Coach had called him over.

"Great race, Brad. You stuck it to them." He nodded his head toward the other side of the field. "It's going down to the wire, and we need you big time for the four-by." He looked across the field. "He *is* fast." Coach didn't even call Carlos by name.

Brad didn't need to hear all this, but he wasn't going to say anything that would get Coach pissed off again. Coach knelt on the grass and motioned to him to join him. It felt good to get off his legs. He hated to admit it, but they were a little wobbly. "Buddy, looks like you're probably going against him in the last leg." Coach picked at the grass. "Got another good four hundred meters left in you?"

Brad couldn't remember exactly what he had said out there, but it was short because by that time, he was starting to get a strong message from his insides.

Inside the locker room, he stood up slowly holding onto the wall for support. So far, so good. With shaking legs, he stepped outside. Heavy afternoon clouds were rolling in over the Siskiyou Mountain range, blotting out much of the sun. The same breeze that brought the cloud cover also whipped around the track, making him feel somewhat refreshed and more alert. Well, maybe. Instead of doing his full warm up routine, he decided to prep for the race by walking.

The stands came alive as kids called and waved to him. The electricity in the air pumped him.

"Way to go, Brad."

"Go get 'em."

"You can take him."

Brad glanced over at a couple of dozen Hispanic kids in the stands. No Juan. They were cheering him and Jesus, who was scheduled to run the third leg of the relay. He was a good choice for that spot. But where was Juan?

A chant rose from the other side of the field "Carlos! Carlos!"

Okay, forget this crap. I'm not letting it lose my concentration. I've got a race to run. A race to win.

Just before getting detailed instructions about the staggered start, he saw a small hand waving to him from in front of the bleachers. Justin. Good thing Mrs. Gargus had given Brad a heads-up about what effect it might have on him to be dumped in the middle of a crowd of screaming kids. They screamed all right! Justin called something, but Brad couldn't hear it over the crowd noise. Next to him was Justin's Dad, and on the other side stood Brad's Dad. Was Justin adopting him and his whole family? Whatever, it felt good to see them rooting for him.

I like being on the field down here with the runners. After Dad told me he would take me to the meet, I worried about having to sit in the crowded bleachers with a lot of kids yelling in my ears. This is one of the noises that hurt my head and make me act funny. Once, when we went to a soccer match, I had to put my hands over my ears and I don't want to do that here because kids will make fun of me I never told Brad that story, so I guess he just wanted me to be here where he could see me. I'm sandwiched between two dads. That expression came to mind because I had heard my dad use it the other night talking about the shirts in his closet being "sandwiched" between his sports coats and his dress slacks. I guess I would be the meat or cheese in this dad sandwich.

Brad is the fastest kid I ever saw. He could have beaten that kid who won, but I think he must have given the guy a chance. In the next race he beat the tar out of all the kids. Well, they don't really have tar in them. I heard that one on *Wheel of Fortune* when Pat Sajak said it to a contestant. It means to beat someone good.

While Brad was running I thought about a song by the famous singer Bruce Springsteen. I kept humming the tune in my head and repeating the words over and over, "We'll run till we drop, baby, we'll never go back, Baby we were born to run … born to run … born to run." It was on an album of the same name, released on Columbia Records, September 25, 1975. That was a long time ago. I think Bruce Springsteen must be very old or dead by now.

The starting gun fired! The first runner for both teams leapt forward to begin one full cycle of the track. The aluminum batons in each boy's left hand pumped forward and backward with every stride, reflecting the dim sunlight that peeked from behind the now fast-moving clouds. Both kids jammed, going for the lead, and just as important, after the first two hundred meters, they went hard for the inside lane. The three remaining runners from each team bounced on their toes, shook out their arms and legs while still focused on the action of the first leg.

While never losing sight of the runners, Brad turned his attention inward. He had trained himself to slow everything down so he'd be as relaxed as possible when the moment came to put it all together. This had worked before, and he prayed it would work again. Now! Slow … it … down. In his mind he played a videotape of a long-ago memory.

The ocean's roar was in his ears, surf pounding, splashing off the rocks and spraying him with cool water. He was seven, maybe eight years old, and while his folks ate dinner at some fancy restaurant, Brad walked barefoot at sunset along the damp sands of Bandon Beach.

Their dog, Sparks, snuffled along, pulling tags of seaweed from the ocean. His red coat, caked with sand, dribbled an uneven channel behind him. Suddenly he was gone, only to return a moment later soppy wet from a quick plunge into the sea. He stopped, shook his body and then wagged his tail and barked, "Come on, let's race."

"Okay, Sparks, stay here so I can get a head start. Remember, you're faster than me." Sparks knew the rules. He sat erect, tongue panting, his large, Irish Setter head cocked to one side while waiting for his master's command. Brad took off, his toes digging into the wet, packed sand, making a trail of small footprints behind him. After he got a little way ahead, he shouted over his shoulder, "Sparks, come!" Each evening Sparks had scrambled after him, but each time it took him a little longer to catch Brad's churning legs.

Back there on the darkening beach, seven-year-old Brad spun out his fantasy: *The moon is a silver disk bobbing far out on the horizon, I can run to it. The ocean covers the world … without air, without tiring, without ever stopping; I can run under the water. And Sparks will chase me forever.*

Sparks was killed the next year by a car, but Brad kept on running. Keep on running. *There is no contest; there is the wind at your back and there is running, just running.*

His pulse was steady and strong. He was ready.

The hand-offs by the second runners were lousy for both teams. When the stumbling baton passes finally got straightened out, Medford had about a five-yard lead. Brad became aware of a pair of eyes boring into the back of his head. He turned. There was Carlos with a smirk on his face that said, "I got your number, boy." Brad considered breaking the stare that linked them, but instead, he held it. Inside, he giggled at a sudden, wild-hair thought. Should he say it? *Shoot, why not? Say it.* "Hey man, ya know, there's a big honkin' hole in the back of your shorts."

Carlos's mouth opened wide, and he whirled around trying to see and feel for the hole. He was frantic until Brad laughed, pointing an "I got ya finger" at him. Carlos stepped forward, red-faced, lower lip jutted out, but the crowd noise erupted, stopping him before he got to Brad. Both of them looked at the other runners: Jesus had caught the Medford kid. They were about hundred yards off, and the starter was calling frantically to Brad and Carlos to get in position. Each wanted the inside lane, but the starter motioned Brad to that spot.

Carlos glared. "You saw what happened in the hundred, man. Different race, same whipping."

Brad bent at the waist, legs flexed ready to spring from the first chalk line, his right arm extended back, palm cupped for the pass. Jesus chugged toward him, trying to hold his speed and at the same time reach out and slap the baton into Brad's hand.

Thwack! He got it. A split-second later, Brad heard the sound of another solid hand-off. Carlos was right on his heels.

There is just running.

His strides were long and easy, so if Carlos wanted to burn it all now and pass, Brad would let him. But Carlos was no dummy. His breathing sounded steady and close behind Brad. He was going to let Brad set the pace and try to pass at the close. Knowing that, Brad slowed ever so slightly, almost inviting Carlos to pass, but trying to conserve the energy he had wasted on that earlier race.

There must have been wild cheering for both runners, but Brad didn't hear it. *There is just running.*

At about the three-hundred-meter mark, the last turn into the finish, Brad picked up the pace. The swish-swish of the other set of running legs shadowed him. Up on his toes, Brad was ready for the sprint home. But his legs began to scream, "We're tired!" They didn't respond with the one-hundred-percent acceleration it would take to win. No cramps, but no great lift either.

They were nearly finishing the final turn. Brad knew he would lose without the closing kick. It would be close, but he … would … lose! There was one small chance. One in a million, and without thinking, he went for it. Instead of hugging the inside edge of the track, he eased out to the second lane, giving Carlos the inside, the shorter distance lane. No runner ever did this – at least no sane runner.

Brad pictured his dad and Coach Goodwin, both with their eyes wide open, screaming, "No, Brad. No!" Probably the whole track team, wanting this victory as much as the state championship, was swearing at Brad.

Sure enough, here came Mr. Carlos. He was burning the track, and Brad knew in his heart he would not have had enough steam to catch this kid. Now in the lead, Carlos's long hair flopped from side to side.

Suddenly he was thrown off stride. Carlos lost his rhythm and fought to regain his balance. In that instant, Brad regained the lead. He heard an explosion of breath behind him and a word Brad didn't understand, but the meaning was clear. Most of the crowd probably hadn't even noticed Carlos's slight stumble on the soft spot in the track.

Brad called on all his reserves.

Pull!

Pull!

Pull!

His legs were not attached, they had no feeling, but they pumped – and they propelled Brad to the finish line a hair's breadth in front of Carlos.

Everyone on the field scrambled to touch Brad, to be a part of his win. His Dad, Coach Goodwin and Pat – who smiled a wide grin and pointed at the new Nikes. Brad nodded, "Yes, your shoes; our win." Justin stood next to his dad, mouth open wide in the first real show of emotion Brad had seen him demonstrate. It was one of sheer joy. Hands tussled Brad's hair, fingers jabbed him, arms hugged him, and wild, excited screams almost lifted him off the ground.

Victory was sweet.

Suddenly a light touch on his face made Brad turn away from his dad. Deep blue eyes pierced him, shutting out the chaotic noise around him. Crystal's look and her fingers on his cheek made him catch his breath. She radiated an indescribable smile as she leaned in close, her breath tickling his ear: "Call me."

It was perfect. Except for one nagging thought.

Chapter 10

"Have you thought about doing a little running, maybe having Brad help coach you?" Dad asks me while he drives us home from the meet.

"You're not answering me, Justin."

It was January 6th of this year that he last tried to coax me to join a physical education program. He thinks I don't get enough exercise and that I'm "a little too heavy." I don't like that push-up and weight-lifting stuff. Feeling sweat all over my body makes me creepy-crawly; besides, it makes me itch.

"I think you should try running the short sprints …" I know his eyes are sliding over to look at me. "I don't think you'd get too overheated."

Up till today, I would have just said, "No, Dad, I d … don't want to do that." But after watching the track meet and how cool it was to see Brad run, I think I could change my mind. After all,

I'm in regular high school now with new classes, and I could get a new attitude. That's a saying Mom always uses to help her change her way of thinking. "Get a new attitude," she says." It sometimes works for her, but I don't think it's ever worked for me. "Dad, I am go … going to change my attitude." When he hears me say this he almost runs the car off A Street, right near the Ashland Food Co-op.

"Whaaat? What did you say?"

I smile out loud 'cause I can't hold back the grin when I see Dad's surprise. I sneak a peek over my left shoulder, pretending not to look at him. "Mrs. Gargus gave out flyers the other day about a Special Olympic track meet in Ashland next month. I could learn how to r … run like a puma or jaguar by then."

"That would be … a cool deal, Justin."

"Dad, you are making fun of me, aren't you?"

"No, Justin, I'm just sharing a joke with you."

During the rest of the drive home, Dad hums the tune that is singing in my head, "Born to Run."

Mom has dinner almost ready for us when we get home at 6:12 p.m. We have to eat right away so Dad can get to work. Some food smells, like cabbage, make me sick, but tonight we have free-range chicken with steamed yams and corn and those smells are alright. And we almost always have a salad with a special dressing Dad makes about every week.

After I wash my hands, we sit down to dinner. I tell Mom all about the track meet and how my friend Brad was a hero, and that he had touched me and I didn't flinch, and …

Dad interrupted, "And Justin is considering, isn't that the right word, son? … considering taking up the noble sport of running."

The serving spoon in Mom's hand stops right over my dish. "Really, hon? You're thinking about that?" I nod my head. "How about if we get that old running movie from Block Buster for tomorrow night and watch it together?"

Taking the spoon from Mom and serving himself, Dad says, "Chariots of Fire." I remember that. Great flick."

My salad is in a bowl by itself. And Mom has put the orange yams on one side of my plate, the yellow corn opposite the yams, and the chicken right in the middle so that none of the food touches. I used to need everything in different plates, but I am getting used to just one or two plates now.

This is my private time. Dad is off to work, Mom is reading, and I don't have to go to bed for an hour and twenty-two minutes. I play my birthday CD as loud as Mom will allow. The speakers in my room are last year's Christmas gift. "Oh, It's Just My Imagination." I sing with Smokey Robinson for three minutes and forty-seven seconds. I love that song because that's what I do, use my imagination. Especially when I think about girls. I saw that girl get up real close to Brad after the race. It looked like she kissed him on the ear. And she was pretty, too. I wonder what that feels like. Do they like each other? I could ask Brad. No I couldn't.

Right after dinner I watched *Wheel of Fortune.* I never told my folks that the reason I watch every night is to see Vanna White. She's a real cool deal lady. A friend at my old school told me that she's over forty, but I don't care. I touch my ear imagining Vanna kissing it.

The song ends, but my imagination keeps on running. I think about that time last year when Lori and I were alone after class. She came over close to me and looked at me like I was her favorite food. "Justin, I really like you." Then she stuck her neck out as far as it could go and put her lips on mine. I didn't know what to do, so I just stood there and let her. When she started to open her mouth a crack, I pulled away. I don't like the idea of her spit in my mouth. That's gross.

Chapter 11

Brad barely heard the TV voices airing bits and pieces about murder, armies and politicians. As always, the six o'clock news invaded the Lockwood household as newscaster Brian Williams (his dad called him Brian) related one tragic story after another. As always, Brad had escaped to his room; it was a place to hide, to stretch out and to think. He sat on his bed, head propped under his folded arms, legs extended in front of him.

Since Thursday was his mom's late evening at the hospital each week, his dad and Brad usually cooked dinner together. His dad saw how tired Brad was from the track meet, so he offered to cook by himself. That usually meant hot dogs cut up into some canned beans with a wedge of lettuce and tomato on the side. Even Brad sided with Amy about their dad's so-called well-balanced meals. His mom and dad. What a pair. To their friends, they looked like model parents on one of those old TV family shows.

Just think, I might have been Ricky Nelson. If I were Justin, I'd be singing, "Hello Marylou, good-bye … Yeah, right. But when nobody was around, Geezo, it seemed like they just couldn't agree on anything, especially the stupidest little things. "Lydia, you know I just can't handle fruit when it's overripe."

Like Dad, get your own melon, why don't you? Brad swore he would never be like his dad. Never!

Brad looked at the giant wall posters of track stars surrounding him. The special one, the most cherished, was tacked to the ceiling above his bed. There, sprinting head-on toward the finish line in his green and yellow track outfit was "Pre," Steve Prefontaine, Oregon's all-time greatest distance runner, one of the best ever in the world. But in the deepening shadows of dusk, the dark brooding eyes of his hero, usually targeted on the tape at the finish, now bored into Brad, asking, "What did you do, Brad?"

A set of H. O. trains and a station sat on the table across from his bed. It had been there since the Christmas Brad was six and his folks decided he was ready for a hobby. That year he had the measles followed by an ear infection. The trains were his relief from the high fever and the echoing, unreal sounds that bounced around in his brain. He spent hours, day after day, putting them together, taking them apart, and running them in circles.

He sat up, reached over for one of the tiny engines, his fingers moving over its fine details. Familiar, so familiar. But today there was little comfort in the touch or the memories. He tossed the engine back onto the table and leaned back against the pillows. Today these little-boy things didn't help with his or "Pre's" question.

Brad tossed a wiffle ball toward the wastebasket. "Missed." His voice sounded like a stranger to him. Shooting baskets or being Ricky Nelson was not why he copped out of helping with dinner.

He thought he understood about winning. And losing too. But today he was not so sure. *I set him up, praying Carlos's foot would find the soft spot and wobble just enough, just enough for me to sneak by and win.* Sneak, that word gnawed at his gut and settled inside him like one of Dad's meals. He locked his fingers behind his head looking up at the poster. "Carlos wouldn't have lost if he hadn't stumbled," he explained to "Pre" as if to excuse himself. But "Pre's" eyes just glared back – he didn't buy his excuse.

Brad lifted his head, sucking in the familiar odor filling his room. There was no smell quite like beans scorched on the bottom of a pot. Burned pot and burned beans. Yum! A glance at the clock on his nightstand told him there was still about five minutes left till the news was over. Five more minutes of hickory bean smoke would gag everyone in the house unless he …

His dad leaned across the restaurant table whispering to Brad, "Thanks for grabbing the beans off the burner and opening all the windows." He covered a laugh with his napkin. "You saved my beans." Another one of his dad's puns that only he laughed at. His mom pretended not to hear him just like she didn't smell the lingering odor filling the house when she got home. Tonight she played it cool. After all, this was a victory day for the Lockwoods. First thing she said when she came through the door was, "Hey everybody, let's celebrate Brad's big win and go for pizza."

Angelo's was the numero uno hangout so even though the four of them wanted some private space, lots of kids and parents came by to say, "Great race, Brad." There was a steady stream of thumbs-up and slaps on the back. It was embarrassing, but Brad began to like the attention. He looked over at Dad tearing into his salad. Yeah, like he said, it was hard to put a single emotion into a little container and be certain that this sensation was exactly the way you felt at that moment. Life wasn't that easy.

But it was good, real good being with his mom, dad and Amy, all together, laughing; Brad's mouth hurt from smiling so much. It was cool that so many people told him, "way to go."

"Hey star, want a slice of my veggie pizza?" Amy asked as strings of cheese stretched from her mouth to the slice she was holding at arm's length. Everybody laughed. "In your honor, I decided to pass up the soy cheese pizza tonight. What the hell, a little cholesterol won't kill me."

His mom raised her glass ready to take a drink. "You could try to watch your language at the table, young lady, and God forbid you should add a pound to your skinny frame. Look at her, Fred, she's all skin and …"

"Tofu!" Brad blurted out, fighting to hold back an explosion of laughter. He just couldn't get a grip. It was one of those times when you couldn't figure out what to do with the food in your mouth. You couldn't swallow it because you were gagging, so along with his raucous laugh, a large blob of half-chewed zucchini sailed across the table and glommed itself to the bottom of his mom's up-turned glass. Splat!

People from the other booths turned and stared at the hysterical, out-of-control Lockwood family.

The drive home later was quieter, his mom reminding everyone that even though they had partied, tomorrow was Friday, a school day and workday. Today was a great day.

Brad sat on the back step, his shoulders hunched low and hands shoved deep into his jacket pockets as protection against the chill April night air. The light from Mrs. Stucky's next door sent a splash of brilliant yellow across the otherwise dark, bare porch. It was too early in the season to put out the deck chairs even though the days were getting warmer.

The frogs didn't seem to mind the cold air though. They chirruped a storm. The far-away wail of a train coming up the tracks near Highway 99 sang a lonely song not unlike his H. O. train set upstairs.

"Brad, is that you?" Amy's voice covered the distant train sound. Wearing her flannel bathrobe against the cold, she stepped out onto the porch. "Super day for you, huh?"

Without turning to her, "Oh, hi. Yeah. I just needed ... eh, I needed some fresh air. Too much pizza to be able to sleep."

"Too much, huh?" She moved a step closer and touched his shoulder. "Seems like you ate only one or two slices, hardly up to your usual half dozen." She gathered her robe around her and sat down beside him, placing her head on his shoulder. The scent of lavender bath water swirled around them. "I know you're my baby brother, but sometimes it feels like you're my big brother. Either way, you are B-B to me." She squeezed in closer.

She hadn't called him B-B (baby-brother) very often since that big-time mess-up. He still remembered the incident. *How* he remembered. He had been playing in the den and his ball had rolled into the garage. Somehow he locked himself in, and Amy, who had her headset on listening to music, didn't hear him screaming and crying. It seemed like hours before Mom heard and came to rescue him. But what Brad remembered most was later that evening. He was still so angry that he threw a walk-man at Amy, popping her on the head.

"Is it about that girl, Crystal?"

He realized that for the first time in weeks, Crystal had not invaded his mind. There were some things more important than girls. He smiled to himself thinking about a guy he used to know, named Charlie. Charlie the Hound they called him because he was always sniffing after girls. If he had heard Brad say there were more important things than girls, he would have sneered and said, "Name two."

"Naw, it's not her." He turned toward Amy, noticing that the light reflected in her eyes was making them "back porch yellow." He hadn't planned to talk to anybody about today's race with Carlos. But the way his head was buzzing, wondering if what he did was okay or if it was plain bogus, he figured, why not talk to Amy? He looked up at the bugs circling around Mrs. Stucky's porch light. They were probably getting up the courage to plunge into the bulb and commit suicide.

Then he looked away and sucked in a long breath. He would like to have as much courage as those insects. Amy took his hand, and soon he was pouring out the whole story of how he beat Carlos in the relay. Afterwards, the stillness of the night held them both in the moment. Amy was thinking – he could tell by that little shape she made with her lips.

"Brad … Brad, I can tell you are really worried, but I don't understand. Carlos tripped and you won. What's so bad about that?" These were not the soothing, compassionate words he imagined she'd say. His mouth was all dry like after sucking on a lemon. "Yeah," he said half-heartedly. "I … I see what you mean." He got up to leave, the wooden deck creaking under his shifting weight.

"B-B?" He turned as he heard Amy stepping toward him. Tears were glistening in her eyes. "I'm sorry. I just don't know how to help. I don't know how to do a lot of things." He hugged her tightly to his chest, like a big brother.

Chapter 12

I spend most Saturday mornings at home working on reading and science with my tutor. I like to read but have trouble with long words or when the print is all squiggly. They call that type of print, italics. It's weird.

Mom called and cancelled the appointment for today because instead of being tutored this morning, I am waiting for Brad with my mom on the field at Pearblossom School. He was supposed to meet me at ten o'clock sharp, but he's already three minutes late. Yesterday when I asked him if he could help me learn to run better, he said he didn't think he'd have time. I bet he wants to spend time with his new girlfriend. Instead of meeting me at our regular spot, he told me to meet him farther down the hall. Because there was so much running and pushing and noise in the halls, I waited with my back pressed against the janitor's door.

I saw him and his girlfriend stop way down by the attendance office. They touched hands for a long time and whispered something no one else could hear. That girl never looks at me, or says hello. I don't know why she doesn't. I wonder if I will ever be touched by a girl the way she touched Brad. Could someone who's pretty and nice put her face up to mine and want to be more than just friends?

I push myself harder against the janitor's door trying to make myself invisible.

The clouds float over in dark waves from the pear orchards that almost surround our school, and there is a cold breeze that makes the dirt on the track blow in little whirlwinds. The wind touches my face and I scrunch down into my jacket. Mom thinks I'm just cold.

"Don't be such a worry-wart, Justin. He said he'd be here."

I'd better change my attitude or Mom will ask me why I have my nose in my coat. "Mom, warts are those big ugly things on witches' no … noses. I don't look anything like that."

She smiles and takes my hand for a moment. "No … no Justin, you don't look anything like that."

"It was a cool deal that Brad called me back last night to tell me he could make it this morning. I think maybe his girlfriend is busy today."

Mom says, "Look, there's Brad on his bike over there across the field."

"I see him. Man, oh man, Brad's going to show me how to be the fastest kid at the Special Olympics."

This was a bad idea. All around bad. It was too darned cold to be out on the track, Brad thought as he rode to the track field. The giant fans placed every couple of hundred yards in the orchards spun loudly, stirring up the air to help prevent the blossoms from getting frostbite. His dad's crew was out before sun-up lighting smudge pots and checking on the fans. He had worked with the crew last spring on the mornings when the frost seemed likely to settle on the trees. He never got used to the frigid mornings, the racket or getting up in the dark at four. Luckily, his dad had said that one season for Brad was enough to appreciate how delicate the blossoms are.

The blades on the fans made a whirr, whirr, whirr racket as Brad dug further down in his windbreaker keeping the spring frost out of his bones. He figured it would be okay working with Justin once they got warmed up and started running. Too bad he'd miss his usual long Saturday bike ride. But that was scratched the moment he happened to mention to Mom that Justin had asked for help … and that Brad had turned him down. The rest of their conversation was indelibly printed in his mind.

"What do you mean you turned him down?" his mom stopped studying her hospital aide manual and drilled him with her eyes. "Where's your head, Bradley. And even more, where's your heart?"

"Mom, I've got a full load; there are track practices, homework, and don't forget my Saturday bike ride." He turned as if to go into the kitchen.

"Don't walk out of the room on me, young man! We're not through here!"

Brad felt like he had been flattened by a sledgehammer. He slowly turned and faced her. "It would be hard to pull off working with him during track season. Honest, I don't mind helping the kid, but …" His breath suddenly disappeared like the air rushing out of a balloon.

"When did you have in mind helping him train for track, during football season? Sit down!" she ordered. He flopped down on the easy chair.

"I'm sorry I got so steamed, but I can't believe you turned him down after our talk the other night about caring and responsibility. Did our conversation just fly out of your brain? Did it mean *anything* to you?"

He really didn't want to give up his ride, or his date with Crystal later in the day, but he didn't think it was a good idea to cross his mom either. Truth was, yesterday's track meet and being with Crystal had sort of jumped to the front of his thoughts.

"You're right, Mom, absolutely right. I'm sorry too. I'll call Justin right now and tell him to meet me tomorrow morning." *And I have to call Crystal and cancel our date too. I'm sure she'll understand.* But somehow, his thoughts didn't convince him. She could be a little possessive.

After the workout and Brad's coaching, Justin lay sprawled on the grass facing the sun with his eyes closed. Next to the bleachers Brad and Mrs. Evans, Justin's Mom, stood quietly talking. She wore a dark jacket with the hood up and scarf around her neck. Her hair peeking out from under the hood was dark, but beginning to streak with grey. She was was probably about the same age as Brad's mom, but didn't seem in as good shape.

"Your influence on him is profound," she began.

"I don't really know what I did to deserve … eh, to have made such a big impression on Justin."

"Well, most times he doesn't show it, but I think just your being with him and caring about him has affected him a lot. And it doesn't hurt that you are somebody important at school. Other kids look up to you, and so does Justin."

Brad turned away, checking out the birds on the phone line, hiding what he was sure was his flushed face. To some degree, he did care about Justin, but not enough to willingly give up a bike ride or spending time alone with Crystal – not without some heavy shots from his mom. He was sure guilt showed on his face like a big red pimple. After a long silence, he asked, "I can see why he wants to learn to run, after seeing the track meet and all, but I've been curious about how Justin got so interested in the details of oldies rock?"

She looked over at her still son and put her hands in her pockets. "Well Brad, you know that many people with autism have the ability to spontaneously remember details and facts about – well, like birthdates, sequences, the order of the U.S. presidents, things like that."

"Yeah, I've noticed that, especially with history dates and other stuff. But what about the music?"

"It was my brother, Justin's Uncle Ned, who was instrumental in steering him to his devotion to early rock music." Brad wondered if Mrs. Evans had used the word "instrumental" as a pun referring to music. Naw, only he thought of strange stuff like that. "He has never mentioned Uncle Ned to me."

"Well, he's sort of out of the picture. We hear from him now and then from some exotic island or Eastern European country. He's been a musician for almost twenty years. Back when Justin was about four, we visited Ned in Marin, near San Francisco. He had a rock group and a little recording studio in his garage. The three of us came in during a rehearsal when they were running through an old Elton John tune called 'Your Song.'" She pressed her tongue out like Justin did when he is puzzled. "Have you heard of him?"

"Eh … yeah, I think so."

"Anyway, Justin fell in love with the lyrics and the melody. He thought Uncle Ned had written the song for him. Then years later, when he heard Elton John on the radio, he got all excited and came running to tell me, 'They are playing the song Uncle Ned wrote for me on the radio.'" He was so disappointed when I told him the truth, but he got over it. Ned sent tapes and CDs of his recordings and lots of other famous artists' albums to Justin who devoured them, and soon it became a natural part of his curiosity to research each of the artists and songs he heard. So that's the story of how he got hooked on that music."

"So what happened to Uncle Ned?"

"He came to visit us three or four times, but then his group, 'The Five Echoes,' had a modest hit. They went on the road, and they've been touring the world ever since. He still sends CDs now and again; in fact, we just got a check from him to buy a belated birthday gift for Justin. But it's not the same, and Justin misses him."

Just then, Justin sat up, arching his back. Soon his mechanical voice boomed over the noisy sound of the fans. "I'm ready to r ... run again."

Brad and Mrs. Evans arched their eyebrows and smiled.

"You got it, Justin."

Chapter 13

Just as he was dressing out for P.E., Brad got the note to report to Mrs. Gargus. At first he thought he'd messed up dealing with Justin, but then he remembered that she wanted to have a conference every couple of weeks with him just to see how things were going. The room was empty except for Mrs. Gargus and Kenny, who were seated at a worktable. As usual, Kenny was whining.

"My mom said I could go." He folded his arms in front of him as though that should settle the argument.

"Kenny, it's not that we don't want you to go, but ..." Mrs. Gargus groped for the right words, "... but only those in the science classes are invited. You remember we talked about this quite a few times?"

"But my mom ... oh, I hate this school. And I hate this class!"

Mrs. Gargus came over and sat on the floor next to Kenny's chair. She took both of his hands in hers and spoke very quietly. "I understand, Kenny. It can be tough and we did our best to get you on this Crater Lake overnight trip. I know there's no way to make it up to you, but our plans are for our class to visit the water slide at Emigrant Lake as soon as it opens."

"You promise?" Kenny said in a hoarse whisper.

"I promise I'll do everything I can to make it happen. Now, why don't you do some Math Blasters on the computer while I speak with Brad?" She went over to her desk to look for some papers as Kenny slowly made his way to the bank of computers at the back of the room.

Brad looked out the window to check on the snowfall. Dark clouds were shrouding the sky, but the ground was covered with a filmy white powder. The snow was coming down steadily. Not in huge puffy flakes, but very cool for a snowfall this late in the year. He pictured the trees around the lake veiled in white, and the fun he and Crystal would have throwing snowballs at each other. He could almost feel the chill of melting snow making little streams of cold water run down his face. It was not just a coincidence that he would be there with a girl named Crystal.

The conference with Mrs. Gargus was easy; they had worked out a sub schedule to help Justin while Brad was gone Friday and Saturday. The science department had scheduled the outdoor activity for the weekend that the track team didn't have a meet.

Justin was disappointed when Brad told him there would be no training this week for the Special Olympics meet. Justin said, "I'll make you a deal, like on the TV show *Let's Make a Deal*. We skip this practice, but you promise to come next month to my track meet, just like I go to yours." Brad had to laugh to himself. *This kid is really sharp, playing the angles, working the deals to get what he wants.* Brad didn't have the heart to refuse. Besides, this would score heavy points with his mom. He smiled and touched Justin's shoulder ever so slightly. "Yeah, buddy, we'll go together, okay?"

The food simmering in the kitchen sent its tangy odor throughout Crystal's house, so when Brad came through the front door, he didn't need any directions; he just followed his nose right to the kitchen. It was so cool that her mom had invited him over to help prepare food for tomorrow's trip. She even picked them up from school, and her step-dad had promised to take him home when they finished.

The kitchen was smaller than at Brad's house, not so many appliances cluttering up the place. There were photographs on the walls – sort of a gallery of Crystal growing up, some with her step-dad, some with what must be her real father. Brad laughed to himself at the one showing her smiling with all her front teeth missing. He would be sure to tease her about that one.

On the stove, a large sputtering pot of thick soup reached out with its moist smell, teasing and inviting Brad. *Oh, if only your dinners smelled this good, Mom. But then I'd weigh two hundred pounds and be a shot-putter instead of a sprinter.* Maybe Brad could wangle an invitation for dinner.

Crystal covered the cutting board in front of them with slices of bread, each desperately wanting a topping to help make its true purpose in life happen.

"These guys want to become sandwiches when they grow up," Brad said.

Crystal raised an eyebrow. "They what?" Her tone was flat, like she couldn't believe he had really said that.

Oh man, when would he learn to shut up? "Oh, nothing. You know, we need to get busy and do the peanut butter. You have to put it on first or you can spoil the best peanut butter and jelly sandwich ever made. I'm positively the world's greatest expert, ya know."

As she smiled, her whole face lit up and her eyes closed down to tiny slits. She wore a bright yellow, cotton apron over her skirt and blouse. It said "kitchen police" under a cartoon of Garfield trying to break into a bulging, locked refrigerator. Even with her apron on, Crystal's curves were curving.

Brad refused the apron she offered even though he wore one at home when he and Dad did the Thursday evening meals. Maybe she would think he looked like a wimp. "So what we do first is glob the peanut butter into a bowl like this. And here's the secret, you have to put it in the microwave on medium for exactly twenty seconds. Any more than that and it gets too runny."

Crystal saluted, "Yes sir, let's go for it." As she took the bowl from him, her hand touched his and lingered a moment. Electricity!

"Brad? Are you going to let me get it in the microwave?"

"Oh yeah, sorry." *Oh, man, she must think I'm such a doofus for holding onto her hand like that.*

She put the bowl in the microwave and turned it on. "Twenty, nineteen …"

And I'm going to be with her for the next two days, just her and me. Oh yeah, and about forty-five other kids and six teachers. Oh well.

"… three, two, one."

The dinger went off and Crystal took the bowl out of the microwave. "Wow. That is super neat. You're right, it's perfect; creamy but not runny just like you said." She twirled the spoon, and with a flourish, smoothed the butter onto the bread. Brad watched every move. "Come on, mister, don't just be standing there like a dork watching me. You do the jelly. There are three different kinds. Oh, and don't mark the sandwich bags; that's so we'll be surprised when we bite into them."

"Listen, I promised Pat we'd bring some extra for him. He's got an appetite like a pack animal."

Crystal's body straightened, and a little twitch etched the corner of her mouth. "Oh, is Pat coming? I didn't know." She went back to smearing the peanut butter, but she did it a little faster than before. When she finished a slice, she picked it up and took a bite. Then she turned the bread around so the part she bit faced him. "Here." She licked her lips slowly. "You taste it."

He did. They faced one another in the middle of the kitchen, each slowly gumming the gooey stuff. Tongues, teeth, lips, all were covered with goop. She looked really funny the way she was trying to lick the stuff off of her teeth. Suddenly she giggled, pointing at him. He must have looked as silly as she did. They both broke up into peanut butter hysteria.

"Hey kids, is everything going all right in there?" Crystal's Mom's voice called. Brad took in a long, deep breath trying to gain control. "I'd better finish doing the jelly."

Crystal straightened her apron and tried to get it together so she could answer. "Yeah, Mom." She struggled to get the words out without cracking up again. "We're doing fine. You can tell Dad that we'll be ready to clean up in a few minutes." She made a face that asked, "Did I do okay?" Finally, she and Brad settled down and made the rest of the sandwiches.

As they bagged them, she asked, "Brad, we're not going to spend time with Pat, are we?" She raised her eyes on the words "are we," emphasizing how much she wanted to be with Brad. Alone! He knew his own eyes went big and fixed on her questioning face.

"Brad?"

"Well, eh …"

Suddenly the deal he had made with Pat popped into his brain. Geezo, Pat was bringing his dad's telescope so they could check out the stars from the utter darkness of Crater Lake. "Sounds cool, bro." Brad had committed himself to working on the science project with Pat days ago. But now?

"Well, what?" She took a wet paper towel, stepped close, very close, and wiped his lower lip. Her peanut butter breath was on him.

"Well, no. Pat's doing this big science thing so he'll be plenty busy. It's going to be just you and me."

He smiled a sickly smile, hoping she couldn't read his mind. Did she suspect he was having a huge fight with himself? "Oh," he justified the unwanted smile with a small joke. "Just you and me and, of course, Mrs. Schofield."

Crystal didn't laugh. "You and me. Kind of like, going steady?" She gave him "that" look. Schofield, Pat and her mom, who was sitting in the next room, they all just dribbled from his mind like melted peanut butter off the end of a spoon. With his heart beating wildly, he leaned over and kissed her mouth. If there was a charge when their hands had touched before, this was an electric storm tingling every cell in his body.

She pulled away from him slowly. When he opened his eyes, there were hers, unblinking, piercing deep into his.

"Hummm?" she asked.

Brad swallowed, hardly able to speak. "Eh, yeah, kind of like that."

I don't take my eyes off the shifting shadows on my wall to make sure they don't turn into monsters or ghosts. I don't believe in that stuff, but sometimes, late at night, if I have a bad dream, the shadows look scary. They change shapes and form things that I don't like. The wind blowing through the leaves of the oak tree outside my window makes a low, howling noise that sounds like the dead. My folks are asleep so I don't want to wake them after a bad dream like I did a long time ago. They had me climb in bed with them, but I'm too old for that now so I just keep my eyes on the shadows.

I was sound asleep, but my dream was so real that it woke me up. I like dreams about being able to hug people and not getting upset. In my dreams I can do that, but tonight I dreamt I was with Brad playing in the snow. The sun was shining, and we were having lots of fun building a snowman, throwing snow, and rolling down a steep hill. We were laughing when suddenly the sun went dark and it got black as tar. Brad called me, "Justin, Justin. I'll take care of you; put out your hand." I did that and we gripped hands so tight it hurt.

"I'm not afraid, Brad, I'm doing good." But even in my dream I felt my stomach almost come up my throat. I could tell I was tangling up in my blankets and knew it was a dream, but I couldn't escape the fear or the dream.

"We'll be okay. I can find our way back to the school bus," Brad said, but his hand lost its grip and slipped away from mine. He was falling down a steep hill and I heard him yell like he fell a thousand feet. Then there was only the sound of the wind. I had lost my friend, and I cried.

I woke up with tears on my cheek and my heart pounding. I know it was only a dream, but I am afraid anyway. I'll watch the shadows the rest of the night.

Chapter 14

Exhaust fumes filled the car as his mom backed the Mazda out of the driveway. "Bradley, would you please close the window? That smell is horrible; besides, it's cold."

Brad heard, but her voice seemed distant. His body was in the car, but his mind was still in bed buried under his blanket. His eyes were closed; Crystal's sweet lips were just inches from his. They got closer, closer. Ohhh, her face was so near, it would be carved into his memory forever.

"Bradley! Hello to earth, do you read me?"

"Huh? Oh, sure." His arms and hands, along with his brain, were not functioning. With concentrated effort, he rolled up the window.

She stole a quick look at her son while steering the car around a corner. "Say, are you all right? You're like a zombie this morning. Maybe you're getting sick and shouldn't go on the trip." She shifted the car into fourth as they drove along Colver Road toward school. There were small frozen spots on the sides of the road, but no snow was left, at least not here on the valley floor. The mountains would be something else.

"I'm okay, honest." *But how okay can you be when you're in love?* Did Crystal feel this way too? Maybe they could talk about important stuff like this on the trip.

"You said something about stopping for Pat?"

"Pat?"

"Yes, your best friend, Pat. Remember?"

Remember? Oh sure, he remembered. He remembered thinking about him half the night, trying to find a righteous way to tell him they wouldn't be working together on the science project. Easy. Like, "You see, Pat, I'm going steady now and the thing is, to be cool, you have to be with your girlfriend. You understand?" Right, and it also meant messing over your best friend. Or how about, "I know I promised, but that was before Crystal. Anyhow, we didn't make enough extra sandwiches for you." That was a real winner. No matter how many ways he tried, all his excuses were lame.

"… on the corner over there. Bradley! You haven't heard one word I said."

"What? Oh, I'm sorry, Mom. What's on the corner?"

"Pat. We're picking him up on Talent Avenue at ten after. And there he is."

Yep, it was Pat all right, waving, smiling and making faces at them. He had a big box at his feet. The telescope! Pat had remembered the damned telescope. Maybe if they pretended not to see him, he would get to school too late for the bus. Sure, without Pat on the trip, there would be no problem. But Mom had already seen him and immediately pulled over.

Pat opened the back door and leaned in, "How about getting off your skinny bottom and helping me with this telescope?"

The answer throbbed in Brad's head. *I'll do it now, but you can kiss off any more help for the rest of this project.* Now there was one Brad didn't think of last night. But like the other excuses, this one sucked!

By nine the two large yellow school buses groaned, straining up Highway Sixty-Two climbing into the Cascade range and on up to Crater Lake. The kids in Brad's bus had finally settled down after a chaotic and disorganized get-away from school. Casual chatter and the loud crunches of tortilla chips replaced the yelling and screaming that happened when some nimrod stole someone's hat and played keep-away with it.

Brad sat in the aisle seat, so his legs had a place to park. The bus came within sight of the Rogue River at the small town of Shady Cove. They were now above the fog-covered valley. The snow level was getting deeper already and would be massive at the six-thousand-foot elevation mark.

A couple more hours – an eternity – until they would be there. Torture! Brad squirmed in his seat, unable to find a comfortable position. This must be what the victors did to punish captured knights in medieval days: Put the vanquished on one bus and his damsel on the other one. Then they let this dude see her whiz by, a flutter of her hankie, a thrown kiss. Then gone. He prayed for a flat tire, anything to stop the bus.

Closing his eyes, Brad took in a long breath and sighed deeply; he could almost smell her rose-water cologne. It was so close, so real, so … Wait a minute, actually the scent was Sarah's, who sat next to him. He had never noticed it on her before. Of course, he never sat this close to her either. As Coach Goodwin's daughter, he saw her all the time on the track. She always seemed to be where she was needed, ready to get somebody water or their starting blocks. She had been a lot of help to Brad and he enjoyed rapping with her. It was like having a junior coach for the team. Really sharp.

Sarah was considered a brain. Her name was always on some list: Leadership, Honor Roll, whatever. Brad glanced over at her as she sat with her eyes closed. Tight brown curls tumbled down, framing her oval face and strong chin. Her nose was tiny; almost not there. She was a smaller, prettier version of Coach. And she had something he didn't have: a dimple on her cheek, but it only blossomed when she smiled. Hey, let's face it, Sarah was cute, but she was only an eighth-grader and not his type.

She opened her eyes and stretched her arms out in front of her. "Ahhhh, that's good. We there yet?"

"Come on, Goodwin. Shady Cove, first leg. We got miles to go before …"

"Before we sleep. Miles to go before we sleep."

"Huh?"

She jabbed him playfully in the ribs. "Get with it, Lockwood. Robert Frost? Poetry? Shoot, never mind."

"Hey, I got it, man. I got it." He should get her together with Pat. They would be so mellow, so right.

"So did you and Juan patch up your blowout yet?" Geezo, Sarah never tiptoed into anything, she just hit the long-jump stripe and leaped all arms and legs into any situation. Of course, Juan and Brad were still science partners and they worked together every day. But man, it was all business: "Pass me the beaker, please; do we have to write down all these notes?" The fun was missing.

Brad had tried to talk to him, explain how he really felt. But every time he said something, it only seemed to make things worse. Like: "Juan, listen, man. I don't even notice when you or Daniel come into a room. Well sure, I notice, but I mean, it's not like I see you guys as different. You're all the same to me." Shoot, it never came out making sense, at least not what he really meant. He just wanted Juan to be his friend again. But Juan would look at him, nod and just go on with the project. He did tell Brad he heard about the race he had won. Right! Great! That was something Brad really needed to hear; what a hero. He beat Carlos, a guy he had practically crippled.

The bus shifted gears, making a loud grinding noise. Sarah sat blinking, waiting for Brad's answer about patching things up with Juan. But instead of answering, he simply turned and looked out the window at the thickening forests closing in on the highway.

The second bus pulled along side of theirs as they climbed the steep canyon road next to Lost Creek Reservoir. As it passed, from one of the windows, Brad saw a familiar smile, a pair of glasses and an exuberant wave hello. Not his lady this time. Pat. Good ol' trusting, going-to-be-sitting-out-in-the-cold-dark-night-at-Crater-Lake-all-by-himself Pat. Brad might as well throw all his friends out into the bottomless waters of Crater Lake.

Sarah looked at him deeply, and for an instant it seemed like she understood what pain he was going through.

The bus doors swung open, and a rush of frosty air tweaked their noses and pinched their ears. Wow! It was a good thing the "must bring" list included long johns. The kids scrambled off the buses and formed into prearranged small work groups. Hats, down jackets and gloves made everybody look like roly-poly characters from a cartoon movie.

Brad and Crystal exchanged a quick hi-five. "See ya at lunch," and then it was off for their late-morning workshops. The kids in Brad's group included Juan and Sarah. Their first assignment was to measure snowdrift heights in various locations around the lodge and lake. Brad was glad he had brought sunglasses. Those who said, "Sunglasses are for wimps" were stumbling around like blind people unable to shield their eyes from the sun's intense reflection off the snow. Brad had been up here before; every year it seemed there was a cousin or somebody who came to visit and they just had to see Crater.

"Hey, come on, everybody. Let's do it," shouted Juan as he scaled a huge fortress-like drift between the parking lot and the rim of the lake.

Brad scampered up after him, hoping for some healing of their friendship in the cold mountain air. "Hey, Juan, how'd you like me to be your personal park guide?" He dug his boots into the fresh snow and scrambled to the top after his used-to-be friend.

Juan stood there facing the lake, tears streaming down his cheeks. "You all right?" Brad said feeling a little embarrassed by Juan's emotional show.

"I ain't ever seen nothin' like this. Never! I seen pictures, but this is so blue, and so big." He sat down cross-legged, shaking his head and muttering, "like a big blue marble."

"I know what you mean, exactly what you mean." And he remembered how he had felt the first time he saw the lake years ago. Brad plopped down next to him and rested his arm on Juan's shoulder. He had never put his arm around another boy before, at least not to show him that he cared about him. Juan turned and smiled, wiping his cheeks with a puffy mitten.

"Thanks, man."

Brad hadn't really needed all those stupid words to let Juan know how he felt about him.

Sarah made it up the rise and stood beside them, her breath puffing as she spoke. "Unreal. Look at the way the rim of snow makes a lace necklace around the whole lake."

"Robert Frost?"

"Naa, Sarah Goodwin. But cool, huh? Whoa, lookee there!" She pointed out the island floating over on the left side of the lake. "That's Wizard Island, and in the summer you can take a boat ride out there. I went on it last year and the guide said this was the deepest lake in the U.S."

Shouts and whoops flew from the parking lot, and so did a barrage of snowballs. "Hey you snow bunnies up there, didn't you hear the whistle? It's time for lunch."

The three of them jumped to their feet and yelled back, "Oh yeah? Not before you guys eat snow!"

"You better run for cover, because you're gonna get it good!"

They fell, rolled and tumbled down the embankment, throwing globs of white puffy "whipped cream" at their attackers.

Brad had been able to avoid Pat during lunch and the afternoon workshops without being too obvious, he hoped. Finding a little snow cave with Crystal to share their peanut butter and jelly sandwiches along with a thermos of hot chocolate was ab-so-lut-ely the best. Wrapped in giggles and laughs, they didn't notice the cold at all.

But now at supper in the lodge cafeteria with a cardboard serving tray filled with food in front of him, Brad had no appetite. Not that the smell of over-cooked canned peas and corn could stimulate it a whole lot. He watched Pat go through the line, piling on the food and finding his way to the small table where Brad was sitting. Well, here's the last meal, he thought. Let the execution begin.

"Hey, bro," Brad flashed a politician's smile.

"What a day! I mean it's unreal. Like everything's going ..." he made his hand into a glider shape sailing it over the soft rolls, "smooooth."

Brad nodded. Yeah, things were going smooth all right. His fingers twisted and untwisted the paper tablecloth.

"You're not eating much – and saying less. What's the matter, lover? Crystal bite off your tongue at lunch?" He laughed so hard at his joke that water spilled from his cup. As he sopped up the table, it was like he got the vibes that something was not right. He suddenly stopped what he was doing and pushed his glasses up on his nose. "What?"

Hearing that simple word "what?" he felt like one of the sharp icicles that hung from the eves of the lodge was plunged into his chest. Brad swallowed hard and looked away, staring at the glass eyes of the mounted stag head that hung over the massive fireplace. "I eh, I got this prob-lem, see. About our plans to set up the telescope ..."

Pat's eyes went huge, magnified by his thick specks. "Yeah, what about it?" His voice suddenly had an edge to it.

"I know we talked about doing this experiment after dinner and all."

"No, we didn't just talk about it." Pat poked his index finger at Brad. "We, you and me, we made plans to set this sucker up and ... you're backing out! That's what it is, isn't it? You're screwing me over, right?"

Brad started to reach for his water, but his hand didn't seem to want to obey him, so he skipped that idea. His mouth would have to stay filled with cotton. "It's not like that. I, Crystal and me, we just need to spend a little time together, ya know, alone."

"Right. You and her, alone. Not the two of *us*. The two of *you*." He pushed his chair back from the table. "When did this hot little plot hatch from the egg? Last night? Or at kissey-kissey lunch? I hope, at least, it was *after* we spent two weeks getting this project ready. Why didn't you just come right out and tell me to forget the telescope, forget our plans? I get it! I see who's more important, bro ... "

Brad closed his eyes, trying to gather his thoughts for an answer, one that would get him out from in front of Pat's firing squad. Pat stood up, his chair crashing down behind him. Every head in the place turned toward them. "Big man! So you're a star now and you can do what you want. You don't care *who* you mess over! Well, I'm sure glad to find out now instead of when I might be needing to trust you with something really important." Pat's jaw quivered, his breath came in short, jagged bursts. He stood there looming over Brad.

How can I explain this? Brad covered his face with his hands, biting his lip, searching for an answer. When he looked up, Pat was gone. Silence. Every eye in the cafeteria drilled him with accusation. Guilty as charged!

The only sound in the universe was the sharp crunch, crunch of the snow under their feet. Small lights glimmered from the far-away windows of the lodge as they moved in nearly total darkness at the far end of the parking lot. Even out under the planetarium-like display of stars, the night was not perfect. Brad thought that walking hand-in-hand with Crystal would be all he wanted tonight. But he was wrong.

Crystal looked up. "They're beautiful. I never saw stars look like this. They're so close …" "… I could touch them," they said in unison. They looked at one another and laughed.

Then Brad thought about Pat trying to focus his telescope. *Geeezo, man. Enough about him. Why should I let him make me feel guilty? He doesn't own me or my life. I want to be with Crystal, and I'm going to enjoy it.*

He turned toward her and put his gloved hand under her chin, tilted it toward him, and touched her lips with his. His lips were cold, but hers, how could they have been so warm in this freezing weather? This was not a passionate kiss. Brad just wanted to say, "I'm glad you're here with me. It's so cool we are together." She gently ran her lips across his as he felt a wool-gloved hand touch on his cheek. She understood him. They stood alone in the world, looking up at the brilliant sky.

From behind he sensed a subtle movement, nothing more than a whisper of sound. Then he heard a low, menacing hiss and a growl. They both whirled, and just yards away, floating in the pitch black, were two green pinpoints of light. The eyes of a cat. A large, predatory cat!

Brad whispered, "Don't move." His heart thumped high in his throat. The eyes out there swam left, then right. The cat's head must have been swaying back and forth trying to puzzle out what was blocking its way.

"Maybe," came her quaking whisper, "we should run for it."

"No," he replied instantly. "It looks like it's curious, not frightened. Just stay put." Their bodies were bonded together, hands squeezed tightly as though to draw courage from one another.

The cat screamed a terrifying roar, shattering the absolute quiet of the night. It's head stopped bobbing and slowly, ever so slowly, crouching just inches above the snow, first the glow of its eyes, then the outline of its smooth and graceful body moved forward. It was coming right toward them.

Chapter 15

The pine needles under the large tree made a soft, dry haven for him and Crystal to sit on. They bundled together against the frigid cold, but still her body trembled uncontrollably. Was it from the plummeting temperature or from fear? It didn't matter much either way. Finally she was quiet, maybe asleep. It was probably only about ten, a long time 'till dawn, but if they were not found or could not make their way back to the lodge before long, they might freeze to death. A shiver sent its message through his body.

At least for the moment, they were safe. Before thinking about their options, Brad tried to piece together what had happened in the last half-hour or so. Maybe by retracing their actions he could somehow find their way back.

He forced the nightmare to play over, to relive it so he might get his bearings. Those eyes. He gasped as he remembered those yellow-green, unblinking eyes. Just when the cat had seemed ready to pounce, to tear them apart, out of nowhere, the second one had appeared, screaming and yowling at the first. Maybe he thought we should be *his* dinner.

The stench of blood and torn flesh hung in the air. His stomach wrenched as he imagined being caught in the grip of those claws and fangs. They had to get away, fast! Holding Crystal's arm in a vice grip, he steered her off the paved area, over a bank of snow, and then into a panic run. They had no choice. They had to head overland across the snow. Sounds of the cats' fight echoed throughout the forest, following them, twisting and turning with every change of direction they made, until, unable to run any more, they crashed down panting and struggling for breath under the tall pine. The sounds of the cats were stilled. In fact, except for Brad and Crystal's heavy breathing, there was no sound at all.

At first they found relief in being safe, not realizing they might be in big trouble anyway. But that was a long time ago. Crystal stirred in his arms. By the light of the faint star glow, he saw her slight smile. "I guess I shouldn't have worn that musk scent. Made them crazy, when it was really you I wanted to drive insane with passion."

Passion was about the furthest thing from his mind at the moment. But humor was better than tears, so he responded, "Bet you never thought a first date could be so exciting." She reached over and tried to tickle his ribs through four layers of clothing. Body warmth from their long run drained away. They were gripped by a deadly chill: numb from the cold and numb from the fear that they were lost.

Raising the edge of her cap away from her ear, Brad said softly, "We can't stay here any more." Crystal nodded. She had also taken the first-aid classes that covered hypothermia and realized that sitting here, sleeping here, meant maybe never waking up.

"They're sure to come looking for us." This was more of a question than a statement. "We could build a fire or start shouting, don't you think?"

He reached over and smoothed her hair, tucking it back under her cap. "They don't even know we're gone. Remember your great plan? How careful we were to sneak out of the dorm rooms so no one would catch us? You're much too clever, my lady queen." His damsel was really in distress. And so was her knight.

She chewed on her lip. "Right. You're right. So how do we know where to go, which direction to head in? Hey, we could follow our tracks back to the parking lot."

Brad made his tone sound light, like it was no big deal. "We could have, except for the wind that came up while you slept. It sort of blurred all the tracks." As casual as he tried to make it sound, it *was* a big deal.

"We could wander all night or we could fall off the bluff into the lake. Brad, I'm scared."

He forced a smile. "It's okay. It's okay." He squeezed her tight. "We're gonna get out of this. I know it." The distant howl of a coyote shattered the silence. Even in this deadly situation, Brad couldn't seem to repress his quirky thought. "Toto, I don't think we're in Kansas any more."

"But how, how will we find our way back?" she asked.

He let go of her and pulled his knees up into his chest wrapping his arms around himself looking in, focusing. He had to shape that small, silent place he reserved for his special moments on the track.

Just … let … it … go.

The night sky shimmered to life in his mind. Not the one overhead, but the one Pat and he had studied for the last couple of weeks. The map with all the stars and April constellations had been on the big table in Pat's front room. Pat pointed out the ones he knew, the ones they would be looking at through the telescope. There was the Little Dipper … the end of its handle was the North Star. "If you know where north is, you always know where you are," Pat had said last week. He didn't know how soon Brad would need to know where he was; Pat wasn't here, but his map was right there in Brad s brain. He stood up and reached down to help her to her feet. "Let's get out of this sleazy bar."

With effort, Crystal grabbed hold of Brad to help her gain her feet. She drew him close to her. "Not yet. In a minute." She put her hands on his cheeks, pulling his face toward her. In a hoarse whisper she said, "In case we never get to do this." Her mouth was warm on his. Their lips touched gently, teasing, then harder with hunger as though trying to hold onto life itself with this kiss. Even through the layers of clothes, he felt the beating of her heart on his chest. She must have felt his too because it was ready to burst.

From a small meadow they were able to see enough of the

sky to find the North Star. The moon was a quarter full so it was not so bright as to blot out the stars, but light enough to keep them from bumping into trees or falling down an unseen embankment. Brad drew a rough map in the snow with a stick. "So we know the lodge is here at the south side of the lake. The long drive going to it runs, as near as I could tell, east and west. So if we go directly opposite of the North Star, keeping it at our backs, we should run into the road." He looked at her trembling with the cold. "I hope."

"At least walking will help us keep a little warmer." She tucked her hands under her armpits for added warmth. "It's getting boring around here. Let's make tracks."

Bad pun, girl, Brad thought. They got their bearings and moved out cautiously. The snow had a light crust at the top but it was powdery just underneath. That wouldn't be too bad except that in a lot of places the stuff was up to their knees. Brad pushed forward, making a small channel for her to follow. His boots were only ankle high, and already they were full of frigid snow from their earlier run. *Don't think about numb toes or being tired. Just focus on climbing the rise in front of us. We can make it.*

"More to the right; we're going too far left." Crystal had taken on the job of checking over her shoulder every few minutes, keeping the North Star right behind them. Her quaking voice hummed a soft melody. It was a sad tune that Brad didn't remember ever hearing before. "Brad," her voice was husky and deep. "I need to stop and rest. You go ahead and find help. I'll just, I'll stay here a little while."

He turned in time to see her body sag down to the white

ground. "No!" he shouted. "Noooo! You can't do this." He closed the space between them in a rush. "I need you to navigate. I could never make it by myself. And I think the road is just over this next hill." He didn't wait for a response; he just grabbed her arms and pulled her up. "You're a runner and in darned good shape. So come on!" he ordered.

Crystal grunted, shrugging his arms off of her shoulders. He could hardly hear her. "I can walk by myself."

They trudged slowly up over the hill and then another, but there was no break in the bleak white in front of them, no dark ribbon of highway leading them to safety. At last they had to stop under a low-hanging cedar tree. He held her to him, as much to conserve body heat as to physically keep her from collapsing. Those extra laps and Saturday runs must have paid off, he thought, because in spite of the stress they were under, his legs were holding them both up.

"One more rise. That's all. I swear." He didn't know if she could understand him or not because his lips and cheeks were so numb it was hard to shape the words. He forced himself to say it again. She shook her head no and closed her eyes, sliding down out of his grasp. "Hey, I got an idea. You don't really know anything about me, and I sure as heck don't know much about you. We'll walk together, arm-in-arm, kind of like the date we planned and we'll talk about ourselves." He nudged her out from the protection of the tree and moved her slowly back into the paralyzing snow.

With difficulty he forced his mouth and lips to shape words. He told her about his family, how annoying it was to have his mom always on the run, yet always available when he needed her. Maybe she heard him; maybe not. But they kept on moving.

Crystal's turn. "My folks ... they split when ... I was little. Never really had a dad." Her voice cracked, a stuttering jumble. Words came, but with long pauses between them. "My step-dad, he ... he's okay. Mom loves him I think, but sometimes ... miss ... my ..."

Brad no longer felt sensations in his hands. They were useless rocks weighing down his arms. His grip on her loosened and she ... slid ... down ... a small, icy ditch. Down, away from him. She was just feet away, but the ice made it too slippery to simply reach in and pull her up. His numb hands could be the start of frostbite.

Her raspy voice called to him. "You, you get help for me. I'll be okay." She slumped down and rolled up into a ball.

Suddenly there was no cold, no paralysis. Brad's body leaped into action, his adrenaline kicked into gear one last time. "No way! No way!" he screamed over and over into the still, frozen night. Then he reached up grabbing a limb. A shower of shimmering snow shook loose and covered him, but did not stop him from forcing the branch down to the ground. It arched lower and lower, but still wouldn't snap. "Break, damn it! Break!" he screamed, willing it to obey him.

Craaack! Next to the trunk, the limb splintered and gave way, sending Brad tumbling backwards. He shook himself off, blood pounding in his head. He would not accept his hands as useless. He lowered the branch to Crystal at the bottom of the icy ditch and commanded, "Grab it.

Now!" Slowly with one hand, then the other, she reached for the branch. She clamped hold. Hand-over-hand Brad torturously hauled the limb up with Crystal just managing to hang on to one end.

At last they sprawled on the snow, wasted, sucking cold air into their lungs. *How much longer can we last?*

He tried but couldn't raise her to her feet. He wondered why he was so weak that he couldn't just lift and carry her to safety. This whole stupid thing was his fault, and he would not let it end like this. One more hill. He had to climb one more hill. At the top he flopped to his knees. He looked ahead for the next hill of white. Was that real? Was that an imaginary dark line winding across in front of him? He rubbed the back of his ice-caked gloves across his face stinging his eyes. The road! The road was just yards away!

Dragging, pulling, pushing, he did anything he could to get her there. "It's really here?" her small voice touched his ear.

"It's really here," he answered. His eyes filled with tears; they spilled over and stuck, frozen to his cheeks. He shuddered in relief. "We made it."

Just down the road to the left, lights streamed from the windows of the lodge. They were only about a quarter mile from warmth, from safety – and from the end of a nightmare.

Chapter 16

I think I'm in love. Every morning in Mrs. Gargus' class I study with Brad, but he's at Crater Lake today. We've been working on the causes and results of the American Civil War, from 1860 to 1865. Abraham Lincoln was our sixteenth president. He was a hero in the North, but a villain to the people of the South.

Oh, I was talking about being in love. Sometimes I start on one thing and then, like my mom says, I go off on a tangent. I don't know what a tangent is, but I'll try to remember to ask Brad when he's back at school on Monday.

Today Mrs. Gargus leads the group because Brad is away and Mr. Hunnicutt is at home taking care of his sick wife. So anyway, this new girl, Elena, is in the study group with me and three others. We all sit around a table and take turns reading from our textbooks, asking questions and having a good time.

Elena sits right next to me while we talk about the war, but I have trouble thinking about anything besides Elena. She has dark skin and really black hair that comes down almost to her shoulders. Right across her forehead she has jaggedy bangs. I don't know why they're called bangs. And just over her left eye on her forehead, right below the bangs, is a dark mole. She has a quarter-inch space between her front teeth that I think is hot. When I look at her, I hum to myself the lines from the song "Yours Are the Prettiest Eyes I've Ever Seen."

Besides being so pretty, her laugh makes me think of the meadowlarks that sing in the mornings by our house. Today she wears a purple sweater over a white blouse that makes her cheeks look like she's blushing. What's funny is that she calls everybody "guy." I didn't think I'd like being called that, but I like the way she stretches out the eee sound on the word "guy-ieee."

"Hey, guy, get on the ball and check out the paragraphs on page 116."

Everybody who comes here to the Resource Center Room has problems with learning. What's good about this room is that nobody cares what the other person's problem is. But that doesn't make me feel better when I have to fight for words or when I stutter. In my mind, I don't stutter, but when I speak out loud I do. I wish I didn't, but I just can't help it. It's worse at our roundtable talks with Elena sitting right next to me so close I can smell the sweet stuff she puts on her hair. I want to be near her, but I get so nervous that I sweat a lot. I wonder if she could love someone who stutters and sweats. Being in love is hard.

The kids in my other classes treat me okay, but when we break into teams, I usually get picked last. I don't always understand the lessons or the questions. When Mr. Hunnicutt comes in he sits right next to me. This is embarrassing. Mrs. Gargus explained that he helps a lot of kids and that I shouldn't feel like I'm being singled out.

I'd rather not get extra help than have him come and sit close to me to explain things. I need to talk to Mrs. Gargus about that. Maybe Mr. Hunnicutt won't ever come back. Because I stutter and talk loud, some of the kids in the regular class think I'm stupid; they talk to me real slow or loud like I'm deaf as a doorknob. Then I say to them, with a harsh tone of voice, but not too loud because others might hear me reprimand them, "That was a very unacceptable thing to say."

Something else that bothers me here at Pearblossom is why the teachers call Mr. Laipply's room a regular class and Mrs. Gargus's special ed. Why aren't they both "regular"? I remember the first day I came into class and all the kids treated me good. I knew that Mr. Laipply had told them that I was different and had to be treated with care. That hurts me. I just want to be treated like the other kids.

"So, guy, are you ever gonna open your book to page 116?"

"Y … you bet I … I am."

"You are one sad-looking mess, Lockwood."

Brad gave a slight nod to Sarah sitting next to him, but he didn't raise an eyelid. Too painful. Besides, he didn't want to get into a big brain-drain conversation with her. Not now, anyway. The bus swayed from side to side as it twisted its way down the mountain on the way back to civilization. His arms, his legs – shoot, his whole body – throbbed with every turn. Even after laying back yesterday and not doing any of the field experiments, he was still wiped out.

The other night was no video arcade party. But he smiled to himself, remembering their final hug and kiss just inside the large doors of the lodge. Then Crystal had shuffled off toward the girls' wing hardly able to move. He stood anchored to the spot for what must have been five minutes, a puddle of melting snow forming at his feet, until he willed his body to trudge painfully to the boys' dorm.

"Got yourself the galloping' crud, huh? No wonder you missed all the workshops yesterday." Sarah uncapped the top of her thermos and poured something that smelled tangy into a plastic cup. "Here, maybe this hot cider will help you stay alive until we get home."

It was useless; Brad knew he was not going to get any sleep, and besides, maybe this stuff really would help. "Man, your face is all red and raw like a boiled lobster. You look yucko." She put her face right up next to his. He smelled cider on her breath. "It's not the flu is it? Something else has happened. The big question, dude, is what?"

He squinted at her, and as she leaned back, her big, brown eyes went wide with concern. The tartness of the cider seemed to have scrubbed a bit of the heavy coating of slime from his tongue. He licked his lips and took in a painful breath. "You wouldn't believe me if I told you."

"Try me. Go on, I dare you." She squiggled her body sideways so she faced him directly, her elbow on the back of the seat, head propped up by her hand. "So?"

They had sworn silence. He promised Crystal, and she likewise had taken the oath, that neither of them would ever tell what happened that night. It would be their private secret.

"Come on, Lockwood. I tell you everything. Aren't we buddies?"

"Yeeaahh, I guess." He gulped at the taste of the cider.

"Come on. I'll never reveal, I promise." She crossed her heart.

"Well . . ." It wouldn't really be telling, would it? He wouldn't be giving any names or say anything about Crystal. Besides, this was too incredible not to tell someone, and geezo, he sure couldn't spill it to Pat. He slid closer and lowered his voice. "Well, after sack time Friday night, I went for a walk ..." He described the face-off against the cats and finally being stuck in no-man's-land in the snow.

Sarah's mouth opened and her head tilted to the side. Believing? Not believing?

"I thought I was gonna become a stiff out there, you know, make the headlines in the *Mail Tribune*: 'Pearblossom track star found frozen at Crater Lake.'"

"But obviously you didn't. So how'd you get back?"

"It was totally amazing." He closed his eyes and thought back.

"I closed my eyes and pictured the whole sky, every star so clear and bright. And then the North Star just stood out and glowed, and when I opened my eyes ..." He opened them looking at Sarah intently. "I used that mental image and the real thing to help guide me. I plowed through knee-deep snow until ..."

Sarah put her hand up, palm out to stop him. "Wait, wait a minute. Don't tell me the rest. I know how it ends."

"You do?"

"Sure. After getting this star message, like from God, and just as you're ready to give up, you look down into the frozen tundra and there at your feet is this beautiful, blonde girl begging for help. 'Brad, oh Brad. Please help me.' So naturally, you just have to save her from the elements and get her back to the real world. You're a gen-u-ine four-star hero."

Now it was Brad whose mouth dropped wide open. "How did you know about ...?"

"You're plowing through it all right, but it sure ain't snow. She shook her head, curls flopping around like little brown springs. "Thank you for sharing this thrilling tale of adventure and romance, 'Lost in the Cascade Mountains.' Film at eleven. Lockwood, you are some piece of work. Go back to sleep, dreamer."

Garlic and onions; nobody could mess them up in a stir-fry. The spicy, sizzling smell filling the kitchen would tempt anyone. Up to a point, that is.

Brad took in a big whiff and glanced over at Amy chopping away on the cutting-board. How was it she could follow the directions on a recipe perfectly, but would get lost just three blocks from the house? She was dicing this slimy, white, gross stuff: tofu. That would be the next ingredient for the big pan on the gas range. Yucchho!

"Hey, quit making faces," she called over her shoulder without even looking at him. How did she do that? "Come on, you promised once in a while to try some of my cooking. And tonight's the night, mister."

"Yeah, yeah, I know, I promised." He started to wrinkle up his nose, but before he could twitch a nostril, she warned, sounding just like Mom, "Braddlllley, cut it out." She turned to him. "You're better at reading the directions than me, so check it out and see if we forgot anything." She stood at attention, spatula at the ready waiting his decision.

"Okay, it says to carefully put all this into the pan. And stir gingerly."

"What does that mean, 'gingerly'?"

"Just be careful not to break up the veggies."

"Got it."

"That's it; gently stir, without bruising the vegetables. Now cover it for a few minutes and let it simmer." Brad was glad Amy could get into cooking and gardening. It gave her pleasure and she was pretty good at doing both.

She stood for a moment trying to figure out what to do next. "There's some early spring parsley and other stuff coming up in the herb garden. Let's go for it."

The sun was going down, but even at seven o'clock, there was enough light to pick herbs. They squatted down in front of the small area that Amy called "my garden." The parsley and oregano gave off their distinctive sweet odors as they pinched a little of this and a little of that. Amy lifted her head, "how'd your field trip go?"

Brad couldn't tell the family about his experience with Crystal, so he played it safe. "It was cold and I might have a little cold." He sniffed to prove his point. And I'm stiff; must be from the long bus ride in that torture machine they call a school bus." He brought some basil up to his nose, "Hummm, great. Coach eased up on me today; I think Sarah must have told him I was feeling crummy. Anyway, Thursday's meet is a soft spot, Rogue River. All we gotta do is show up. So I'm penciled in for just two races." He stood up, arching his back. "Ugggh, stiffening up again."

As they started toward the house, Amy touched his shoulder, halting him at the door. She leaned against the house, "You really like Crystal, huh? I heard she called you the minute you got home."

He licked his lips and shrugged. *How do you talk about stuff like this to your sister?*

"You sounded pretty lovey-dovey on the phone, Romeo."

"Well, yeah. It's going great. I mean we like each other."
He knew he shouldn't get embarrassed talking about
this stuff with Amy. Would she get it? Had she ever had
a crush on a boy? Had she ever kissed one? She always
asked about his experiences with girls, but somehow he
never got around to asking about hers … he could hardly
say it even in his mind, *her love life*. Sure, she had dated a
few times, but that was always kind of a group date. The
folks kept a pretty careful eye on who she went out with.
He should ask her about … Well, not tonight. He looked
at the dying sun sending its red streamers through the
young leaves of the oak tree in the front yard.

Was Crystal looking at the same sunset? They had talked
on the phone, like it must have been forty-five minutes.
About nothing, maybe about everything, but he couldn't
remember what. "You kiss real good," she had said to
him. Twice. And all he could mumble was, "thanks." He
should have told her how warm her lips were and how
good she felt even through all those clothes. Naw, he
could never say something like that to her.

"So what do you guys talk about?" Amy asked. He hoped
she couldn't read his mind. Geezo, why did he blush so
easily? It was a curse. A curse to help keep him honest?

When they returned to the kitchen, Amy crushed some of
the herbs in her hands and sprinkled them over the vegetables, sending off one pretty incredible smell. Maybe the
tofu would dissolve or something. And maybe he could
get the conversation away from Crystal.

"Ohhh yeah, Justin is going to sing at the school concert next Wednesday evening. I might go see him. Besides, I have a lot of friends in the choir."

She checked the rice pot, turning the heat down a smidgen. "What do you mean, you might go; it should be fun." He stirred the veggies without purpose. That wasn't exactly what Crystal had said to him an hour earlier. "Everybody is going to think you're like married to the little twerp. If you ask me, his folks should hire somebody to be with him all the time. Besides, from what my friends in choir say, he'll probably do something embarrassing."

It bothered him that she called Justin a twerp. Oh, he could be a royal pain all right, but it was upsetting to hear somebody put him down, especially Crystal. Anyway, she said Justin took up too much of Brad's time and energy.

"Don't let that burn!" Amy's voice cut through his thoughts.

"What?"

"Come on, sleepy head, move over and let me finish this so the folks don't end up with one of Dad's Thursday night specials.

Later, when dinner was over, for the fifth time that evening, he tried to call Pat. But it was always the answering machine or his dad. "Oh, didn't Pat call you back? Must have slipped his mind. I'll make sure he gets the message. And how's track season going, Brad?" Yatta, yatta, yatta.

More of the same on the next try. He flopped down on the couch, relieved that he didn't have any homework. While holding the phone, it rang. It had to be …

"Hey, Pat how goes it?" Instead of Pat's hoarse croak, "Hey, Lockwood. Do I sound like our pal, Jesse James?" It was Sarah. She hardly ever called anybody by their real name.

"Oh, hi, Goodwin. Sorry I couldn't go those laps with you. Maybe tomorrow?" He stretched his legs out and put them up on the couch.

"No problem. Say, you haven't told anyone else that wild story of yours have you?" Before he could answer that he hadn't, Sarah blasted in. "I've got this paper to write for my creative fantasy assignment. I wondered if you'd mind if I bor …"

"Funny, very funny. What did you call about, anyway?"

"Oh yeah, you got to hear this. You know your buddy Justin is in art class with me. I was just coming out of the supply room and I heard him tell Mr. Whitford that he's going to sing at Pearblossom Special. And you know what else he said? 'My friend Brad Lockwood's going be there to w … watch.'" She imitated Justin's stutter. "Is that ever cool?"

He closed his eyes and shook his head. "Oh yeah, Sarah, that is really cool."

Chapter 17

I don't need help finding the cafeteria any more, but I wait until the crowd of kids finish their race to get in line. They make so much noise and they push and shove like it's a football game or something. It gets a lot quieter when everybody is eating; that's when I come in with my blue and green insulated lunch container. I always sit at the end table on the right side, the one that has "Chicken bones are bad for your dog" written in dark black ink on it.

Each school night I look in our refrigerator and pick what I want for the next day's lunch. I put each food in its own little plastic box and eat each one separately. I used to bring a different spoon or fork for each food, but now I'm okay with using the same one for all my lunch. Sometimes I eat with kids from Room Thirty-Two, but today I am alone. It's common for people to feel lonesome for periods in their lives, because, like that hit song written by Jule Styne and sung by Barbra Streisand in 1964 says, "People who need people ..." My dad always asks me if I have friends, or if I eat lunch with other kids. I usually just tell him "yes" so he doesn't get all cranky. (I like this word "cranky" because it sounds like the feeling.) But here's the truth: There are times I just like to have lunch by myself and think.

On the other side of the cafeteria I can see Brad eating with a bunch of the Hispanic boys. They are laughing and joking and one of them pretends to throw Tater-Tots at the others. Brad usually sits near the gym doors with his girlfriend, Crystal, but I think she's absent today. Nancy, the helper lady, comes to my table every day to bring me juice. She knows I am not comfortable waiting in the service or checkout lines, and today she brought me pink lemonade. Lemons are yellow, so I wonder how do they make the lemonade pink?

Some girls are sitting one table over and across the way. Elena is the prettiest one. I try really hard not to let her know I am peeking at her, but sometimes she spots me and, like now, she smiles back at me. "Oh no!" I spilled my cup of soup all over the table. What a mess!

"Having a bean burrito today, Brad?" the cafeteria lady asked, smiling at him from behind the glass partition. He started to reach for the platter she had in her hand, then the memory of scorched beans nibbled at his nose. "Eh, no thanks, Nancy." He slid his tray along the metal skids, "I'm having the salad and a cheese sandwich."

He checked out the milling crowd of kids; some sat, some had their bodies kind of slopped over the blue plastic benches attached to both sides of the plastic tables. Crystal was usually waiting for Brad, but not today. And Pat was nowhere to be seen either. He'd been absent all week. Over at the end of the farthest row he saw Justin sitting all alone. Brad was tempted to join him, but another idea had been sneaking into his thoughts. Well, actually leaping out at him like that cougar almost did the other night.

He steered himself over toward Juan, trying to look casual. "Hi Juan, mind if I sit here?" This was the table that many of the Hispanic boys had claimed for their own. The unwritten law was: Nobody with lighter skin joined them. Most of the other benches were filled with either boys or girls, sitting apart from one another. A few times Juan had joined Brad's track bunch at their table. Sometimes he called over to Brad to come join him, but Brad felt uncomfortable being with Juan's friends and told him, "no thanks." He was sure Juan felt the same way about eating lunch at Brad's table.

"Sure man, come on in. Hey, Francisco, slide your behind over so Brad can park himself." Several pairs of dark eyes glanced one way, then the other. Brad pretended not to notice. At first there was small talk across the table about Brad's win at the track meet and the science field trip that some had gone on. Juan tried to include Brad in their conversations, but slowly the exchanges returned to Spanish. Brad laughed when they did and ate his lunch in silence. Maybe this is what Justin feels like being alone in his corner.

At the front of the cafeteria, arms crossed in front of his chest, stood Mr. Fischer. He laughed and joked with kids, but the "Fish" was always checking for troublemakers. His periscope was up and scanning. "Booeep, Booeep, Booeep" alarm sirens signaled that the enemy had been discovered. The "Fish" set his radar on Tony, the dreaded Tater-Tot-tosser.

A moment after Tony launched his missile and splattered on a loud-mouthed kid named Danny, Mr. Fischer stood in front of Tony, finger in his chest. "You report to me after school young man." Then the finger swiveled toward the doors. "Now get your tray and finish your lunch in the office." Tony slouched down pretending he was sorry for what he did. "Yes sir, Mr. Fischer." But on the way out, he smirked and winked at his buddies at each of the tables.

Brad's mind drifted to his last scene with Pat when – geezo speak of the devil – there he was. Pat had just gotten his lunch card stamped by the cashier and was heading toward a newly vacated table. "Hey, nice to have lunch with you," Brad said to Juan and his friends, as he got up. "See you around."

He got some raised hands and nods in response and took his tray over to where Pat sat nibbling at his food. Maybe Pat had thought about their fight and understood why Brad absolutely had to be with Crystal Saturday night. Yeah, Pat would say, "It's cool, I'm sorry." He'd push his glasses up further on his nose. "I blew the cork clear out of my bottle."

"Hi, Pat. How ya feeling?"

Pat put his fork down and pushed his glasses back. "Feeling better. I, eh, had a pinch of the flu, but I'm outstanding now. Just outstanding."

Wait a minute. Same voice, same weird guy, but there was something different, something not … well, not Pat about him. "I tried to call you."

"Sorry, man. I just couldn't make it to the phone." He nudged the burrito with his fork, staring at his food. "Look, I'm sorry I got so busted up on the trip. About you and Crystal, I mean. I understand."

Brad's gut tightened. Good thing he didn't get the beans. This was exactly what he wanted. Right. Pat understood about Crystal and him. But before he could recite the response he had practiced for three days, accepting Pat's apology, a stream of unrehearsed words tumbled out of Brad's mouth. "Hey, no, no, no, it wasn't you out of line, it was me, and you had a right to get pissed off. It wasn't your fault, I swear."

What was he saying? He felt little beads of sweat on his upper lip. Wait a minute; Pat was the one who needed to apologize, not Brad. And he did. The whole thing was Pat's fault. It was, wasn't it?

Pat sat up straight looking Brad in the eye. "You mean it? You honestly mean you're sorry?" There was a kind of glow around him.

Brad felt lighter than he had since they got back from the trip. What was it about making somebody feel good that made you feel good too?

"How about timing my sprints today at practice? Let's see if I can finish two-hundred without cramping up."

Pat picked up his fork and dug into the burrito like he hadn't eaten since the Chicago Bears were in the Super Bowl. "You're on, bro."

Brad gets up from Juan's table and heads toward me like he's going to say hi. Good thing I had enough napkins to wipe up the soup mess. The kids around me laughed when I spilled, but I didn't think it was funny, especially since Elena saw me. She didn't laugh.

Brad stops at his other friend's table and sits down with him. I understand though; they have been friends for a long time and I'm just a new friend. They have important things to talk about, but probably Brad will stop by before he leaves.

They get up together and … and Brad puts his arm around the other kid's shoulder … and they walk by my table. I want to say, "Hi, Brad," but they walk right out of the cafeteria together.

I don't understand. Sometimes Brad acts like my friend, and other times he doesn't even know I am here. I am here! Why doesn't he see me?

Chapter 18

"Hey Brad, Lydia; wait up!" Coach Goodwin stepped out from behind the car in the school lot, stuffing his keys into his pocket. He gave Brad's mom a quick hug and Brad a thumping fist to the arm. He was wearing his usual shorts and one of his hundreds of marathon t-shirts. This one had a silk-screen picture of a sand dune, the ocean and a bright, red line – a road meandering across it like an artery slashing through the mountains. The writing on the shirt said in jungle-green lettering, "Petaluma-Winter Marathon." Probably Sarah will be wearing it by this summer, Brad thought.

Coach's chewing gum cracked as he spoke, "Glad I caught up with you." It was almost dark; the headlights of the cars pulling into the lot spread their beams of light over the three of them. Coach and Mom leaned against a car and gabbed about Dad who was up in Portland on business. Coach had asked if he'd be able to pick up some stuff for the track team while he was there.

Brad soon lost interest in the conversation. He thought about Crystal instead. She had missed school all of last week, but at least they had talked every night on the phone. "My ankles look like bowling pins," she complained, "they're so swollen. And my face, uccch, it looks like I was a spectator at a nuke explosion. I don't want anybody seeing me like this!" But now she was back at school. And she looked fine. Yeah! Too bad she's not coming tonight to the Pearblossom Special.

"… not to worry about that kid, Carlos." The name spoken by Coach grabbed Brad by the neck and shook him. What about Carlos?

"By the time the district meet comes up next month, Brad will be back in top shape and peaking. I think he can take that kid in at least two of the three races."

A sour taste filled Brad's mouth. Yeah, right, he thought. Now all he had to do was dig a small, unnoticed hole in the all-weather track at Medford High School. "No way, Jose!'"

Coach boosted himself up, sitting on the hood of the car. "So Sarah came early with my wife to check with a few teachers on some missing assignments." He went on and on. Mom smiled and did that lip thing of hers. She really didn't care at all about Coach's predictions for the track season. She was bored out of her skull. That made two of them.

Her hand was on Brad's arm. "Thanks, Stan. I'll try to make it to at least one of the meets." She shoved Brad in the direction of the main doors. "Freedom, at last," she muttered under her breath. "Now let's see about those algebra grades of yours."

Finally, they got inside the building to visit some of Brad's teachers before the program in the gym. The hall was packed. They had to say "excuse me" about a zillion times, cutting past kids who tried not to hang too close to their parents. How bogus to be seen with your folks. "That was awfully nice what Mrs. Gargus said about you." Mom messed with his hair. That's what she did when she was proud of him. Brad pictured her doing that at his wedding. "I do," he will say, and she'll come running down the aisle to muss his hair. Geezo, when would she grow up?

"Compton's algebra class is down this way."

"*Mrs.* Compton."

"Right, *Mrs.* Compton." She should hear what some of the kids called Mrs. McMeen, but not to her face, of course. They crashed their way through the crowd like they were in those cool amusement park bumper-cars.

After the teachers' conferences, the crowd started to trickle into the gym. Soon it grew into a flood, filling every bleacher space and spilling over onto the hardwood floor. With so many people, it was hot and steamy like the kitchen at Angelos. Of course, the school air-conditioning system was scratching its vented head, "Dah, what do I do?" Brad and his mom sat sweating right across from the choir stands.

This was it; the big night. Parents had aimed for it, some even writing it on their calendars at the beginning of the school year. All the work done in the past five months had been collected, laid out on tables, hung on walls, printed, painted, graphed and displayed in the large glass cases. Every comma ever written, every math problem solved, every line drawn by hundreds of kids was examined and "oohed" over like a brand-new baby. But several times Brad had overheard some of the teachers talk about Pearblossom Special as they came out of the staff lounge.

"… another three-ring circus."

"… so where are the parents hiding out during the rest of the year?"

"… why is it the parents of the kids who do good work who are usually the ones who show up?"

For Brad and a lot of the ninth-graders, after three years of coming to Pearblossom Special, it was just plain boring, except for the concert.

"Is that Justin over there waving at us?" Mom asked, pointing toward some people at the door. It was Justin all right standing next to his folks, the Evans. "He looks just like you described him, Brad. He's a good-looking boy."

They came up the bleacher steps and sat in the row right in front of Brad and his mom. Brad thought Justin looked more like his mom than his dad, but he was built stocky like his dad. They chatted, waiting for the awards and concert to start. Justin turned his head toward Brad. "Wait till you see the surprise Mrs. Robinson is going to spring on the audience. You're going to like it. I …"

"Shhh, Justin, you're going to give it away before the show even starts."

"You'll see it," he said as he turned back to the gym floor.

Right in front of the bleachers, some kids were assembling the choir risers, so it shouldn't be too long now. Better not! There was a ton of people fanning themselves with their programs.

Mr. Fischer stood at mid-court with a mike in his hand waiting for the crowd to quiet down. It took forever. He couldn't give parents his "look," so he stood, arms folded across his chest, waiting. When it was quiet, he introduced everybody on the staff. Man, it took three weeks!

"… fortunate enough to have Mrs. Robinson and her choir to entertain us tonight. If the choir members will come down quietly and take their positions." Justin tried to whisper to his mom that he was going down now to sing. Of course, everyone for five rows around heard him.

When they were in place, Mrs. Robinson leapt forward to tell the audience about the choir and what it was going to sing. Her voice was so loud she didn't need a mike. She had admitted to her classes that she could do the P. A. announcing for the Portland Trailblazers even without the mike. Justin looked calm standing in the front row down at the end of the baritone section. The audience was silent for the first time tonight. Mrs. Robinson raised her arms, nodded toward a girl to start the accompanying music on the CD player, and the concert began.

The first song was up-tempo, and everyone swayed in rhythm and clapped on the word "jump." Justin was doing a good job, a little behind the beat, but not bad. His voice was piercing, and he sang pretty much the same pitch for the whole song. He had a huge smile on his face and was enjoying himself. The Evans nudged one another. Then Mrs. Evans leaned over to her husband and said, "It's too bad Uncle Ned isn't here to see him, isn't it?" She had the same big smile on her face as Justin. Bet she would like to reach down from where she was sitting and tussle his hair. Brad's hand twitched, almost doing it for her.

"Who put the Ram in the Ram-a-lam-a ding-dong?" asked the choir in unison. The audience clapped along with the kids on the risers. They made some good noise and could have been on MTV. Well, almost. Man, having an audience was just like having spectators cheer at a track meet. It could lift you off the floor.

During the verse, Justin had quietly walked up to Mrs. Robinson and turned to audience. What the heck? They looked like they knew what they were doing, so maybe this was going to be the surprise. Mrs. Robinson moved over, allowing room for Justin to mount the podium alongside of her. They both waved their arms with a flourish, conducting the seventy voices for the rest of the verse. Justin was really into it, pointing at the altos, then the tenors, following Mrs. Robinson's cues. When the verse ended, he took the mike from the stand and spoke the words in his resounding voice, "Just who p ... put the bop in the bop-she-bop-she-bop?" The song ended, and the entire choir cheered for Justin. Everyone in the bleachers stood and applauded. *Way to go, Justin!*

I can't sleep. I am still too excited from the concert. I know I did good because everybody said so. My pillow feels like it is stuffed with … harmonicas. That's pretty dumb, but in the middle of the night, I can't think of a better … what's that word? Sim-i-lie? Something like that. A lot of people tried to shake my hand, but I kept them in my pockets. I was so proud, especially when Brad and his mom came up to me and said, "That was awesome!" I could see Brad starting to hug me, but he stopped and just clapped his hands in applause. I think that was a cool deal what he did to not embarrass me.

Elena waved to me, and I thought she might come over to talk to me, but she was with her folks. Besides, there were a lot of people in the way. While I try to sleep, I picture her – she's looking right at me. Then she pushes her way through all those people until she stands right in front of me, and she puts her mouth up close to my ear and gives me a soft kiss, whispering, "I love you, Justin." That's the way it is in my dreams.

Chapter 19

Brad sang to himself; it was the new song that was getting so much play on KTMT, *"Ohhh Baby. Life Is Sooo Sweet."* Yeah, dude, ain't it soooo? Even the bus ride to school that morning was smoother and quieter than usual. Most of the kids were mellow, looking out the windows at the green pastures and budding pear trees. With the windows open, the sweet smell of cut hay, the first of the season, came wafting into the bus, mixing with the putrid exhaust fumes. What a freaky blend.

Just a month ago he had sat on this bus, in this very seat, rapping with some dumb kid about who knows what, all the time watching Crystal's blonde hair bob up and down a few rows away. He had dreamt about sitting with her, holding her hand. He saw himself holding her, kissing her. That was then. And now is, well … Her fingers were curled around his hand, giving a little squeeze as she turned her eyes from the pasture to look at him. Ohhh, man, now those dreams were real.

The bus bounced over the railroad tracks, and a boy wearing dark shades and a big, knit hat called out to the driver, "Hey Bob, floor it, man. Let's get up to orbit speed." Without turning around, Bob yelled back, "Chris, settle down. And stay in your seat. Got it?"

The boy scrunched down, snickering into his hands while the guy next to him gave him a playful elbow shot to the ribs. Those kids were so young, Brad thought.

"Brad, I feel really stupid about not coming to school last night." Crystal's lips pressed together pouting. Did she know how much he'd like to lean over and kiss them?

"Look, I told you, it's no big deal." Her excuse, something about doing her hair, seemed kind of lame, but, girls, what are you gonna do? "Hey, do you mind if we make it a little later on Saturday evening? In all the excitement, I forgot to tell you, I can't make it till after eight."

She opened her purse and took out a package of gum, slowly unwrapping a stick. "Sure I mind. I want to spend the whole day with you." A small, teasing smile crossed her lips, and she folded the gum into her mouth. "And more than that." Brad turned to look out the window afraid she'd see his face blossom crimson. "Kidding, I'm just kidding. So what's the story on Saturday?"

"Oh, I've just got some things that need to be done at the house and Saturday's, you know … Saturday ..." Why did he feel embarrassed to admit what he was really doing that day? It was not like he was going out with another girl. But … but he felt Crystal, and even some of his friends, would think he was being a dork hanging out with Justin. After last night's concert he had promised Justin's folks, with a little prod from his mom, that he would go with him to the Special Olympics meet over in Ashland. He turned back to Crystal. "Hey, how'd you do in your computer test?"

She looked at him funny and silently offered him a stick of gum.

"If you please, boys and girls, I'd like you to open your notebooks." Compton's voice belonged to a little girl, maybe like Lucy in the *Peanuts'* comic strip. It floated delicately over her algebra 2 class like a gentle mist. Her voice was elegant, but she was big; very big. Brad thought that she must have played basketball because she must be over six feet tall. Everything about her was big, except her voice. Talk about a mismatch.

"Boys and girls," she said pulling a marking pencil from out of her thick, dark hair; that's where she always kept it. "Here's tonight's assignment. Please copy it and have it completed for me tomorrow. Thank you, so much." She neatly wrote the page and problem numbers on the overhead projector. Brad scribbled the assignment down, hoping Pat would be able to spend a few minutes with him later going over the processes.

The class had only about fifteen kids, mostly brains like Pat. But there were a few like Brad, who sweated and groaned, just managing to get by. He stretched his legs out into the aisle thinking about what Mom had told him last year. She busted him good when he told her he wasn't going to continue with algebra. She was ferocious, even threatening to yank him from track because algebra was one of the few middle school courses that counted toward college entrance. Man, did she and Dad have some bruising rounds over that one. Finally, when Pat said he'd be Brad's unofficial aide, the white flags flew. If he didn't pass, he would be dog food. Walking between the rows Compton came to Brad's outstretched legs. She stopped and tilted her head slightly. It meant, "Move your big feet, buster!" but she would never say it like that. Brad reeled them back in under his desk. Her tiny voice sang, "There's only about ten minutes left, so you may work on your homework or visit quietly with one another."

Pat immediately slid from his seat two rows over. "Yo, can I have your autograph, star?"

"All right, nerd breath, enough already."

"Okay, okay." He moved his chair closer. "Remember that girl, Linda?"

Brad remembered all right. "Yeah, the one that came to my party." And he remembered how Pat got slam-dunked that night too. "The good dancer, right?" That was a safe thing to say.

"Uh huh. Well," he licked his lips and fidgeted with his pen. "Well, when you mentioned about going skating Saturday night, it sounded pretty cool. So I, eh, I asked Linda if she would go with me." He took in a deep breath. Brad felt himself matching the breath with one of his own. "Do you think we could maybe double? Ya know, go together?"

Not a good idea! In fact, it was a terrible one. Crystal and Brad, Brad and Crystal! Now that sounded super cool. Not Brad and Crystal and Pat and Linda. But the whole scene over the telescope up at Crater still stung. He knew what he had to do. And maybe it wouldn't be so bad. Actually, once Linda warmed up and smiled, she was pretty nice. Sort of.

Brad punched Pat, almost sending him off the chair. "Darned good idea, bro. A double date. And maybe one of our folks will drive us. It'll be great!"

The metallic voice of the office secretary came over the speaker system. "Mrs. Compton, would you send Brad Lockwood to the office, please? Thank you."

Pat fixed his glasses and sat back upright in his chair grinning like he just got another straight "A" report card. "Sooo, the sport's press is here for pictures and a front-page story."

On the way to the main office, Brad cracked his knuckles; the only time kids got called out of class was when they were about to get a detention or somebody in their family had died. Neither one sounded acceptable. He rounded the corner to the administrative area and there was Dad. Brad sucked in a quick breath. God, something had happened to Mom or Amy. But the big smirk on Dad's face immediately said, "Good news, not bad!" Brad knew Dad had flown home from Portland that afternoon, but he usually went right back to work. Something was really in the breeze here.

They hugged, said hi to one another, and then went into the empty counselor's office. It looked strange seeing his dad sitting at Mr. Reins' desk.

"Yep, the trip was fine. I got to my meetings okay and got the equipment for Coach. And, oh yeah, one other little thing happened." The way Dad squirmed in his seat and fooled with Mr. Reins's family pictures on the desk meant this was not "little." *Come on, Dad, come on, already.* "I didn't want to say anything about this before I left, because, if it didn't come through, I knew you'd be disappointed. And frankly, so would I. There was this meeting at Portland State about scheduling an all-state summer track seminar. Well, more than a seminar, more like an all-star, coach's training session with only invited athletes from around the state attending." Brad leaned forward, his heart pumping a faster rhythm. "Anyway, the decision was made to hold this invitational at Autzen."

Autzen Stadium, Eugene, The University of Oregon, Prefontaine's school, all those magic names floated to the front of Brad's mind. He swallowed hard.

"And a few middle school kids will be invited." Dad stood and pointed at Brad. "And if there's no mess-ups, you will be one of the few fifteen-year-olds to go!" Dad grabbed Brad's hand and pumped so hard his teeth rattled. "It's a once-in-a-lifetime opportunity, and you've earned it. Congratulations, son." He came from behind the desk and they hugged.

Incredible! He could hardly breathe. Was it the hug or the excitement? He could hardly wait to tell Pat, and Crystal, and Coach and Sarah. And everybody! But what was that Dad had said about, "… if there was no mess-ups"? What did that mean?

"No biggie. Look, you've won just about every race so far and with great times. Sure, it would be best if you could break a state record in one of the races, but really, it's not that necessary. Just run for fun." His dad playfully poked Brad's shoulder.

How come Dad didn't say anything about Carlos? *What if I don't beat him? What if I lose two or even three events at the district finals? Who are they going to invite, me or Carlos?*

A new pair of running shorts, that's what I want to get with Uncle Ned's birthday money. I'm going to surprise Brad at the meet on Saturday. Mom and Dad had picked me up from school so we could come to the Big Sport store at the mall. I don't mind the mall too much if we come during the week and not on holidays. I walk between my folks because sometimes the crowds and noisy kids make my breath come in short puffs like in the hallways at school. I used to hold both their hands, but that was when I was a little kid.

Dad asks, "How'd you like to stop for an ice cream, Justin?" Mom looks over at him, and Dad adds, "We can get the really good soy cream – the kind that you like so much."

"That would be a nice way to top off the afternoon," Mom says, guiding us over to the Scoop. After we sit down, I "chow down."

That's what they call it when someone really enjoys his food.

My folks look pretty happy now, but they were mad at each other for a few days. They didn't tell me why, because they never do when they have an argument. When they get on each other's case, I feel like I have to be the one to act like I'm in a good mood. I know everybody has disagreements and feelings have to be let out, but when they argue, it seems like I have to be the parent and tell them to "cool it kids." I never do say this to them though.

This time I heard Mom on the phone with Grandma, and she said that Dad didn't want me to run in the Special Olympics. "Oh sure, it was okay for Justin to run with Brad, but suddenly if there's competition … Mom, he's just being an over-protective dad."

I know what that means. I stood outside the swinging kitchen doors and heard her and Grandma on the speakerphone. "He has trouble learning to let go, Mom. Remember when we had that terrible time last summer about Justin going to the water-slide park?"

Grandma's thin voice answered, "Lori, you know I agree with you about most issues regarding Justin's safety, and I backed you a hundred percent on letting him go to the water-slide park. He did fine there, but kids get awful wild on a field and …"

"Mom, he's not a baby! And if I left it to Jerry, Justin would still be at his old school, and we'd still be dropping him off and picking him up."

"Well, you may be right about that, but you did ask my opinion …"

"When did I do that? I simply mentioned that we were discussing …'"

"You said, arguing."

"Alright, arguing. Jerry was really bugged that I had set up Justin's training program and planned for him to go to the meet without talking to him first. He's being an unreasonable …"

I put my hands over my ears and go outside to the backyard. I hate it when they fight about me. It makes me feel like I'm the one who caused the argument. I remember on the page of drawings I used to look at to help me understand what people are thinking, there was a face labeled guilt. That's the face I wore when I sat out there by myself.

I'm glad Dad changed his mind about letting me go on Saturday. I didn't tell him I knew why, when he told me, like three times, to be very careful. Maybe from now on he'll treat me like I'm fifteen years old and not still his little boy.

Chapter 20

Brad sat cross-legged on the infield grass, scoping out the nearly empty Ashland High bleachers. They must seat about a couple of thousand, but not today. This was less crowded than for an average middle school meet. There were maybe fifty parents and friends in the stands. Brad had expected more since Mrs. Evans had told him that the district Special Olympics was some kind of big thing.

Patty, a pimply-faced girl in her early twenties, the mini-van driver who picked him up that morning, had told him that some kids lived in foster homes or group residences. Justin was lucky; he lived at home with his mom and dad.

Off by the jumping-pit, all the participants gathered around the coaches getting instructions for the day. There were maybe ten adult volunteers altogether that coached, got the events going, recorded the results and took care of a bloody nose now and again. Pretty thin. Brad stretched his legs forward, bent at the waist to inch down and touch his nose to his knees. Feelin' good. He sniffed the sweet aroma of the new-cut grass, reminding him of the summer two years ago when he had tried out for five-man, tackle football. He ate a lot of grass strained through a facemask before he decided that he didn't have to run with a football to be an athlete.

He relaxed out of his stretch. No body aches or cramped muscles during last Thursday's meet, so he had opened up during his races. Good times too, but not the record-breaker Dad was looking for. Brad itched to leap up and do some sprints, especially on Ashland's new surface. Maybe before lunch break he could at least do some laps to make up for missing his Saturday 5 K's.

The kids had all kinds of disabilities, and some of them needed a one-on-one aide. He was asked to keep an eye out for one of the wanderers who could get lost under the stands, or stroll across the field while somebody tossed the shot-putt in his direction. There really wasn't much that Brad could do to coach, so aside from being a spectator, it seemed like this would be more or less a wasted day.

"Whoooeee!" A loud shriek echoed off the stands as the kids broke their huddle and got themselves ready for the meet to start. Brad stood up, brushing the grass clippings from his jeans. A couple of boys with Down syndrome walked toward him laughing and gesturing wildly. Brad recognized their features because he had seen an item on the news about a family with Down syndrome kids. Even though they didn't know Brad, they stopped. Wall-to-wall smiles spread across their faces. One of the boys spoke loudly, "Hey, buddy. Hey, it's good to see ya." He put out his hand to shake, but the other boy stepped right up and gave Brad a bear-hug. The first one said, "Gimme five." There was no way Brad, or anybody, could ignore this straight-up greeting.

"Hey, my name is Brad. What's yours?"

They introduced themselves as Donny and Pete. Donny lifted his chin, "You came to see us race right, Brad?"

Pete nodded, "Right?" Brad agreed. "Brad's our friend, and he's going to root for us." They quickly walked back toward the track, arms waving as they argued good-naturedly with each other, "I'm gonna win," Donny's voiced trailed after him.

Brad moved toward the group of kids to look for Justin. A boy, actually a youngish man, walked the center of the track toward him. His head tilted off to one side and every few seconds it twitched. As he came closer, Brad saw drool dripping from his mouth. He waved at Brad and made a thumbs-up sign. A girl with her legs in braces was riding an electric wheelchair. She motored along the track behind him. "Roger, Roger, wait up. I got a kiss for you at the finish line." One thing was obvious: These kids, these people, whatever age, they were geared up for this.

The weather had warmed up a lot since a cool, foggy start this morning. When the mini-bus picked him up about nine thirty, it looked like the meet might be canceled because of the heavy overcast. Justin, the driver and five other competitors were in the bus, too. On the way, they went to the local Subway drive-through for a free breakfast. Patty mentioned that several merchants donated food to the Special Olympic participants. Justin munched on a hard-boiled egg he had asked the voice in the machine for. "I can eat eggs, all I want," he called to Brad over the back of the front seat.

The girl sitting next to Brad smiled a crooked grin. "I been practicin' all week and I know I'm going to win my events." Patty turned and in a quiet voice said, "All the kids feel like they win – everybody gets ribbons and medals."

A familiar penetrating voice called out from behind Brad as he headed toward the mob of athletes who jogged across the grass infield. "Ooooh Brad, Braaaad." It was Justin wearing a brand-new pair of bright blue shorts. He jogged up and down in place. "What d … do you think?"

"Unreal. You look like a real pro, Justin."

"My uncle Ned sent me the money for them as a belated birthday gift." Suddenly Brad was aware that standing just behind Justin was Juan, his science lab partner.

"Hey, what you say, man?" Juan had a big smile on his face. "So your ol' lady let you out for the day?"

Was it that obvious that we were welded together? Guess so. "Well, actually I invited Crystal to come today, but she couldn't make it." Brad didn't want to admit to Juan, or even to himself, that the word was *wouldn't* come.

"Anyway, it's good to see you here with Justin."

Justin took Brad's hand and imitated Juan; "Good you're here with me to … today, Brad."

"Thanks for finding my all-state sprinter here." Brad was glad to have some company for the meet, and especially glad it was Juan. They had gotten somewhat closer, but not like they once were. Brad was about to ask what Juan was doing here, when over a hand-held megaphone a raspy voice announced the red heat for the hundred meters. Justin had a red tag stapled to his shirt and was scheduled to run in the next race; everyone was grouped to compete with those of about the same ability. Brad put his arm around Justin, "Listen, Juan. I'll make sure Justin has warmed up, and then maybe you want to take some laps with me? Or maybe we could just talk."

"That's cool. First I got to go take care of my little cousin, Rosa. She's over by the refreshment table. Meet you there," he said to Justin. "Hey, good luck, man!"

Brad guided Justin to the starting line where a dozen or so boys and girls all wearing red tags were stretching their legs. The boys had met Justin earlier in the locker room and waved to him when they showed up.

"Hey Justin, how ya doin'?"

"It's good to see you, buddy."

Justin laughed and announced to everyone with his megaphone voice, "This is my coach, the famous sprint champion, and he says I'm ready to go." He was really one of the gang here, Brad thought. But as far as being "ready to go," Justin had speed all right, but he looked like a young giraffe, arms and legs flailing about. It's a wonder he didn't trip himself at every step. But the rest of his red group was probably no different.

Justin joined the others and started the routine of warm up exercises Brad had shown him. All of the red-group runners accepted one another without pointing or making fun of each other. They were a group without judgment.

It feels good to stretch my legs in my new shorts, especially now that the fog is gone and the sun is warm. I thought I'd be nervous coming to my first Special Olympics meet, and I wondered if I'd know what I'm supposed to do. But there are lots of people here to help me. And I'm not the only one who asks where to go and what to do. When I came out of the locker room, I forgot where I was going to meet Brad. Then I saw Juan, that friend of his, over by the long-jump pit. First he introduced me to his cousin, I forget her name, and then he said we'd check out the field to find Brad. When we did, Brad's mouth just opened up like he was at the dentist's office. He was so surprised at my new blue shorts that he said, "Justin, you look like a real pro."

This is the first race of the day for me. It's a hundred meters long, just like the race that Brad runs. We have to go straight down the track and follow the white chalk lines, called lanes, that show us where each runner has to stay. No one tells us what will happen to us if we run outside the lines. The red-tagged runners line up at one long chalk line and a man stands next to us with a gun raised over his head. It shoots blanks. He tells all of us to listen up while he gives us directions. I've been to a Pearblossom track meet so I know what he's telling us.

"Runners to your marks." A few kids stand with their hands on their hips but most of us crouch down low, like Brad taught me.

"Get set." I raise my butt up high.

Bang! The pistol shot scares me, and some of the others too, but half of us start to run and the rest of us follow them. I try to remember Brad's coaching, "Stay low, swing your arm out … left leg, right arm … right leg, left arm." I can't get my arms and legs to work right, so I just move my legs as fast as I can … and I look down at the white stripes trying to stay between them. I pass some girls and I feel like I'm going fast, faster than I ever ran before. My shorts flap against my thighs and it feels good. Now I know how Brad feels when he runs. During practice I thought to myself, "One-thousand-one, one-thousand-two …" to count the seconds. But I don't do that today; then suddenly, the race is over.

Brad and Juan and his cousin, I forget her name, cheer as I cross the finish line. There's a mob of people yelling and cheering everyone, even the few kids who are just now finishing. I don't know who won.

I jog over to the stands where Mom and Dad are yelling too. I'm too excited to stand still so I run up the bleacher steps. I wish Uncle Ned was here to see me in my blue shorts. And I wish Elena was here to whisper to me.

Brad noticed that Justin started out like he hadn't remembered one word of training they had gone over the past few Saturdays. He felt compelled to close his eyes, but when he looked up again, Justin was really moving down the track and gaining on those who had started when the gun went off. He finished tied for third with about six other kids. He was super happy and took off to see his folks. Then he just sprinted up and down the bleachers.

While Justin hung out with his folks, Juan and Brad watched the mob of green-tagged kids in their heat. Rosa, Juan's cousin, a frail, dark girl of about ten, stood at a distance not really watching the race. It took about a week to get them all sorted out and facing in the right direction. Finally, the gun exploded and almost all the boys and girls moved out like a bunch of puppies headed for the chow bowl. Some took a full ten seconds to react to the gun, and then, at last, they were off. One boy ran a few yards, but then stopped in his lane to tie his shoelace. Near the finish, Donnie and Pete bumped into each other. Donnie stopped and laughed, pointing first at himself then at Pete. Everything cracked this kid up. Then they saw others still running and bolted for the finish line.

The runners finished, but the exact order was not really important. Pete was a winner. And so was Donnie – and so were all the rest.

Later as Justin and Brad sat and sipped juice from their paper cups, Juan and Rosa came over to join them. Rosa stopped a few feet away, standing off by herself brooding and sucking her thumb.

"Rosa has got some problems." Juan shrugged, "I don't know what." As they talked, a woman wearing a Special Olympics t-shirt walked over, nodded "hi" to Juan and went over to Rosa. She took her by the hand and led her toward the refreshment tables. The woman spoke in Spanish, obviously inviting the little girl to have something. But Rosa leaned her head into the woman, and with her thumb in her mouth she just stared at Juan.

"I take her every time, but no change." Juan looked down, tossing a small clod of dirt. Brad hurt for Juan and for Rosa, but didn't know what to say. "My uncle, he brought her from Mexico a couple years back. He thought she could get, you know, some good treatment here in the U.S. But she hasn't changed much." Rosa walked back to Juan, took a drink from his cup and nestled down, resting her head on his leg.

Justin tugged at Brad's shirt. "I'm tired!" Then he threw his body down on the grass, whacked out from the sprints, jumps and hurdles. The kids could participate in as many events as they wanted; most didn't seem to know when to quit. He closed his eyes and was quiet, as the noise level in the whole stadium seemed to chill.

Brad sat looking at the kids scattered about in their colorful t-shirts with "Because We Care, Special Olympics" written on the front. A few kids looked like, well, they didn't *look* challenged, as Mrs. Gargus would say. She had mentioned that some special ed. kids had emotional and learning difficulties, stuff that kept them from being considered "normal." Well she didn't say "normal," but that's kind of what he thought she meant.

It was weird. Aside from Amy, he had never thought much about kids or grown-ups like Justin. Sure, they were at school and they acted different and all, but they were just those "out-there kids," not in Brad's crowd or in his life. But lately, he had paid attention to Justin, and to a lot of others as well. And today for the first time, Brad was in the minority; he and Juan were the ones who were different from the others.

Brad sipped on his juice, and Juan played quietly with his cousin. Her large, dark eyes lost their dull look as she wrestled with him, but she never really smiled. A month ago, would Brad even have noticed her at a restaurant or at the mall?

Justin's Mom had told him there were over three hundred special ed. kids and adults in the area. So where were they all anyway? He put the icy cup on his forehead so the cool beads of moisture rolled down his face. Had he seen them and just tuned them out? He closed his eyes, feeling the wetness like teardrops sliding down his cheeks. Yeah, oh yeah, just a few weeks ago there was some guy in a wheelchair at the Jackson County Court House. Brad had to move way back in the elevator so the man could get on, but Brad hadn't said anything to him. The guy could have been totally invisible. And at the Saturday Grower's Market, those people who sold veggies to Amy, they had metal braces on their legs. Brad hadn't looked right at them. Instead he checked them out real quick from the corners of his eyes and then left to go taste the baked goods. Invisible! And there were others, lots of others who suddenly projected themselves onto his brain like characters from a movie. Sure, he lived with Amy's problems, helping her work out her frustrations, like when she'd freak out just because she couldn't get an electric plug into the right socket. But others, he never saw them as people; not really.

Did we just tune in on who we want to see and tune out others just because they seemed too different? In spite of the warmth of the afternoon sun, Brad's body shivered, a chill sprang from somewhere down deep. *What if all these people knew that most people didn't really give a crap about them? How would that make them feel?*

The sun hung low over Ashland High stadium, making the kids laugh at their elongated, toothpick shadows. Brad made a funny shadow hat with his hands and fingers over Donny; he and Pete pointed at each other's shadows and giggled.

"I'm all stretched out."

"I'm twenty feet big."

Over the megaphone, the judge announced, "Winners, all the winners please line up by the refreshment stand for the victory lap." Every participant had blue and red ribbons pinned to their t-shirts. And almost everyone had silver or gold medals hanging from around his or her neck. They gathered on the track near Brad, Juan and Rosa, their arms waving, bodies bumping each other and big smiles sketched on their faces.

The gun fired its last shot of the day. They were off with a loud whoop chasing their dark, shadow-selves stretched out on the track in front of them. And as they jogged past Brad, every one a winner, each waved and shouted "hi" to him. Brad looked at each one, catching their eyes as they moved by. And he saw *every one* of them.

Chapter 21

Of all the Saturdays in my entire fifteen years, six weeks and two days, today was the coolest deal ever. The track meet was more fun than conducting the choir at the school open house. Brad is a good coach; even though I never ran before today, I won medals. The silver one for finishing second in the two-hundred-meter run is the one I'm proudest of. After I showed it to my folks, I went over to Brad. We stood on the grass in-field with people running, shoving and yelling. I stood there quiet and couldn't speak; Brad asked me what was wrong. It was like the scene from the *Wizard of Oz* when the Wizard gives the Tin Man a heart, the Cowardly Lion, courage, and the Straw Man, a brain. I pretended to blow a trumpet fan-fare and put the medal over Brad's grey sweatshirt for being the best coach in the world.

This was my first Special Olympics, and even though I thought I'd be scared, I got comfortable as soon as I met some of my friends from my old school in the locker room. Right then I forgot to be nervous. Everybody I met stopped and said, "hello how are you?"

That's really different than a lot of other places I go to. When you pass somebody, like in the hall or on the street, and you say "Hi," they say, "Hi, how are you?" But they don't really care how you are because they just keep on walking away from you. One time I stopped a girl when she said that, and I said, "I had trouble sleeping last night, but I felt better after my mom fixed me a protein drink and toast in the morning." The girl's mouth opened wide and she muttered, "Whatever!" and then she went over to her friends and they pointed at me and laughed. Nobody laughed at anybody else today.

Dad and I are walking in Lithia Park along the creek and I point out all the different colors of the rhododendrons. "That one's fuchsia, and that one I think is ver-mill-ion. That's a funny name, Dad." The flowers are just starting to bud out and in the light of the setting sun, they light up and kind of glow like the Chinese lanterns I saw on the boats on a lake near Portland. It was Chinese New Year. I need to find out why they don't celebrate New Year at the same time we do.

The snow run-off makes the current flow high and fast. I'll try to remember the sound the rushing water makes for when I'm in bed and can't sleep. We stop on an old wooden bridge that crosses the creek to watch the branches and twigs wash down under us. This is the coolest day ever.

"I ran good today, d … didn't I Dad?"

He puts his arm around my shoulder and squeezes me. "Yep, you did a fine job today. You know, son, we are proud of you every day."

I throw a small stone into the water and watch it float downstream before it sinks. I am sure he's in a good mood and not mad at Mom any more, so I say, "The Special Olympics state meet is coming up later in the s … spring. Dad, I really w … want to go."

Dad stands with his arms folded on the top of the bridge. "Will that be in Ashland too?"

I knew he would ask where, and I don't want to answer because it might make his answer bad. "N … no, it's going to be in Eugene, but there will be a bus taking the com … competitors, and we'll all stay in dorms at the University and …"

He turns toward me and puts a finger to his lips, which is a sign for me to be quiet. I can see the cuticle on his index finger where he has chewed on it. I don't like being told to be quiet, but I have no choice. His voice is hard and low like the one he uses when wants me to focus and control myself.

"Then the answer is no." He puts his hand on my arm. " I know how much you want to go … look I'm sorry, but Justin, you know how I feel about you taking trips away from home. You're still too young to put yourself at risk being with all those kids who can't always control themselves." I bite my lower lip so hard I can taste the blood.

"I made a concession and let your Mom talk me into today's meet, and we were lucky, nobody got hurt, but who knows what will happen the next time? Anyway that was the deal we made."

He rubs my arm. He wants to rub away the hurt I feel, but it's not working. If I cry, I show him that I am too young to go on a trip. But if I don't let it out I will explode! I grab his hand and push it away from my shoulder

"Don't … don't treat me like I can't take care of myself." My words come yelling out of my mouth before I can stop them. They splatter Dad with their ugly sounds. His face looks like a painting 'cause it's got all these little red speckles from my bloody spit on it. I hear myself yelling with a voice I don't recognize. "You don't know wh ... what I can do. In fact, you d ... don't know anything!"

Dad doesn't wipe his face. He just stands there looking at me with pain in his eyes.

People walk by fast and don't look at us. I can't stop what is coming out, what I feel. "It's you who t ... treat me like I'm handicapped, more than the kids at school! It's you who wants ... wants to keep me locked away where others won't see me! You don't know anything! You don't know me!"

I don't move and I don't breathe. My heart pounds like it will come out of my chest. Dad just stands there and looks at me.

He slowly puts his hands up to my face and pulls me to his chest, holding me tight like he will keep my heart from popping out. His tears are warm on my neck. "Justin, Justin, Justin," he says over and over.

I have hurt him. Suddenly I am sorry for yelling at him like I did. I am the child and he is the father, and I know I have to respect him; not hurt him. I pull away.

"Dad, I ... lost my temper, but this is the last minute of our argument. It's over. I'm ... I'm so sorry I screamed at you like an animal. I have aggressions and I couldn't control them, but I shouldn't have let them out so ... so destructively. Do you understand?"

I could see his Adam's apple move in his neck as he swallowed. "You are not an animal, you are a sensitive, caring, loving boy; no, young man. Justin, I think I have a lot of things I need to understand about you, and about myself. Let's talk in a better time and place. And now, I think I'd like to walk quietly and enjoy the creek and the park."

He took my hand and we walked up the dirt trail facing the last rays of sunlight.

Brad walked into the living room dressed for his date, and there was Amy, kicked back on the couch listening to a blues CD by some old guy he'd never heard of. Another Saturday night for her at home alone with her music. He wished he could fix her up with some good-looking guy, but he didn't know anybody around her age. Seeing her staying home another weekend night took some of the joy out of his own expectations. Amy looked up and checked out his new jeans and tight fitting tan t-shirt. She whistled.

"Awesome. My brother's a stud."

Yeah, he thought, what did she know? He plopped down next to her and put his arm around her shoulder. "Nice music. It's mellow, you know?"

The folks would be back soon from the Carpet Mart, and then his mom was going to drive him to Crystal's house. From there it was an easy bus ride to the Rollerdome. When he had mentioned to Crystal that Pat and Linda were joining them, she said it would be fine, but the way her voice sounded made it seem like it wouldn't be too cool. Well shoot, it wasn't like we were going to the senior prom or something. It was just skating at the Rollerdome with about a million kids. No problem. It would all go smooth. So what was he worried about?

Amy's voice broke into his thoughts. "Want to tell me about today's happenings over at Ashland High?" He popped a Blue Ice mint into his mouth, saving one for later, and told Amy about Justin and the track meet, Juan's cousin, and especially, the victory lap. "It was really a super day," he concluded.

"How'd you handle being with so many gimps?" Amy asked out of the blue.

The hairs on the back of his neck stood up and his hands clamped into fists. "What do you mean, 'gimps'?" He glared at her.

"Whoa, slow down, Brad. I don't mean to dis anybody ..."

"Well, what do you think calling them gimps is? Total disrespect!" His voice was a lot louder than he had expected. "It's a damned insult; that's what it is!"

Whew, since when did he feel this heavy about special ed. people? *Like, how about today, Brad?* "Just because some of 'em are in wheelchairs or aren't too smart ...!"

"Testing, just testing. Don't forget, I'm one of those gimps. And you're right; it is disrespectful, especially if someone who is not challenged uses it, but here's a clue – it's what many people, especially those in wheelchairs, call one another."

"Amy ... Amy ... you drive me nuts, you know that?"

Just then Brad heard his folks' car pull up. He immediately jumped up to get his sweater and headed for the door. "I'll get even with you Amy, just you wait and see."

They stood at the entrance of the Rollerdome shivering in the evening chill. Neither of them said a word, but the memories of their frozen night clinging to each other up at Crater Lake were just below the surface. Brad tried to focus on the good parts – cuddling in the small snow dugout they had made. *Where is Pat, anyway?* He said to meet him at 8:30 and they were already ten minutes late. Finally, Brad spotted Pat's arm waving from the back seat window of the James's Buick. The car pulled up to the curb, and out jumped Pat rushing to the other door to open it for Linda. Brad waved hello to Mrs. James and just before pulling away, she called to the kids, "See you at 10:30. Have a good time."

Linda wore jeans that were like from a K-Mart special rack, and over it she wore a faded pink blouse. Her hair was cut shorter than at Brad's party, but her glasses, geezo, they were still mounted on her like a pair of headlights. At first the four of them stood in an awkward silence. Finally, Crystal broke the impasse, her voice sharp, her tone, brittle. "Hey, Pat, come on, move it, will you?" She could easily be a physical education teacher.

Pat's eyes narrowed. "I don't know if you two have met; Linda, this is Crystal; Crystal, this is Linda."

Linda licked her lips and swallowed hard. "I … I'm pleased to meet you." She put out her hand, but Crystal ignored it. The evening hadn't even started, and Brad already felt like crawling into the gutter. Sometimes he just couldn't figure out what was bugging Crystal.

Pat looked squarely at Crystal, "Nice to see you too."

Without another word they walked into the arena in pairs. At the rental counter Pat ordered two pair of regular skates.

"Oh, aren't you two getting blades?" Crystal asked. "They're so cool and everybody wears them."

Linda smiled meekly and shook her head. "I, eh, I've never skated before." Looking at the floor, she explained, "I'd better stick to regular wheels."

"Well, I guess you'd better do that." Crystal made it sound so super sweet, it almost made you barf. Brad couldn't stomach Crystal's ugly mood any more. "Cool it, will you? Get off their case!" he hissed.

Crystal glared at Brad for a quick moment, then her expression softened. "Right, you're right, Brad." She turned to Linda and Pat, "I apologize … really."

Pat put his arm around Linda and with his voice trembling, he said, "Apology …" There was a pause long enough to run fifty meters, "… accepted."

Angry and confused, Brad didn't know what to do. *Get out of here, quick!*

"I'd like a Coke before we skate. Come on, Crystal."

His words were sharp enough to cut someone's throat. Without waiting for her response, he moved her through the crowd of kids toward the refreshment stand, leaving Pat and Linda at the desk.

A few minutes later the two of them sat in a booth across from each other sipping their drinks. The music, especially the beat, was a thunderous disco song from the seventies or eighties. Justin would probably know all the words, he thought. As kids zoomed by, they waved to Brad, and another group called to Crystal, but neither of them paid the slightest attention or waved back. Coming out of the crowd of skaters Brad suddenly saw Sarah headed for the booth. She raised her arm to wave hi and came over to them. Brad waved her off with a small wag of his head, and she put on the speed and skimmed by. Crystal and he hadn't spoken since the scene at the rental booth. Brad tightened and released the grip on his napkin. He was afraid to speak because he might explode. The way she treated Pat and Linda. His fingers smashed the straw, then drummed on the table.

Finally, he swallowed hard. "Just what is your problem, anyway?" His voice was demanding. "What did Pat or Linda do to get you so p.o.'d?" Her head snapped back like she had been slapped, like she never expected to hear Brad speak to her so harshly. Her eyes flashed like they could start a fire twenty feet away. But then she slowly fell back against the cushion in the booth, the energy drained out of her. She bit on her lower lip, still not speaking. Brad spoke softer now, "Crystal, I deserve an answer. What the hell is going on?"

Her jaw trembled and her voice came out soft and kind of shaky. "Brad, I didn't mean ..." She looked straight down at the table, ignoring the hellos from kids who skimmed by. "I thought we'd ... I wanted us to be together. You know, just the two of us, not ..." She looked up, tears bubbling from the corners of her eyes. "... I was pretty mean, huh?"

Oh, man. Brad sucked in a long gulp of Coke from a fresh straw to moisten his mouth. How did she do that to him? She made him feel like he wanted to move across to her side of the booth and hold her and tell her it was okay. But instead, he reached out and took her hand.

"Brad, I'm sorry. Honest, it was just a mistake." She wiped the tears from her cheeks before he could take his napkin to do it for her. Then she put her tissue down and covered his hand with hers. It was warm and soft. "You know, it's partly your fault too. You really shouldn't have asked them to come with us." She stroked the back of his hand. "You won't do that again, will you?"

They sat in silence for a few minutes until Brad finally decided to let go of the evening's rocky start. "Come on, Crystal, let's show everybody how the champs skate." And off they went. When the music stopped, they glided over where Pat and Linda sat talking.

Crystal must have taken Brad's words to heart because she was so smooth to both Pat and Linda as the four of them sat together on the benches that edged the hardwood floor. Crystal and Linda even went off to the bathroom together. That was when Pat whispered his throaty, "Thanks, dude."

The voice over the PA system echoed round and round the Rollerdome. "Ladies and gentlemen, your attention pullease." He sounded like the ring announcer on an old prizefight movie. "This is lllladiesss choooiiice! Sooo gentlemen," the voice blasted on. "No winks, nods or come-onsss. Ladiieess, rope 'em, tie 'em, and get 'em out on the floorrr." Without missing a beat, the guy cranked up the music, *"Pretty woman, don't walk on by …"*

Crystal's cheek was against Brad's, her warm breath caressed his skin. "Brad, come on, let's go for it." The next moment they were linked arm in arm, floating along the boards. Her full smile and grace took his breath away. Soon all the garbage that had gone down before was erased by these most excellent moments.

They were at the far turn when Pat and Linda appeared just ahead of them. Linda was clutching the railing as Pat wrapped his arm around her to help keep her balanced. As Brad and Crystal skated up alongside, Linda tried to put on a brave front. Smiling her timid smile, she let go of the rail for a second to wave. It wasn't a good idea. She lost it. First she lurched to the right, one arm out behind her waving in the air, then her feet slid out in opposite directions. At the same time, her other arm gripped Pat's waist, tightly pulling him toward the rail with her. There was a tearing sound of cloth as her fingernails ripped through his shirt. "Oww," Pat yelled, losing his grip. Linda tried to hold on, but it was no use. Pat, torn lose from her grasp, catapulted toward and up over the rail while Linda spiraled in the other direction slamming into Brad low across his legs – a perfect, but illegal body-block.

"Brad!" Crystal screamed in one ear.

"Brad!" Linda screamed in the other.

Ohhhhhhh man. They were a tangle of arms and legs as they bounced off the rail and slammed to the floor. Whoosh! Brad gasped for breath, the wind was knocked out of him. *Oh God, if I'm hurt. Don't let me be hurt, please!*

It seemed like about a week later, when at last he gasped in a ragged inhalation. Don't let me be hurt. He stretched and poked his arms, legs, ribs and feet to check for broken bones. He had done this body check before after a few bad spills on his bike so he knew the routine. So far, so good.

Crystal was on the hardwood next to him rubbing her elbow. She looked okay, so he rolled over to check out Linda, who was sitting with her legs stretched out in front of her. She didn't look hurt, but she was crying.

"Ohhh, what have I done?"

Geezo, Linda, good question. He swallowed his comments before he could blurt them out and really shoot Linda down. He rotated his shoulders left, then right to check them out.

A crowd from school collected around them as he, Linda and Crystal slowly untangled themselves. At first, there was a ton of laughter. It must have looked really wild to watch them bail out like that. Yeah, right, like the Three Stooges.

Pat's head and shoulders came up from where he'd flipped over the guardrail; then he began to slowly make his way toward them.

"Hey it's Brad Lockwood," a girl yelled.

"It's the runner."

A couple of kids skated in close to help them.

"You all right, man?"

"Crystal, are you okay?"

"Nuthin' broke?"

Brad got up slowly. He felt shaken, but not too bad, except for a bruise on his hip. "Naw, nothin's busted." The girls were up. Linda was held by Sarah and a boy from the track team. Crystal skated cautiously up to his side. A wave of relief poured over him. Oh man, this could have been all there was to his track season, the district finals and summer training camp. He twisted his body left then right to be doubly sure.

Seeing there was no blood or exposed bones, the crowd drifted away from the scene. Sarah brushed the flakes of ice from Linda's skirt and tried to dab the tears from her eyes. Linda lifted her head, but didn't look at him. "I … I'm so sorry. It was all my fault."

He felt guilty for all the things he had thought about her. "It was an accident, okay? It just happened, that's all." But his voice was far from forgiving. He tried to soften his tone. Taking her by the hand, he tried to reassure her, "Hey, hey. It's all right. No harm. It was funny. Really, it was a crack-up. Get it?"

Sarah glared at him with a look that said, "Not funny, Brad." He forced himself to laugh, but Linda's face was deep red and streaked with tears.

Pat finally made it over to them. "You dudes all right?" His shirt was torn at the shoulder and his glasses were bent some, but his pudgy body must have absorbed the crash and bounced like a rubber ball. "Linda?" He smiled trying to soothe her. She reached out for him like a drowning person clutching a lifeguard.

"Got ya. You're okay now, I promise."

"It's all my fault. Brad, I'm … I'm sorry. You could have been hurt bad. Crystal, I'm …" She cried again, wiping her cheeks with her sleeve.

"Come on," Pat interrupted, "Let's find a place to relax for a while." They started off gingerly. Sarah forced a smile and waved, "Adios, amigos."

All this time Crystal had been standing with her arms folded across her chest. "Linda!" Crystal pointed an accusing finger. "You are one clumsy bitch! Keep your hands off of Brad. You hear me?"

Pat didn't pause for a second. He kept moving with Linda toward the exit and croaked out over his shoulder, "I'll call my mom for a ride."

Brad's body was not hurt, but deep inside he felt an intense pain.

Chapter 22

Brad hardly noticed the slight pain in his hip, even after having finished his Sunday morning stretch-out exercises. And now he was flying on his bike, with the breeze at his back, covering the course he had laid out along the back roads in the hills above Talent. It had been four years since he decided not to sleep in on the weekends. Saturdays he ran; Sundays he biked. And during the weeks of track seasons, he won races. That was the pledge he made himself when he found out at eleven that he could beat most thirteen- and fourteen-year-olds in the sprints.

As the years went by, he made his course longer and harder; it hurt some, but not as much as losing. There was more to riding than just conditioning – freedom, the electric charge both his body and his spirit got from the two hours or so of intense biking. But today he needed time alone to clear his head and to think about a ton of stuff that was coming down. There was the district meet in just over two weeks; the leering look of triumph on Carlos's face after the race he won; the summer training camp that he desperately wanted to be selected for; and then, there was Crystal. Yeah, there was a whole lot of Crystal.

He stopped at the top of a rise at about halfway through his course. His heart thumped from the uphill climb and he felt a dampness of sweat clinging to his arms and chest. He usually stopped here to take a swig of water and check out Mt. McLaughlin. There it was in the east, towering above the valley, still covered with snow on its northern slope. The morning was clear and cool, as yesterday's fog had crept back to the coast where it belonged. Off to his right he heard the sounds of a tractor putt-putt, doing its work on a pasture as the cows watched and chewed new grass. The pungent cattle smells drifted over the fence on an easy wind. This was a perfect spot, a perfect morning. Almost.

Before putting on his racing togs and helmet this morning, Brad had demolished three platters of Mom's special, whole-wheat pancakes. A great Sunday breakfast tradition! He managed to hide the bruise and slight limp from the family.

A cow that had wandered over to the fence by the road looked up at him. "Hey, what are ya looking at?" She mooed in response. "Thank you ma'am."

He rubbed his hip, easing away the last twinges of pain, but the ache from the way Crystal had behaved, that didn't go away so easily. Linda had reason to cry, the way she was put down just for being, well … Linda. Odd, he suddenly pictured her, tears streaming down her face, wanting to patch up the evening, but helpless to do it.

And at the same time, she needed help. Not just from Pat, but from Brad and Crystal too. So what could Brad have done to help? He just didn't know.

Sure, Crystal apologized with moist eyes on the way home and promised to call Pat and Linda to tell them she was sorry. But it all seemed kind of bogus. Questions, so many questions scrambled around in his mind; it was like taking a test that he hadn't studied for. He should know the answers, but none of it made sense.

Was he really in love with Crystal? He was pretty sure. But could he love her and at the same time be so bummed by what she did? Like how she treated Pat and Linda, and even Justin. He probably wasn't even aware of how she was avoiding him.

Brad thought back to the super times they had shared: How did they manage to get involved in such weird situations? Sure, there was lots of fun, but too often when they were together, something had gone wrong. That was not the way going steady was supposed to be, was it?

He stretched his arms high over his head and took in a deep breath. Over near Mt. McLaughlin's peak, a dark cloud was forming. It snaked its way, slithering down the slopes to make stormy weather for later in the day. "Doesn't look so good. Not good at all."

The cow answered with a long, plaintive mooooo. After his customary rest stop, Brad slipped his feet into the peddle-straps and checked that his water bottle was secure. "See ya." Off he rode, skimming down the hill, gaining speed each second.

I'm as excited as the time Dad took me to a Blazer basketball game. Not as excited as I was a few days ago for the Special Olympic meet, but today is really a special day. I'm having lunch with Elena. Just me. She has a therapy appointment early this afternoon and her mom is picking her up from school. That's why she's got first lunch today instead of her regular second lunch period. I think Pearblossom Middle School has two lunches because there are too many kids to fit into the cafeteria at one time.

Elena and I were sitting next to each other in Mrs. Gargus's class this morning like usual doing our history research – we're up to the Rest-o-ration. It started after the Civil War, but I forget exactly what it was. Next thing that happened was that we went on a bathroom break. In the hall, Elena stopped me and said, "Guy, where do you eat your lunch today?"

"I brought it and may sit in the caf with Kenny or one of the other kids," I answered. I wondered why she asked me. So I said, "Why do you want to know?"

She brushed her bangs to one side and looked around, like to see if anybody was watching us. "Listen ..." and then she giggled, "maybe we can have lunch together over on the picnic tables behind the gym? Are you up for that, guy?"

I thought that over for maybe two point three seconds. "That would be a cool deal!"

"Okay, then it's a date."

A date? Is this like a real boy-and-girl date? Or did she mean like marking a date in my calendar? I've never been on a date before. I went to the school dance at my old school, but the girls all stood on one side and the boys on the other. I remember nobody smiled or danced. I don't think that's a date.

I asked Brad to take me over to the benches before he went to the cafeteria, and now it's 11:07 and Elena still isn't here. She's two minutes late. Oops, I see her coming around the corner of the gym with a girlfriend. I think her name is Joanne. I am going to be disappointed if she brings Joanne to lunch. This is not a date. But now Elena points at me and hugs her friend goodbye. My disappointment disappears like the computer drawings when I hit delete. It's gone, but I don't really know where.

"Hiya, guy." She plops down next to me just as calm as sitting down next to a dog. Maybe that's the way she thinks of me – just a friendly buddy. I'm sweating while she opens her lunch bag and spreads her food out on the napkin she brought. I try to be cool, but I think I have too many thumbs because I knock over my juice bottle and spill mashed potatoes on the table. Before I can stop myself, I blurt out, "You m … make me n … nervous!"

She smiles but doesn't look at me. "Do I? That's nice. I'm nervous too. My armpits sweat. See?" And she raises both arms to show me the damp spots.

"Wow! You are the first g … girl I ever made nervous," I exclaim. After that we both eat our lunches and laugh and joke like we really know each other. I never felt this way about anybody before and I don't know how to describe it. Everything seems shiny and everyone I see smiles and I want to bust out and shout like it's New Year's Eve. I don't do that. Instead, I tell her about Saturday's track meet and that my folks are thinking about letting me going to Eugene to the state Special Olympics meet.

"I'm really impressed, guy."

"I like it when you call me 'guy,' but you call everybody that. Elena, I think I'd like it better if you call me Justin. She puts her hand on mine, and I feel tingling going up and down my arm. I don't pull away. And it's not at all like when Mom touches me.

"Justin," she whispers so only I can hear, "Justin."

Chapter 23

Wednesday the cafeteria's lunch special was good ol' pork hoagies. Brad never had the courage to ask what that was, let alone try one. As they sat on the lunchroom benches, Pat made a big thing of pretending to gift-wrap a hoagie with a white paper napkin.

"Hello, U.P.S.?" he mimed into an imaginary telephone. "I'd like to send a package to a friend, Amy Lockwood, and she's dying to get her gums around the genuine thing, the real article, a perfect pork hoagie. Can you deliver it immediately? It'll make a big impression on her." His foghorn voice and performance even cracked up the kids two tables over. Pat could really be one funny dude.

Sarah sat with Brad and Pat while Justin ate by himself a few tables over. After Brad had made sure he got through the food line okay, Justin was on his own. He looked so all alone that Brad couldn't help but feel a little guilty. Maybe he should go sit with him for a few minutes. *Why should I feel that way? As Crystal reminded him often, "You're not his keeper."*

"So Dad's been checking up on brother Carlos's times for the past couple of weeks," Sarah commented while waving the remains of a pizza slice in front of her. "Let me tell you, buddy, this guy's fast."

"Faster than Brad? No way, Jose. You saw the way Brad took him in the first meet. Listen, Sarah, my man here is the fastest. Right, Brad?" Pat pushed his glasses farther up on his nose.

"Right, right. Nobody can take me. Nobody!" Brad tried to sound convincing, trying to convince himself as well. A couple of weeks would tell.

"Hear anything about the summer camp selections?" Sarah asked between bites.

Before he could say anything, he noticed Crystal had come in and sat down at the table across from them. Pat and Sarah swiveled their heads following Brad's gaze. "Not yet," he managed to mutter.

Pat belched as gross as he could. "Okay, lover-boy. We know when we've been aced out. Go join Juliet … but no kissing in the cafeteria, hear me?"

Brad smiled sheepishly, picked up his tray and walked as casually as he could over to Crystal. He was still furious with her, but he missed her, and when he dreamt about her, it was never a dream about them fighting. He focused on the way her nose crinkled when she bit into a roll. Had he ever noticed that before? Suddenly a loud noise erupted from the kitchen. It sounded like a huge pot had leaped from the stove and committed suicide by smashing itself on the floor. Mr. Reins, who was on duty in the cafeteria, bolted for the kitchen.

"Bye bye, Mr. Reins," some boys called out while waving their napkins good-bye. With Reins gone, the noise level increased, but who cared? Only teachers and bus drivers got bummed over too much noise.

The trash barrels were in the middle of the floor so kids from both sides of the double row of tables could dump their stuff on the way out. A guy named Danny Macintosh bullied his way past a few Latino girls to throw his garbage in the barrel. "Out of my way, beaners!" Some kids called him Big Mac. Geezo, he was about six feet tall, his hair hung down around his face. He wore a long, black leather coat and was constantly scowling. Summer or winter, Big Mac was ready to rumble.

Since Reins was in the kitchen, Big Mac tossed his trash from about ten feet. "He scores!" Mac hollered. Not! He missed with his milk carton and made a gross mess with what must have been his half-eaten hoagie.

Immediately, Justin stood up, fearless. "Hey, you s … should put your garbage in the can. We all have to be care … careful about the environment."

Mac looked at Justin and sneered. "What did you say, butt-head?"

"I …I t's not cool to trash the school grounds.

Brad held his breath. Big Mac didn't look like he was in the mood for advice.

He swaggered over to Justin and bent down; his head came right to about Justin's eye level. Mac looked straight at him. "You want it in the can so much, you do it."

Brad couldn't just sit and watch. "Hey, Justin, come here a minute will ya?" He hoped to defuse the situation by getting his friend away from the action. "Don't worry about it, Mac. We'll get it cleaned up later, okay?"

But Mac was not biting. "Now, you little bugger, I said, pick it up now."

By this time, nearly everyone in the caf was tuned to the scene. Out of the corner of his eye, Brad noticed that Pat had inched his way back toward the end of the bench close to Sarah. They both looked pale. The noise level had dropped to zero. A bomb was about to go off, and Justin seemed determined to stand up for what was right.

"You d ... dropped it, and it doesn't seem right for me to have to pick ... pick up after you. Now, does it?" He shoved his hands deep into his pockets, but Brad could see Justin's face twitch with ripples of fear. Mac reached one large hand out and took Justin by the shirt front, lifting him up off the bench.

Justin cried out, "You think m ... might is right? Well, it's n ... not!"

Where in the world had Justin picked up that expression? Brad got up, his heart pounding hard, his neck tight. "That's enough, Mac. Leave him alone. I said I'd take care of it, and

I will." He moved toward the two of them. A hand grabbed his sleeve holding him back. It was Crystal's.

Her voice shook and she spoke low enough for only Brad to hear. "Hey! Don't. Don't do it!"

Brad shrugged her hand off. "I gotta do something!"

Big Mac held Justin in his grip while his eyes zapped Brad, nearly pushing him back with the sheer power of his look. Crystal now was grabbing Brad by the forearm. "Don't be an ass. What will the kids say about you getting decked just to save … him! If you get caught fighting, it's an automatic suspension. That means you're off the team. You hear me?"

Pat rushed over to put in his two cents. "Listen to her, man. She's right! Back off, and I'll run to get Reins."

It must have taken a lot of courage for Pat to come over and side with Crystal. It didn't take a mental giant to figure out which way Brad's decision would go. Attack and get his face altered big time and be thrown off the team as well, or wait it out and let Reins deal with it. He dropped his hands and took a small step back, but the blood was still pounding in his temples.

Pat scooted under the tables and headed for the kitchen. In the meantime, Justin was being pulled up almost off the floor by Mac. Nevertheless, he managed to choke out a last defiant challenge, "You think you are right about e … everything just 'cause you're big … bigger than everyone else. Well you … you're … not!" Then he spit a big wad right into Mac's face.

The teasing was over. Mac became a ferocious bulldog that had been taunted beyond what he could take. "You're the one that's getting' thrown away!" he shouted, picking Justin up with both hands about to push him headfirst into the trash barrel.

Electricity jolted Brad to action. His strong legs carried him across the table in an extended leap. Sailing through the air, he landed on Big Mac's back with a bone-jarring thud. Mack screamed and dropped his arms, while Justin hit the floor with a thump. Brad struggled to hang on, his arms clamped and fingers locked around Mac's beefy neck. But Mac started to pry Brad's hands lose; he felt them, one finger at a time, bend backward, forcing him to release his grip. His hands slid down the slick leather coat. In that awkward position mounted on Mac, who was still thrashing about, Brad grabbed hard at the collar and arms of Mac's coat. It pulled down around the big guy's upper arms and chest, binding him in his own trademark.

Brad knew without looking that there had to be a zillion kids watching the fight. This was the big one, the one everybody had been waiting for. Someone had finally taken on this big turd. The kids' screams and shouts bounced off of the cafeteria walls. Could he hold on till Reins came? Surely, he had heard the racket by now.

Suddenly he felt the pressure of fingers on his hands and arms trying to pry them off of Mac, and he heard a voice shouting right in his ear. "Let off, Brad! It's okay. It's Mr. Reins. Let go of him. Now! "

Finally, he allowed himself to be pulled off the big guy.

Reins's voice was blotted out and replaced by Mac's animal screams. "Let go of me. I'll kill him. I'll kill the …"

Brad fell to the floor next to Justin, who had curled up under the table with his eyes clamped shut. He squinted one open, then reached out and touched Brad's arm. "Are you all right, Br … Brad?"

Brad could hardly catch his breath, but he managed to get out these few words. "It's been a tough week, Justin. A very tough week."

I don't mind sitting by myself at the lunch table. Even though the cafeteria's noisy, I can sit and replay yesterday's lunch date with Elena. As I eat my cold noodle salad with sunflower seeds and oregano, I "hear" everything we talked about. I can do it in my mind like it's playing on my DVD. I have kind of like this special file where I hide old memories, and any time I want, I just hit the play button in my mind to hear and watch.

Last night before dinner Dad had to go to work, so I told Mom the story of my date, word-for-word. She took my hand, sighed and smiled, but she looked kind of sad at the same time. Sometimes I don't understand my own mother. It's funny that I think that because she's said that about me a hundred times.

I am finishing my noodle salad when there's a big crash that sounds like it comes from the kitchen. The noise is so loud it hurts my head, so I put my hands over my ears and shut my eyes till I have counted to fifty. When I open my eyes and take my hands away, I look up and see this big kid standing near the cashier like he owns the place. He wears a long, black coat and has greasy hair that seems like it's been cut jaggedy with a bread knife. He has a crooked grin on his face that makes him look really evil. I don't need the face cue drawings to tell me what his emotion is. This guy reminds me of "Big Bad, Leroy Brown" in person. Jim Croce, writer, singer … top-ten hit in the summer of 1973 on ABC-Dunhill Records.

Then I remember: The kids call him Big Mac. He pushes a couple of girls out of the way and yells, "Out of my way, beaners!"

His eyeballs roll one way and then the other, like he's checking to see if Mr. Reins is around. Then he tosses his trash at the garbage can. "He scores!" Mac hollers, but he misses and his mess splatters on the floor, on the tables and on the salad bar too. Strings of gooey mashed potatoes ooze down the can, making these little spiral shapes. This is not right, and it makes me mad. My ears ring and my breath comes in short gasps. I tell myself, *walk away, Justin.* I should think about Elena. But something takes control of me, like when I saw a man shaking a little baby in the supermarket. I told him he should stop doing that. He just glared at me and told me to shut up.

"Hey, you s … should put your garbage in the can. We all have to be care … careful about the environment." Mac looks at me like that man did, and I knew immediately I had made a bad mistake.

"What did you say, butt-head?"

I try to think about Elena and the way she laughs, but all I can see Big Mac's face in front of me. I tell him, "I … it's not c … cool to trash the school grounds."

He stoops over and I can feel his warm breath and smell his stink. He really is "the baddest man in the whole damned town."

He growls, "You want it in the can so much, you do it!"

Brad's voice is behind me. "Hey, Justin, come here a minute, will ya? Don't worry about it, Mac. We'll get it cleaned up later, okay?"

Before I can back up, Mac shouts. "Now, you little bugger, I said, pick it up *now*!"

I am so scared I can't talk or move. My eyes are glued shut and I wish my dad was here. Mac pulls me up by the shirt; it hurts bad. Then I remember what my dad said to the man in the market. I yell out his exact words: "You think m … might is right, mister? Well, it's n … not!"

I don't remember much after that but I think … I think I spit right in Mac's face. I know now that was the biggest mistake of all because I hit the floor so hard my teeth rattle and my shoulder hurts where I land. I will just lie here and rest.

Something thuds hard down right next to me. I open my eyes and I can't believe it. It's Brad! "Are y … you all right, Brad?"

Brad pants like a dog that's thirsty, and his voice doesn't sound like his. "It's been a tough week, Justin. A very tough week."

The milk from Mac's smashed carton oozed onto the floor right in front of Brad's face. It drained out, a sickly, dirty liquid pooling in a low spot, going nowhere. Brad closed his eyes. His track meets, the season, the training camp, like the spilled milk, all were going nowhere.

Chapter 24

Suspension! That word should be changed to plain boreing, Brad thought. Two days canned from school, two days in prison here at his dad's office. What a total drag. His mom and dad both came close to agreeing that Brad had no choice but to fight Mac. And then the idea to have Brad sentenced to work at the plant with his dad, well they both hopped on that one like it was the best idea since jockey-shorts.

Brad glanced at the open window looking out on hundreds of acres of pears, nothing but pears. How did his dad handle the gagging odor every spring? Brad thought back to when he had choked on Schofield's science class projects, the ones that went wrong. The bags of chemical mix on the loading dock they used to keep some bug or other from nesting in the pear blossoms reached out and grabbed him by the throat. He rubbed his stinging eyes and blinked hard making them tear. Geezo, he hoped he didn't get another headache like yesterday.

Looking up from his book and peeking out through misty eyes, Brad checked the clock on the wall of his dad's office. It was a pear-shaped clock, as if anybody needed to be reminded that pears were their business. Ten thirty. His dad was on the phone laughing at some industry joke that Brad wouldn't get even if he was listening.

A few minutes later he hung up and said, "How about if we spend some time together, just you and me. We'll go for lunch and maybe we can talk about the orchard business." Great. That was really high on Brad's list of stuff he wanted to discuss. It came right after taking lessons on how to drive a tank on the freeway and how to knit left-handed.

"Let me take care of a few things and we'll leave pretty soon." His dad went back to his computer and settled in.

Brad liked to read, but not for two straight days. At least he was kept entertained on the phone by friends' calls and, of course, Crystal. She was great. He thought she might have gotten on his case for having jumped Mac, but she was totally supporting him. Maybe she was changing her ideas. She said that kids at school were behind him too. Shows you how much they knew; they weren't the ones sitting on their butts here in jail. In seven hours and fifteen minutes he'd be finished with today's suspension. Tomorrow? Man, Saturday school; six more hours of brain-sucking, nothingness. Well, that was the deal and it had sounded pretty all right in Reins's office two days ago. Not too bad compared to what might have been.

"Brad," Reins had said in his most serious voice after the lunch fight on Wednesday. It was hard to take him seriously. He looked like Spiderman with his twenty-foot legs propped on the corner of the desk right in front of Brad's face. "I've heard every excuse and reason over the last eight years from hundreds of kids why they got into fights." He ran his hand over thinning black hair and flopped one size thirteen shoe over the other forming a large "X" in front of Brad. He ticked off the excuses on his fingers: "The other guy stole my homework or my watch; he put down my sister. Oh, those are the most popular ones. One bozo even told me a voice inside his head said to hit this other dude, because he was *thinking* about spilling his nachos in the first kid's lap. You believe that?" Brad didn't think Reins wanted an answer. He was right. "But nobody, I mean, nobody's ever said they banged heads to save someone else's life." Reins laced his fingers together behind his head. "Mr. Lockwood, you are a prize."

Brad had to admit it had sounded a little strange when he told Reins why he leaped across the table smack onto Big Mac's back. But shoot, he didn't make up the story. Justin was going to be potato salad.

"Wait out in the front office while I interview some kids who saw the incident. I need to get all the facts before deciding what to do with you." Reins stood and pointed to the door muttering to himself, "Hummp, jumped a giant to save somebody from being thrown away. I gotta remember that one."

Of course, the story was true, but Reins had to come down hard on anybody caught fighting in school; there was mandatory suspension, no exceptions. This was especially bad because there was such a big audience. *Great ratings, Brad!* The verdict: Suspension and two conference meets gone. He'd also have to sit out the practices, but at least he could compete in the district finals.

There was some satisfaction though: Mac had to face the cops and was charged with assault. That would keep him clear of school and he'd have a long time to think things over at juvie detention. Toooo bad.

Mr. Reins did something that really surprised Brad. By the time he got home after school, Spiderman had called the folks and told them the whole story. He even went to bat for Brad so the folks never came down hard on him. They just said, "We'll discuss it later." Of course, big-mouthed Amy, she kissed him and made him feel like a freak hero. "I'm really proud of you. I can't handle fighting, but sometimes you gotta step out." The problem was how did he feel about the whole scene? Bummed out? Proud? What?

"Hey, how you doin'?" His dad came over to sit on the chair next to Brad. "Ooooh, your eyes look terrible, like you've been swimming in a chlorinated pool for hours. Sorry about the chemical storage being so close to the offices."

"Not your fault, Dad."

"Listen up. How about we get out of here soon? We'll go to an early lunch and then hit some balls on the driving range. You said you'd like to try my clubs."

Even if this was part of the father-son bonding program, it sounded pretty darned good. "Boy, am I up for that. I'm going loony-tunes around here, in case you hadn't noticed."

His raised spirits almost lifted him right out of the chair.

His dad started to get up, and then plopped back down. "Something I need to tell you about the training camp selections. I know this is a pretty low time for you, missing two weeks of the season and all." He fidgeted with his tie, his fingers running up and down the length of it. Brad was aware that he was staring at the large, ugly tree on his dad's tie. His fingers tightened around the wooden arms of the chair. This was not going to be good.

"The selection committee is going to wait till after the district meets around the state to make its choices. They, eh, they want to see how the candidates make out. Brad, I won't minimize the difficulty of the situation. They want district winners."

Brad loosened his grip on the chair and spread out his fingers, trying to stretch the tightness away. Winners, they wanted winners. That was just what he might have been. He was just starting to peak: faster times, more confidence. Something inside him told him that with every race he ran, with every lengthening margin of victory, he could beat Carlos. But now, what kind of shape would he be in? How would he compete after a two-week lay-off and still be a winner? The summer camp selection was slipping right through his outstretched fingers.

"Runners, to your marks." The familiar, croaking voice of his friend sent Brad to his starting blocks. "Get set."

Head level, tail up, steady, easy breath in. Wait for the gun, not for the sound, to actually register in your brain. You gotta sense it to get off to a rolling start.

Alongside of Brad were the other sprinters on the Pearblossom track team. Standing on a little stair step, just beside the track, was Pat holding two blocks of wood above his head. His face wore a smirk. He must really be digging the role of starter. Down past the finish line of the hundred-meters, way back by the gym doors, was Coach Goodwin. He had a stopwatch cupped in his hand, but no one would know it if they just walked by the middle school track. It was after the official practice, and most of the team had showered and gone home. But a few guys hung around getting in some extra laps. Sure, Brad didn't mind helping them out. After all, it wasn't a regular, legal practice. No coaches were around, just a few of the guys doing some extra laps. Nothing in his suspension about a few sprints with his friends.

It had been over a week since the cafeteria fight with Big Mac, and a few days since Brad had been doing these late, non-practice, practices. Pat and Sarah had thought up the scheme; Coach Goodwin just hung out by the gym chewing his gum and secretly timed Brad.

The air moved slightly. He pushed off with his trail foot. Bang went the two slats of wood that Pat slapped together. The sprinters were out of their blocks.

Brad tried adjusting his stride, lifting his knees a little bit higher, gauging his breathing cycle, trying to get a fix on the perfect race. As he moved into a glide at the sixty-meter mark, he began to feel that old boost of energy again. Not just the physical, but also the emotional, the part that said with each footfall, "I can beat Carlos, I can beat him!"

He had started feeling good about himself when he returned to school last Monday. Kids, some he hardly knew, gave him a thumbs-up sign. A few of the Latino kids stopped him and said, "Way to go, man." All this for pounding on Big Mac's head. The dweeb had been known to put his hands all over some girls, especially the Latinas. They must have felt Brad had done his part to even the score with Mac.

Across the finish line, he easily beat his teammates. But that was not the challenge; it was the clock, the stopwatch hidden under Coach's workout jacket. Sarah strolled by her dad, paused a moment, then continued right on until she came to Brad at the finish line. Her eyes shifted first one way, then the other.

"Neat day for a run, huh?" She looked down, picked up a blade of grass and under her breath, delivered the coach's message and Brad's time. She stood up again and blew the sliver of green from her hand. "How about taking a shower, oh smelly one?" That meant the session was over. Brad stuck out his tongue at her. That was for the "oh smelly one" comment.

Some of Brad's best workouts were not even on the track. The late May sun got pretty hot during the day, but now after dark, the weather was excellent. It was about a three-mile run to Justin's house so the roundtrip of six miles was a fine conditioner.

Brad waited at their front door drinking in the sweet smell of the blooming lilac bushes. A lot better than his body funk. He hoped the Evanses could handle his odor. Mrs. Evans opened the door, greeted him with a smile, and invited him in. The house wasn't as big as his family's, but it was neat and homey. There were paintings on every wall and statues of naked people on most of the tables. Justin's Dad was in the art business buying or selling, or whatever it was that people did with art. Justin had told him that Mr. Evans worked mostly at night on computers making overseas deals of some kind. Guess he was off tonight. Brad was shown to a wooden, straight-backed chair. Looking around, he noticed all the furniture was old, made from dark wood. Must be antiques. He squirmed on the hard seat. Uncomfortable was what they were.

The big clock against the wall sounded a single chime. Eight thirty. On the way over, Brad had wondered why Mrs. Evans had called and asked him to come by. She said they wanted to discuss something important with him.

Mrs. Evans sat across from him on a larger model of his chair and said, "Justin is still working with his speech pathologist, but he'll be done in time to pop in and say hi." She sat upright, away from the chair's back. Brad straightened up too. Nobody slouched in this house. The sound of glasses tinkled from the kitchen. "We're in here, dear. Are the drinks ready?"

Justin's Dad's voice called from the other room, "Yes, be right there."

"Well, make yourself comfortable." With torture chair furniture like they had, Brad could hardly believe she really said that. "We'll have some cold juice in a minute. You look like you could use a cool drink."

Did her nose wrinkle a little when she said that? How could he hide the smell of sweat? "That sounds real good, Mrs. Evans, thanks." At that point Mr. Evans entered with a tray of glasses. He was thin like a pencil and looked like he could slide right between the support posts on the backs of his chair. Brad pictured the man slipping through to the floor and immediately being carried off by a big dog and buried in the backyard. He tried hard not to smile at the image.

After the drinks were served, they talked about how much they appreciated him defending Justin in the cafeteria and how pleased they were that he had coached Justin for the Special Olympics a few weeks ago.

" . . . So we hoped that you would be available to join Justin and us at the state Special Olympics competition this summer," Mrs. Evans said as she put her glass down on a fancy coaster on the table. It took a moment for Brad to get his head back into the conversation. Special Olympics … this summer … Corvallis. That was it, that was why they had invited him over.

"Of course, we'd pay all the expenses." Mr. Evans' voice was as thin as his body. "And we think we could manage to pay you something as well. Say, a hundred dollars for the four days?"

A hundred bucks and a trip up north. Not bad, not bad at all. Brad couldn't think of a single reason why this wouldn't be a super summer vacation trip.

Then they went on to discuss Brad's responsibilities and the details of the track meet. "Oh yes, the dates." Mrs. Evans opened a cabinet door. Instead of a bunch of stuff tumbling out, like at Brad's house, everything was sorted and neatly arranged. Mom said this was evidence of a sick mind. Pulling a calendar from the cabinet, Mrs. Evans checked that everything was in its correct place, and then she closed the door.

"All right now, let's see. Yes, here it is. It's the second week of July, Thursday through Sunday. I hope there won't be a conflict. Why Brad, what's the matter, dear? You look absolutely white."

Chapter 25

I love the smell of cinnamon. It climbs up my nostrils and blanks out any unimportant thoughts that are running around in my brain. My doctor calls it aromatherapy. I went on line to find out what I could about this kind of treatment. There's a ton (well, that's just an expression, it's not measured in weight) of information about it. I read it all in six hours and twenty-two minutes. The articles say, "Certain odors taken from oils stimulate the olfactory system and enhance health and beauty." I don't know about the health part, but I don't think the beauty part of it is working on me. The cinnamon smell is from the apple cider my mom is making for the party we are having at my house today. She thought it would be a good idea to invite some kids from my class so we could, how did she say it? "Enjoy one another's company." That's not the real reason. She wants to meet Elena.

It has been over three weeks since my date with Elena, and we meet at school every day. We can do this because I ride the regular bus now; it is number sixteen and it parks right in front of

Elena's bus, number seventeen. We stand and talk every day until the buses leave. I am proud of myself: I don't sweat or stutter very much any more when I am with her.

I wanted to invite Brad, but my folks said it might not be a good idea. I think I know why, but that gets very complicated. He still hasn't made up his mind about coaching me at the state Special Olympics. He told me that he had to think about it. I'm worried because whenever someone says that, it means they probably won't do what you are asking.

I put out the plastic plates and settings on the dining room table for each of the six kids who are coming. I like folding the napkins just right and lining up the cups with a fork standing in each one. Everything is perfect like a row of soldiers standing at attention.

When I'm done, Dad comes over and sits down on his favorite antique rocker; I sit cross-legged in front of him. I know what's coming: The rules!

"Remember, Justin, gatherings like this are for people to exchange ideas, so don't 'monopolize' the conversations." We had discussed this before, so I know what monopolize means. "And please, don't make a face if somebody mixes cake and ice cream into goop. You can keep yours separate, but don't make a scene."

We have two kinds of cake and two kinds of ice cream, one for me and one for the others. Mom called all their mothers to check on special diets. Mom is a cool deal; I know she is because when I go to other folks' houses, mostly they don't check to find out if I can eat what they are serving.

After everybody gets here, we sit in the living room, and Mom asks each one to introduce himself and tell what he likes the most and what he likes the least. I think this is interesting, but Kenny and Melanie make faces like it is boring. I think Melanie is boring. She never says anything in class, and sometimes she puts her head down and falls asleep. Mrs. Gargus told us that it was okay because she's on heavy medications. I'm on medications too, but I don't fall asleep in class. Kenny acts like he never sleeps.

I do my best to listen to the others as each one talks, but I can barely wait for my turn. When it gets to Kenny's turn, he pops up and his lips fizz with spit like he's a can of Pepsi. "The best time I ever had was last summer when I went to visit my grandparents' farm in Nevada. Feeding the animals was the most fun, but I didn't like having to get up at the butt-crack of dawn every morning."

I'm last, and finally I tell everyone about my Uncle Ned and how he tours the world. "He sends me neat stuff from places like China, Europe, Alabama … I get little African musical instruments and pictures of waterfalls and big lakes and rivers and …" I get the cue from my mom, her finger raised to her lips, that I've talked enough, so I shut up.

Kenny leaps up like he's sitting in an electric chair and somebody has just pulled the switch. Then he shouts in a harsh tone, "When do we eat?" That finishes the game.

"The dining room table looks fabulous," says Elena looking right at me. I think Dad must have told her I did it.

Little orange and blue cardboard nametags are set right in the middle of each dish. This tells us where we are to sit down. Melanie sits in Rebecca's seat, but when Rebecca whispers to her, she turns red and moves over one place, where she was supposed to sit. After that, she just nibbles at her dessert, so Kenny reaches across the table and says, "Can I?" But he doesn't wait for her answer before he scoops her cake onto his plate.

While I eat my gluten-free sponge cake and Rice Dream™ dessert, I look over at Elena. When our eyes meet, I stop chewing and drop my plastic fork. Now I feel like I'm in Kenny's electric chair!

When everybody is finished, Elena offers to help Mom clean up, so they both grab an armful of used plates and stuff and head for the kitchen. Kenny starts checking out my father's big glassed-in cabinets with all the statues and figures in them. Dad drifts over to stand next to him to be sure he doesn't touch anything.

"Wow, look at the boobs on this one!" Kenny turns toward Melanie when he says this. She bites her lip and gets up in a rush. "I'm going to the little girls' room," she says and is gone in a second. Kenny's eyebrows rise, touching his shaggy hair. "Now, what did I say?"

Mom and Elena have been in the kitchen a long time, and I wish I knew what they were saying about me. I feel all squirmy.

Later in the afternoon, the sun shines through the front windows making long shadows on the floor. I am able to see floating dust particles when the sunlight is just at this angle. It's almost time for parents to pick up their kids, so I walk with Elena to the closet to get her sweater, and for a few minutes we are alone in the front hall.

"Guy … eh, Justin, I had a fabulous time." She takes my hand and we stare into each other's eyes till mine start to tear. She touches my cheek, and then presses her lips up to my runny eyes. It is like a butterfly wing on my face. I can't breathe. I raise my face and our lips touch. I don't know what to do! This is the first real kiss I ever experienced. My eyes are squeezed shut, so my nose bumps into hers. What do I do with my lips? Then it's over, and we do a quick hug. I thought being in love was a special feeling that you kept inside, but I was wrong. It makes me want to explode.

The boys huddled around Coach Goodwin as they prepared for today's final full-speed work out before the district finals on Saturday. The feeling in the huddle was that they had a great shot at winning the district title for the first time ever. Even the seventh-graders who had never won a race during the season, who always trailed the rest of the pack by a mile, were hyped. Brad could almost feel the electricity come in waves from the team. As he looked around, he saw the glances, the eyes of the guys focused on him. He knew that the victory lap would depend on his wins – or his losses against Carlos. His heart was filled with a mixture of pride and dread.

Sweat poured from the faces and backs of the boys' team as the late afternoon heat sapped their strength. The girls just went through the motions since they didn't qualify for the district meet. Once in a while, while bent over gasping for breath, Brad noticed a blonde ponytail bobbing across the field. Then it was back to business.

On the way to the locker room, Sarah stopped him in the shade of the gym. A slight breeze came across the nearby pear orchard, bringing the refreshing scent of pear blossoms and a cooling break from the heat.

"Good workout today, Lockwood. Seems like you finally put some punch into the sprints."

"Don't I always?"

"Not these last two weeks you haven't, dude. Something's been chewing you besides just racing against Carlos. Even Dad noticed it." She tilted her head sideways like she was asking for an answer. During today's practice, he had totally forgotten about the sore spot he had felt since the conversation with the Evanses. Should he go to the state invitational, if invited, or buddy up with Justin at the Special Olympics meet?

Brad knew that no one could really help him with the decision. But like the Crater Lake adventure, here was Sarah to turn to, again wanting to know what was going on with him. He squatted down, leaning against the cinderblock wall of the gym. Sarah took this as an invitation and sat next to him. She didn't say a word, not pushing him to talk, but ready to listen.

Brad carefully told her the story and about being torn between the two options. She listened with her full attention focused on him. He could tell that she took serious matters seriously.

"Look" he said, "I don't expect you to give me any answers, but I think it made me feel better just talking to you."

She looked away, and then back at him. She moved her hand toward his, about to touch it … but then it fell back to her lap. She whispered, "Thank you." Then after a moment, "Tell you what, Brad …" *She actually called me Brad!*

"I agree, this is a tough one to crack and you're right, there's no one who's going to see this the way you do. People will have an opinion about which way to go, but it will come down to this …" She jabbed him in the middle of his sweat-drenched shirt, "Listen to your heart."

Right now his heart was saying, "Focus on Saturday and don't waste energy or sleep worrying about what might be."

I can do that!

Chapter 26

Waiting for the district meet to start this afternoon was a lot like having poison-oak rash itch: No matter what you did, you couldn't get your mind off of it.

It seemed like everybody who knew him had called, either last night or early this morning, to wish him luck. All right, so it was the biggest meet of his life, but talking about it over and over, that wasn't the way to prepare for running his best. He just had to escape.

Brad walked slowly in the orchards, hearing only the steady chug-chug of the ten-o'clock freight train as it ground along about quarter of a mile away. Since talking to Sarah, he was amazed at how he had been able to focus on today's meet, watching his carbohydrate and fluid intake, doing a modest stretching program and watching horror videos at night until he got sleepy. Except for a minute here and there, he hadn't thought that much about Justin wanting him to come with him to … That's enough!

Today: The district finals.

He spotted a familiar ridge near the pump house where he could lie back to look up and name the shapes of clouds drifting overhead. He leaned back and propped his legs against an old cement block. Puffy faces up there and weird animals kept on changing. A breeze out of the south sent the tree limbs and leaves into a shimmering dance. Nice. Even so, lurking behind the fluffiest cloud, negative thoughts peeked into his mind: What if his secret was discovered, that he was really a loser lucky enough to win against weak competition. Maybe he shouldn't even be in the finals. Stupid thoughts. Luckily, this dark image disappeared behind the next cloud, and he was totally cool again; no two legs in the state could take him. Just fire the gun and watch him kick butt.

Time to go. Brad got up and walked the rutted ground between rows of trees stretching out as far as he could see. He trailed his hand along the young leaves and inhaled the dark green smells of new pears and dense weed undergrowth. The day was perfect for walking, and very soon it would be perfect for the track meet.

The visitor's dressing room at Medford High was crammed with finalists from half a dozen middle schools in the district, but the normal locker room buzz was missing as the athletes leisurely went about the business of changing into their track clothes. There were a lot of guys, but no loud noises, towel snapping or joking. Each boy was into his own anxious thoughts.

Brad was glad that Carlos had already changed and left the locker room. Better to meet him only on the track. He finished dressing, pulled his sweats over his running gear, and then Pat's gift, the Nikes; first the left foot, then the right. Then he laced them, first the right, then the left. That was the prescribed order since he started running. This was not the time to change routines. When he got outside, he would do a single warm-up lap, clockwise. That was opposite of the way the races were run, but that was his thing. He was sure it had nothing to do with helping him win, but just the same, that's what he would do.

Coach had done a super job this year. There were enough guys qualified to have a great shot at the district title. A shot, yeah, but nothing was for sure. A lot of them would have to get their season's best times or distances to pull off a win, and as he had seen so often, most of them looked to him to lead the way. As they started out of the locker room, he and the members of his team looked down at the grimy floor, and with newfound intensity, they made their way through the double doors to the track.

It was early, but the stands were already starting to fill. The flags on the mast at the entrance to the stadium fluttered. Should be just fine for both the runners and the field guys. Off to one side was a bench and tables for the Pearblossom equipment, coaches and go-fers. Sarah and Pat were busy sorting out relay batons, shot-putts and other materials. They waved hi, but they knew better than to come over and start up a conversation. Some runners could handle it or even liked to rap. Not Brad.

His dad was also over there holding a clipboard with dozens of sticky-notes attached to remind him to do something or other. He had a ton of organizational stuff to handle. They made eye contact and exchanged a short nod. They had talked last night and again this morning so there was really nothing left to say. It took his dad about forty-five minutes after breakfast to tell him, "Just do your best and know we love you." That was what his mom and Amy told him too, but it took them only about a minute. They didn't make too big a thing of the track season so they sat way up in the stands. They supported it, but didn't want Brad to feel like that was what school, or life for that matter, was all about. It was important, but not any more so than finishing a tough assignment with an exceptional grade. He had thought about this often, and in his head, he agreed with them. But right now, his heart and gut screamed that this was a heck of a lot more important than getting a B-plus in Schofield's class.

The team gathered without Coach for its warm-up stretches. Everybody knew the routine, and without needing to select, somebody always stepped up to lead the cadence count: "Hup, two, three, four … hup, two … "

Brad's body did the stretches, but his mind was inspecting the area. Six groups of boys dressed in different school colors were gathered in separate locations around the field. They were all doing pretty much the same as the Pearblossom guys. Carlos was in the group way over by the ticket booths. Bet he was looking over this way to see if he could spot Brad. He'd be saying to himself, "Only one of us dudes goes to the summer camp. And it's going to be me." *Don't count on it Carlos, don't count on it!*

Too bad the girls' team wasn't in the meet; Brad wouldn't mind the "distraction" of Crystal jogging by in her shorts and smiling at him. Oh, she will be here, probably with her mom sitting low in the bleachers where he could see her later on. Once when he was waiting at her house for her to get ready for their date, her mom had said, "I think you're really good for Crystal, Brad. Sometimes I worry about her being, you know, kind of superficial." Straight shot, Mom.

Come on, Brad. Long, slow extension. Get your head back to Medford High, buddy.

The noise level rose as the stands started to fill.

"Go, big blue!"

"Get 'em, Robert. Number one!"

Brad aimed himself for the side of the track without stands to do some last-minute wind sprints. With each forty-yard run he focused on a different technique: quick, choppy start, head and eyes level, arm pump relaxed. *There's no contest; there's just running. Run 'till I lift off the ground.* He was nearly ready.

Over in front of the stands checking out his starting position was Carlos. As though there was no stress, he talked to kids who jogged by, to people in the stands, anybody. At his feet was a fanny-pack and from it, he pulled his comb. Then he strutted in front of the bleachers combing his long, dark hair. For a moment, Brad pictured himself going over to wish the dude good luck. Forget that!

After the team introductions by the announcer on the P.A., Coach Goodwin gathered the team in a circle around him. There was no big pep talk or phony-baloney.

"We've all worked a long time to get here, and I know each of you wants to do his best and would love going home with a medal." Coach sat down on the ground giving the impression he was relaxed. But he was not. Some of his words were a little garbled because he chewed so hard on a huge wad of gum. "But I want you all to remember this day ..." He took in a breath and scanned his athletes, "... because you had fun. You are young, and this is a game. Games are for having fun. That's it; that's all I got to say." He waved his hand like he was shooing away a bunch of flies and the team yelled, "Go," and then scattered.

A lot of the guys on the track team treat me like I'm one of the team now. After being on the field and close to them all for four track meets, some of them come over and talk to me about school, and music and other stuff they are interested in. I'm really glad now that I'm in regular school, especially since Brad asked me to stay on the field. I can't disturb him now; no one talks to him before his races. Sarah told me that at the first meet I came to. I still don't like the loud noise the crowds make when they cheer for their team, but I'm getting more used to it. I learned a new technique from my mom. She told me to think about something that's soothing and the noise would get less and less in my head. She thinks I'm concentrating on ocean waves, but I'm thinking about kissing Elena. It's not soothing, but it works just the same.

"Hey there, Evans. How are you doing, buddy?" Sarah comes over and plops right down next to me on the team bench. She does not do the rules of getting to know someone a little at a time. Our legs touch, but she doesn't mind at all. I do! "You're sitting too close to me, Sarah." She moves over a tiny bit and starts a conversation in the middle of a sentence.

"… really focused today, don't you think, Evans?"

I like Sarah, but she makes me feel she's going to crush me. I go back to thinking about Elena.

"You sure gave the guy some tough choices," Sarah says while watching some kids throw the shot put. "Follow through" she shouts at them.

"Huh?"

"Oh, sorry Evans." She turns toward him, shoving some curls out of her eyes. Freckles dot her face and make a dozen little designs on it. "I mean asking him to go with you to the Special Olympics the same weekend as the coaches' invitational. If he wins today, I mean when he wins, that's going to be a toughie for him." She looks back at some of the guys by the long-jump pit and yells, "Hey you bozos, take your third warm-up jumps now, will ya'? Oh man, they can't hear me. Talk to you later." And off she goes, leaving me with a gigantic empty space in my gut.

Brad and Carlos were qualified in the same three races: The hundred, two-hundred, and the sixteen-hundred meter, four by four hundred-relay. The crowd quieted, and it seemed like most of the competitors in the field events had stopped to watch as the six of them lined up at the start for the one-hundred-meter race.

Carlos posed and strutted, but said not a word to Brad. That was just fine. The starter peered through thick glasses at his group of sprinters. Brad swallowed a laugh, half expecting Pat's foghorn voice to blast from this guy. After all, that was what he heard, even in his sleep, for the past week and a half.

"Runners, to your blocks."

But this was not Pat's voice. And it was not a practice run. He shook out the last of his tensions and crouched into position.

"On your marks."

There was no tiredness today. Brad knew his legs would do whatever he asked of them. The tunnel ahead of him closed down to a single lane. That's all there was between him and the finish.

"Get set."

Rolling, rolling forward and almost out. The gun fired, and Brad was gone before anyone else. He sensed it. And he sensed victory.

Before Carlos could make up for Brad's incredible start, the race was over. In a flash, one hundred meters was behind them. And he had won!

Crystal's voice. He heard her scream, "Brad, Brad," as he jogged past the stands. He stopped and waved to her and her mom. Oh, this was good, sooo good. Up there some-where were his mom and Amy, but their voices were lost in the general cheering. Seemed like Carlos must have made some enemies around the league, because everyone except Medford Middle fans were on their feet cheering for Brad. He raised his hand high over his head in a vic-tory salute. The crowd responded, sending a rush of elec-tricity through his body. Yes!

Half-hour later, Brad sat on the end of the team bench. Enough of handshakes and slaps on the back. It was great, but the two-hundred was another race, and it was just minutes from starting. Focus. Focus on the sand under his feet, the wind at his back and the lift from running.

"Hey." Sarah stood in front of him with a water bottle. "Don't forget to give those muscles plenty to drink."

He sipped at the water. "Thanks, Coach."

She laughed, crinkling her forehead. Her short brown curls bounced as she shook her head. "Go get 'em, Gonzo."

It was time. Just him, Carlos and four others. Two hun-dred meters.

This time when the gun went off, Carlos was not left inspecting his shoelaces at the starting blocks. From his staggered, outside position on the track, Carlos was off and moving. Down the first straightaway, Brad could see he was not making up any ground. Pump-and-breathe, pump-and-breathe, establish and keep the rhythm.

They were in the turn before the long drive to the finish. Brad was in the inside lane; he caught and passed everyone, everyone but Carlos. Now the curve straightened and there were just the two of them running flat-out for the finish. Pump-and-breathe.

This time the walk back to the bench was quieter. Taking second place by a hair was no disgrace. But …

A while later his dad came by to give Brad a hug. "Darned good races." That was what he always said, win or lose; that is, if Brad had run good races. The afternoon events were ticked off on his clipboard. The meet was close, and once again, the relay would decide the district's number-one team. And it might decide even more for Brad.

Two relay teams scratched, leaving only four to compete. The runners for the opening leg got instructions from the starter as the mob of twelve, including Brad and Carlos, stood clear, waiting on the infield. All this time, Carlos hadn't said a word to Brad. Brad cracked his knuckles; he hadn't said anything to Carlos either. This didn't seem right. He took in a long breath and walked up to the lanky kid from Stockton.

"You were tough."

Carlos looked at Brad with eyes of steel. He didn't budge, but Brad could see the guy thinking. Will it be, "Go to hell," or what?

Carlos licked his lips. "Yeah, thanks." He broke off his stare. Then, just like that, he walked away.

Brad thought, why did he even bother? The guy couldn't accept a compliment, and he sure couldn't give one. Carlos was an A-number-one-jerk. Brad shook his head and came back to his teammates. It was time to stop thinking about Carlos; there was only running and soaring across the sand. The crowd noise faded, and only the steady beat of his heart was in his ears.

The relay started, and the first two-hundred-meters told the story of the race. The Medford and Pearblossom runners were close, but way out in front of the others. The Medford team had a new kid running second, and this guy was fast. He opened up a few meters' lead, and when the third Pearblossom runner, Jesus, almost bobbled the hand-off, Medford had some real space. The judge yelled out to Brad and the other three to get in position.

Here they come! Carlos had the inside since his team was ahead. The Medford kid was sucking and blowing hard. He didn't let up as he raised the baton for the hand-off to Carlos. But here came Jesus about three strides behind, straining, neck tendons protruding, his arm reaching out for Brad. He was trying to make up the distance magically by making the pass before he even got to Brad. Brad was moving, no longer looking back. It had to be there, had to. Thwack! In full stride, Brad was in pursuit.

His legs lifted and drove him forward without conscious thought. About eight meters in front of him was the blue-and-gold jersey that he must catch and pass. If he even thought that beating a runner as strong as Carlos was impossible, he would never catch him. Brad had the wind at his back and four-hundred-meters to fly. He would catch Carlos!

The first turn, usually he saved a little here. Not today. Inches were gained on the lead runner. Breathe, relax and kick! The blue jersey was closer. Carlos couldn't see Brad gaining, but he knew, he knew. The long straightaway, *time to accelerate*, but there had to be another gear, one that Brad had never shifted to. Let it just happen, don't force it. The blood pounded in his head, but his breathing was even. *Keep the breath and the stride steady.*

Suddenly a surge, an extra burst of power propelled him closer, closer. Each stride, each breath trimmed more from Carlos's lead as they started into the last turn. Brad's inner voice yelled, *"I got you, man. Move over, I'm coming by!"* And Carlos's mind yelled back, *"In your dreams!"* The distance between them was less than a meter as they headed for the final sprint home.

His legs and chest cried in agony. He'd never pushed so hard and for so long before. But he wouldn't accept pain, not now, not when the jersey was so close he could reach out and touch it. Carlos dug into his reserves for the kick to the finish. If Brad even thought about what little he had left, he would have pulled up and quit. But he was on automatic. When he saw the tape stretched across the finish line, he leaped into over-drive.

Ten meters from the finish and they were dead-even, stride for stride. On his left was a moving blur, blue-and-gold, gold-and-blue. Catching Carlos was a victory in itself. Finishing in a tie would be enough.

Just … hang … on.

No! A tie would not be enough! He hadn't punished his body for four-hundred-meters to settle for a tie. He heard Coach Goodwin's voice in his head, "There's always just a little bit more." So even though there was no energy or strength left to spend, he found some. And he spent it. Brad lifted his arms and his chest, surging toward the finish.

Everything drifted into a hazy fuzz after that. There was not much of reality after that. Pain. Arms catching him, holding him before he fell. Pain. Faces swam in the darkness.

"Did … I … win?" he gasped.

"Don't know yet."

"Maybe a tie."

"Judges meeting."

These bits of words started to make a little sense. Still groggy, he sagged, starting to collapse to the track.

In the haze he heard Sarah's voice, "Walk it off." A lot of hands helped him stay on his feet, but it was no use. His legs were worn-out elastic, unable to support his body.

Down he went in a heap. Slowly the jagged, tearing sensation in his chest that came with each breath diminished.

It was quiet at last. The stands were empty and the soft, late-afternoon breeze lifted the flags and pennants posted around the stadium. Brad heard them snap, crack-crack as he sat alone on the team bench. He was feeling better, especially after his puking session in the bathroom. God, that was gross.

The quiet tread of steps behind caused him to stand and turn. Still with a swagger, it was Carlos. It must have taken a lot of guts for him to step up to the guy who came from behind to beat him. Brad wondered, *what do I say to him?* Then a thought inched down from that funny spot in his brain. He pointed a finger. "Got your sweats on in-side-out."

Carlos snapped his head down, then up again with a slight nod as if to say, "You got me again." Brad wiped the sweat from his forehead. "Good races, buddy."

The nod became more pronounced. "You were fine." He tugged at a small stud earring. "Hey, my old man is heading back to Stockton, and me with him." He looked around checking out the flapping pennants. "But I'll tell the dudes down there that there are two fast hombres in Or-ee-gone." The faintest of smiles crept across his face, "Me and one, okay brother." He put out his hand and shook Brad's with a firm grip.

And as they parted, Brad heard these intense words, "Hey, man, what do you say? Show them all in Eugene for me."

Chapter 27

I don't know what to feel. My room is filled with music and I have my Sunday afternoon fun games up on my computer. But I'm not having fun. I am puzzled. How I feel now reminds me of when we're up at this lake in the Cascades that my folks take me to each summer. When I swim in it, sometimes the water is so cold my skin gets bumpy and my teeth chatter. Then the next second, a wave of warm water covers me like I'm in a bathtub. It goes back and forth … hot-cold … hot-cold. It confuses my body like my feelings today are confused. Am I sad or glad or both at the same time?

I cheered for Brad to win his races yesterday and when he did, I went and stood near him and I wanted to tell everyone, "Brad is my friend and my track coach." When he got to his feet and looked a little steadier, he saw me, and I stepped toward him.

Then, for the first time I can remember, I put out my arms to hug somebody besides my folks or Uncle Ned. He looked surprised … and I was too. We hugged for a second and pulled away before I was ready to. His odor stunk up my shirt, so I smelled it till I got home and showered.

"Gr … great race, Brad. You did all … all the things you showed me just r … right." He looked pale as a ghost … that's what I hear people say, but I don't think most of them have ever seen one. He laughed and thanked me and then he was swept away by a bunch of people like he was a stick going downstream in a fast creek.

I'm really happy for him. But I'm sad for myself. If he had lost, he would be disappointed 'cause he wouldn't be invited to that training camp next month. Then he could go with me. But he did win, and I really wanted him to. Thoughts and words are jumbled in my head. I try to figure it out. I want him to go with me because that's what he wants, whether he won the races or lost them. I sit on my bed and rock back and forth, back and forth. No, I didn't want him to win … I wanted him to come with me no matter what! That's what I wanted. "No it isn't!" I yell over the music. That's a mean and selfish way to feel. But still, I do feel that way … or do I? My head is all mixed up.

"I'm Mister Blue … da, da, da, da …" Million-selling single on 45 RPM by the Fleetwoods on Liberty Records, summer of 1959. The song on my CD makes *me* feel blue!

I curl up on my bed and push my head into my pillow to hide from everybody. But I can't hide from myself, or my thoughts. I can't stop them from pulling me down. Why am I autistic? Why did I have to be made so different than other people? Kids talk about me and laugh at me. I know it's wrong for them to do ugly things like that … it hurts me so bad. Other kids don't need therapists, or have to be in the special education room. They don't know what it's like to be thought of as a freak.

I do.

Warm tears spill from my eyes and soak into the pillowcase. I don't want to cry … I don't want to feel sorry for myself, for who I am and what I am. I can't help it. I don't want my folks to hear my sobs, so I wrap the pillow around my head and cry … and cry. "They call me, Mister Blue …"

Chapter 28

Pat's glasses slipped down his nose as he bent over his golf ball on the Putt and Roll miniature golf course near his house. Brad and Pat were hanging out together after school, counting the days … no the hours … until senior ditch-day and the dance that night. Less than a week to go!

Pat sank the six-foot putt. "He scores!" he yelled, and he can really bellow. "Top that shot, if you can, oh buddy of mine. You don't have this much of a chance." He put his thumb and finger up close together.

Brad lined up his shot, timing it to go through the wind-mill blades, up a slight hill, and to the cup. He had made this shot a dozen times before, mostly playing with Amy. Taking a touch off the speed, he gave the ball a solid thwack, but not too solid. The ball rolled up to within inches of the hole. "Oh no, I thought I had it made."

Pat couldn't hold back his horsy laugh. "In your dreams!

That's it, you owe me a double-chocolate milk shake, and I intend to rub it in with every slurp of my drink."

They sat at the soda shop sucking in too many calories. Pat did rub it in, but then he turned serious. "You're gonna get the invitation, no question about that. I'm sure you raised a lot of eyebrows up at state with your finish and your times. When those coaches check you out in the flesh up north, and then when you slam-dunk the sprints in high school, you'll be able to name the university you want with a full athletic scholarship."

Brad just said, "hummm."

"What's that supposed to mean? You're not seriously considering going to the Special Olympics with Justin, are you?"

Another "hummm." Brad had not mentioned this double invitation possibility to his folks. He could see and hear Dad if he told him he might turn down the invitation. He would rant and rave, turn red, and sputter all over the living room. After coming down off the walls, he'd try to get his breath and say in a quiet, intense voice, "Get that nonsense out of your head right now. We're talking scholarships and careers here. I don't even want to discuss it, or have you consider that as an option."

On the other hand, if he talked it over with his mom, she'd say nothing for a good minute. Then she would ask if Brad had weighed the merits of each choice and that whatever decision he made, she would support him. Mom.

Pat gave one last slurp and turned toward Brad. "So

what's cooking in that pea-brain of yours? 'Hummm' is definitely not a profound answer."

"Well, of course, I'm not seriously thinking about going with Justin, it's just that … that I feel kind of dishonest. You know I never told him about the state invitational coming the same weekend."

"But shoot, he knows now. Everybody knows; it's the big story all over school." Pat framed the headlines with his hands. "'Lockwood invited to state.'"

"Yeah, he knows now all right, but I should have been the one to tell him. I never said anything even when he asked me about it few times. At first he was all gung-ho about wanting me to go with him, but for about the last week or so he's avoided talking about it."

"But dude, it really doesn't matter, he'll be disappointed for himself, but he'll be happy for you. Straight ahead, game, set and match!"

"Right, Pat, you're right, man. I just have to be up front with him and he'll be so happy for me he'll forget all about the Special Olympics." That should have sounded right, but in Brad's mind, he still said, "hummm."

While Dad reads the newspaper, sitting in his spindly rocking chair, he hums with the music playing on his old L.P. turntable. When the song gets to the chorus, he sings along with Jackson Browne, "Running on Empty." Mom comes into the living room wiping her hands on a dishtowel since tonight was her turn to do the dishes. I have every third night, so tomorrow night and three nights after that will be my turn.

She sits on the chair next to Dad singing with him and Jackson Browne. Dad puts his paper down on his lap and she asks him, "Remember that concert back in, when was it, '85, or was it '86? when we saw him in San Francisco?

"We were just a couple of kids then ..."

They hold hands for a moment, and then Dad lifts the paper and goes back to reading. Mom comes over and sits at the table with me. "So what is it that was so important you had to talk to me while I was chopping onions and crying?"

Well, you ... you know I talked to you about inviting that girl from school ..."

"Yes, dear, I know. Elena."

I wanted to be sure she knew exactly what girl I meant, so I guess I repeated myself ... maybe more than once. I do that when I want to be sure people understand me. I guess it annoys them, but I can't help it. "Elena, that's right. She said she wants to come with me, but her m ... mom won't let her go on a date. She says she's too ... too young to do that. I'm not too young, am I, Mom?"

"Well, this is a very special occasion, dear, and Dad and I both think it would be all right for you to go." Dad grunts his approval. "Maybe she could just meet you there?"

"Elena asked her mom, but she doesn't want her go ... going at all. She thinks too many bad things could hap ... happen there. What bad things happen at dances, Mom?" She makes a funny face that I don't understand. "Why did you make that face, Mom?"

"Justin, there are some things I just can't explain. But as far as bad things, I guess she's thinking about alcohol, or rowdy boys fighting or inappropriate dancing … I don't know what she's thinking, but she probably has had a bad experience herself."

Dad threw his paper to the floor. "Maybe she's just an uptight old biddy!"

"Jerry! That's a really rude thing to say." But I could tell she covered a smile with her hand, hoping I wouldn't see it. "Well Justin, you just may have to face it. You might have to be content seeing Elena at school until her mother thinks she's old enough to date."

That didn't make me feel good at all, and I don't think changing my attitude will help me. I feel a dark place inside me starting to grow and I feel like I have to throw up.

Dad stands up and comes over, kneeling at my side. He puts his hand around mine. "Hold on, son. I've got an idea … and it just may work."

"Ohhh hey, cut that out! The water's icy," Crystal yelled. But that didn't stop her from splashing back. "You won't get away with that stuff, you dweeb."

Brad sent a tidal wave of water at her. "Water fight, water fight, and guess who's gonna get wiped?" They sat on a low bank of Ashland Creek way up where the tourists never went. Brad scooped up another handful of water, sending a shower over her head. She laughed and held her hands up in mock surrender. "Okay, okay, I give up. But you don't fight fair." Droplets of water flew from her hair as she shook her head. A splash of sunlight peeked through the leaves making dozens of tiny, instant rainbows around her.

It was Friday, officially senior ditch-day, and tonight was the senior ball. Nearly everyone in the graduation class met for breakfast at restaurants around Talent or Ashland, and after that, it was kick-back time. Since Brad's Mom needed to do some shopping, she offered to drop Crystal and him off at the Ashland Plaza. It was a cool place with a lot of neat shops and artsy-crafty stuff; and it was also near the park and creek where the two of them could be alone.

His mom was buzzing around for a few hours getting some things for his trip up to the coaches' camp. The official invitation came yesterday by registered mail. Brad had never received a registered letter before … made him feel important. He could hardly believe it, only a few days until graduation, then two more weeks until Eugene. Tomorrow he'd have to tell Justin and his folks why he couldn't go with him. It would be hard, but what else could he do?

Sure hope Mom remembered to pick up the corsage he had ordered for Crystal and hid it where she couldn't see it. After she had left them off earlier this morning, Brad and Crystal hung out for a while at the Plaza, got a frozen yogurt and tried on some hippie clothes at Renaissance Rose. "How do you like this on me?" Crystal asked while posing in front of the full-length mirror. She put on a wide-brimmed straw hat with a tie-dyed bandanna around it. In a broad accent she said, "Heey man, prepare to get with it."

"You are one foxy lady, but Schofield would crush you to get that hat for herself. So what do you think of these threads?" He tried on a multicolored vest with fringes all the way around and made a peace sign with his fingers. "Far out, dude."

She laughed, and her eyes closed to slits the way they always did. "We are like two, way-out dudes, brother."

That was an hour ago and they hadn't stopped laughing since. With their shoes off, they dangled their feet in the frigid water. The babble of the creek flowing down from the mountain watershed cascaded over the rocks making little waterfalls. "This is the best, isn't it?" he asked.

She didn't answer with words. One hand squeezed his and her other touched his cheek. It was so soft and caring. He looked at his rippling reflection in the water and smiled at himself.

Even though his feet were getting numb in the freezing water, he didn't move, afraid to break the spell. "You know what I did?" Crystal asked as she finally pulled her feet out and scooted her knees up resting them under her chin. "I cut out pictures of you from last week's newspapers and circled your name with a red marker, and I sent them to my dad in Denver." She never mentioned her dad, only to say that he left them about five years ago. "I want him to know that I'm going steady with somebody special." She looked at him intently. "You're special, Brad."

Holding hands, they slowly wandered down the path that led back to where his mom was going to pick them up on the Plaza. They walked by a children's play area with swings, slides, little plastic horses mounted on springs and lots more. Over by the see-saw was a huge woman, she must have been about three hundred pounds, and with her was a little boy with a deformed leg. Brad guided Crystal to a bench close-by where he could check out the little boy.

"Aaron," the woman said in a tired voice, "I can push you on the swings, but that's it. I just can't never get on that thing with you. Shoot, boy, I'll break the dang contraption." Aaron looked to be about seven. His eyes were big, brown saucers that seemed not to blink at all. He looked at her a long time before speaking.

"Mama, please?" His arms reached out to her like he expected her to pick him up and put him on the board. He held the position, unmoving, unblinking, waiting. Brad was reminded of the invisible people he and Amy had talked about.

Although this short drama had taken place right in front of them, Crystal was busy looking into her little mirror checking her lipstick and hadn't noticed any of it. To her, Aaron was one of those invisible children. "Ready to go?" she asked pleasantly, snapping her compact closed.

Didn't she see him? Didn't this scene rip a piece of heart out of her and hurt like hell? "Ready?" His voice was flat as he tried not to let his frustration show. "No, I don't think I am. And it beats the hell out me that you're ready to just pick up and leave! "

"What?" Crystal reacted with great surprise. "I don't …"

Brad got up abruptly, leaving her on the bench. He smiled and opened his arms to the reaching boy. "Hi, Aaron, how'd you like to play on the see-saw with me?"

After he had see-sawed with Aaron for a while, Brad turned back to Crystal. His jaw was clamped so tight his face hurt. Crystal sat where he had left her… and she was fuming. "What did I do? Why did you treat me like that?"

He tried, but it was too hard to explain how he felt at the park, and especially, what he had expected her to feel. All he could say was, "I'm sorry." Why had he talked to her like that? And why had he walked off and left her sitting on the bench after he had played with Aaron? As they neared the Plaza, he realized he had spoiled the mood and the great time they had, but he really wasn't that sorry.

While driving home, it was obvious that his mom knew something had gone down between them. She had let them off near the house to give them some room. So the two of them sat on the curb a block from home, Brad explaining, Crystal crying.

Chapter 29

"It's beautiful, Brad. Thank you."

He pinned the corsage on her just before they went into the dance. "Gardenias," he said, leaning close, inhaling their sweet fragrance. They had managed to patch up the afternoon's painful fight. He agreed that some of what he did was stupid, and she agreed that when he got his head on straight they would talk it out. He would definitely need to unload to her about her insensitivity to others, especially people who were different. He thought she would understand. No, he was positive. But tonight was not the time to talk about that. He leaned into her ear. "You look awesome." Her head rested against his shoulder.

She wore a shiny, black, tight-fitting dress that left her shoulders bare; her neckline was cut low, but acceptable for a school dance. Her blonde hair fell around her neck and shoulders, forming a striking contrast against her dark dress. Brad couldn't take his eyes off her as they walked into the commons, the entry to the dance. In his letterman jacket and Dockers, he felt like he was going to a ball game, not his senior ball. But none of the guys were in suits even though most of the girls were totally out there, dressed up.

They moved slowly toward the gym, which was supposed to look cool with banners and signs on all the walls, "Senior Class Rules, Pearblossom's Best" and stuff like that. It looked like MTV advertising junk. Suspended from the ceiling was a spinning mirrored-ball with colored spotlights focused on it making ghostly red, blue or green spots floated across the kids' faces. The DJ's music was ear-crushing loud. This was too cool. Lots of seniors came without dates, so like at most of the school dances, girls danced with other girls or kids formed group dances.

The music blared out, *"Y Emm Cee Aaay ..."* Everybody jammed and sang the chorus to this one. Crystal and Brad raised their arms high over their heads and swayed to the heavy beat, joining a couple of hundred other kids. They rocked out and the whole gym shook.

"You are one mighty good dancer," Crystal shouted to Brad as she was almost run over by a line of dancers. It was like a giant snake slithering its way around the entire gym. When the song ended, Mr. Reins and Ms. Sesock cruised by to make sure nobody had smuggled in beer or was doing dope. Some couples got into making out behind the folded-up bleachers. As Mr. Reins spotted them, he stopped the action but tried to keep his comments light. "Hey, kids, save something for when you're grown up, will you?"

Before they danced again, Crystal took him by the arm and they cruised the gym. She made a big deal of reminding every girl she had ever met for the tenth time: "This is my boyfriend, Brad. You know, the track star." Geezo, it was embarrassing. But as they walked, every guy stared at Crystal. She was on *his* arm. And *she* was not letting him go for a minute.

Brad spotted Pat and Linda talking to a group of kids. He wasn't going to ignore them. No way. "Come on, Crystal, let's go say hi."

Crystal's body stiffened. "I'd rather not. Do you mind?"

Well, yeah, he minded. After all, they were his friends, and even though he had promised Crystal they would come alone tonight, he still wanted to see Pat and Linda. "Just for a couple of minutes, I promise."

"Brrraaad," she whined, tugging on him.

She was one hard case. "All right then, you go get us something to drink and I'll be right back." He tried to say this without any edge to his voice. This was something else they would talk about.

"But Brad …"

For the second time that day, he walked off and left her. And for the second time, he felt he had done the right thing. Pushing his way through bodies, half of the kids slapped him on the shoulder or high-fived him on the way, he finally made it to where Pat and Linda were standing near the photographer's booth. Brad hardly recognized Linda. Her hair looked cool, and was there a hint of red in it? Her braces were gone, and she wore makeup that made her look pretty darned good. Pat was beaming and waving to friends – checking them out to see if they were checking him out.

"Hey bro. Great gig, huh?" He didn't wait for an answer.

Linda gave Brad a self-conscious smile before her eyes dropped, staring at her blue, almost-in-style, dress. "Hi, Brad. It's really nice to see you." Her eyes glanced up, probably to see if Crystal was nearby. "You look very … very …"

Stuck for the right word, Pat butted in. "Cool! My man here is cool."

"Yes, that … that's right. Would you excuse me, please? I've got to use the … the bathroom." Immediately, the tidal wave of kids moving in the right direction swept her away.

"Isn't she neat?" Again, Pat hardly ever waited for an answer when he knew what the answer was.

Brad put his hand on Pat's arm. "She looks great. What happened to her?" Suddenly Brad realized this didn't come out the way he intended. It made her transformation seem like an impossibility. "What I mean is …"

Pat laughed. Don't sweat it, I know what you mean. Linda came over to the house last week for dessert, and my mom asked her, subtle-like, if her mom had, you know, helped her with girl stuff. Linda doesn't see her mom much; I guess they're not close. Anyway, one thing led to another and Linda came over after school yesterday and again today for one of those deals like on TV, a complete makeover."

"She sure looks great." Brad wondered if her new look would help her get over her shyness. "Gotta go, Pat. Catch you guys later, okay?"

Pat's smile froze on his face. "I get it, bro. I understand." And he walked away headed toward the bathrooms.

His meeting with Pat and Linda took a little longer than Crystal had probably expected. Too bad. He took a few more minutes to look around the commons to see if Justin and Elena had really come to the dance. Justin had mentioned that Elena's Mom thought she was too young to be out on a real date. Maybe that's why he had been acting a little strange lately. Brad smiled to himself as he realized that a few months ago, Justin would have seemed nothing but strange to him.

As he and Crystal met at the soft drink counter, the lights darkened, a cue for everyone to get out their colored light-ropes.

"Whoa. In-cred-i-ble."

The gym was a sea of waving blue, orange and yellow glowing lights. It was unreal. It suddenly hit Brad that this was it, his last dance, and his last days in middle school. In a few months, there would be a whole new life. Scary, but exciting.

A slow oldie, one of his favorites, played over the system. This was one of the tunes Justin always hummed while he tugged at the formulas in his algebra lessons. The Drifters sang to them, *"So darlin', save the last dance for me."* The overhead ball poured down its shower of light and the colored ropes whirled as they danced, pressed together by the crowd. They were close. Real close. Rose and gardenia scent covered them. It couldn't get much better than this.

Crystal hadn't said a word about being bent out of shape because of his visit with Pat and Linda. Instead, she whispered, "We'll be together all summer, won't we? We'll do all kinds of fun things, just you and me, and we won't need anybody else."

"So darlin', save the last dance for me . . . "

After the dance ended they walked hand-in-hand to the commons. Brad spotted Justin and Elena – they had made it after all. Walking behind them pretending to be just another of the parent chaperones, was Mrs. Evans. So that was the deal. It was cool, but all the same, he was glad it was not his mother at the dance with him and Crystal. He started to point them out to Crystal, but decided not to.

"Brad … Brad," Justin's metallic voice called out over the noisy crowd. Heads swiveled – first toward Justin and then back to Brad and Crystal. Crystal's hand tightened sharply around his.

Elena's hand tightens around mine as she tugs me to hurry through the commons and into the gym where we can dance. I told her I didn't know how to dance but she just laughed and said she didn't either. "We'll just be two more bodies swaying in the dark." I'm getting better at letting people touch me now – at least some people. After we got out of the car, Mom gave us a head start, so it didn't look like she was really "with" us. But she had promised Elena's Mom that she wouldn't take her eyes off of us. It's kind of weird, but it worked because here we are.

"Hey, there's your buddy, Brad, with his date, what'sername."

"Her name is Crystal. C … come on, I'll introduce you to her."

"Brad … Brad," I call out. Brad looks at us like he's trying to recognize me. He raises his arm to say hi and then it looks like he and Crystal start to go back to the gym. He says something to her and they stop right in the middle of the commons, making the people behind them bump into them like amusement bumper cars.

Elena has seen this too. "What's with your friends … I mean have they been drinking, or what?"

"Hi Justin, hello Elena. It's great that you were able to make it," says Brad looking over my shoulder. "I see you brought backup." He waves at Mom and in the reflection of the door I see that she makes a small wave and turns away to talk to one of the teachers.

"Crystal, I w … want you to meet my *girlfriend*, Elena. This is Crystal." This is the first time I have introduced Elena as my girlfriend. It's the first time I have ever introduced any girl as my girlfriend. I must be wearing the biggest grin since I'm so proud to say, 'my girlfriend.'"

Crystal puts on a smile and nods to me. Brad gives her a nudge with his elbow that I don't think I am supposed to see. "Hi, Justin." She says this like she's spitting out bad-tasting food. I don't like what is happening, but I will do my best to "bite my tongue" like my mom says.

Elena puts her hand out to shake. "Hiya, guy," she says.

Crystal stands like one of those life-size store dummies with the painted smiles on their faces. She doesn't say anything. Nobody says anything. We all are frozen wax dummies. Just when I think I'm going to say something mean to Crystal, my mom comes over and says hi to everyone. I am glad for the interruption because what I am thinking almost saying to Crystal might make Brad not like me any more.

"Have you decided yet, Brad, about the Special Olympics meet in Corvallis, I mean …?"

Mom doesn't know about … Thoughts race through my brain, thoughts that I couldn't admit till now. It was cool of Brad to tell my folks that he'd think it over, but he's a hero now, and he's invited to a big-deal event. It was selfish to want him to come with me to a special ed. track meet when he's been invited to a *really* special state meet. I have been like a little kid wanting him to give up what's most important to him. I bet he thinks I'm not a very good friend. I want to be a real friend.

My mind settles down, and I focus on one thought that is very clear to me. I understand something about myself, something very important. I can change my attitude. I know exactly what I have to do. "He's not coming with us to Corvallis, Mom; Brad's go … going to the coaches' state invitational meet in Eugene!"

Suddenly the noise in the commons seemed to disappear and all Brad could hear was Justin's words that cut through him like a saw blade. He knew how much Justin wanted him to go with him and that he was giving up his dream so Brad could have his. He had never realized what a true friend he was.

Crystal leaned down close to Justin, ignoring the fact that his mom was standing next to him. "That's right! Brad is going to a real track meet." Her words were poisoned darts, and each sharp tip was aimed right at Justin. Mrs. Evans's mouth dropped open, and Brad was unable to speak.

Justin lowered his eyes. Then he looked up with a big smile. "You … you know, Crystal, I don't l … like you very much at all."

She straightened up like someone had punched her. Her voice was like liquid poison. "How about a Coke now, Brad?"

Brad knew exactly what he had to do. He couldn't believe he'd ever hear himself say these words: "Justin, maybe I *will* come to Special Olympics with you after all."

Crystal's hand fell from his arm as she stepped back, eyebrows raised about a mile. "Brad, you can't be thinking seriously about this. I mean, your dad's made all the plans, and everybody expects you to go." Her face turned red and her lips quivered as she spoke. "What … what will I tell all my friends?"

Chapter 30

Even though the hill was steep and Amy had to shift her bike gears way down, she managed, with some heavy huffing and puffing, to make it up the unpaved dirt trail. About three miles into the mountains Brad and his sister were in the heart of an extensive forest of pines, cedar and spruce, and here and there, an old, shaggy oak or white-blossomed dogwood tree. Wagner Creek flowed to the right of the bumpy trail and the water rushed downhill white and foamy.

The folks had gone to Sunday church services about nine thirty, and that was when Amy popped her head into Brad's room. "Hey brother, what do ya' say, am I invited to come with you on your cross-country bike ride?" Brad was kind of expecting her. There was no way she would let him get away with the mummy treatment he gave her last night after he had come home early from the dance. It was obvious to anyone that there was disaster in the air.

"Come on, spill it," she had demanded about a dozen times last night. But he couldn't talk about it. When he finally got to bed, he could not sleep. His head hurt, his eyes burned and his stomach – ugh. Now he knew why Country and Western songs had so many "pain-in-ma'-heart lyrics." Feeling like this was the pits. Pounding his pillow into marshmallow fluff didn't help; his brain kept singing the same two songs: Had he really meant what he told Justin about maybe going with him? And as far as Crystal was concerned, just where was their relationship headed? He didn't want to stop seeing her. He couldn't do that. But what was he supposed to do?

They slowed and plopped their bikes down at a wide spot tucked next to a meadow. At its far edge, a pair of deer was grazing: a doe and a fawn. They raised their heads as if to check out the humans, seemed not to be spooked, and then bent their heads back down into the tall grass. It would be neat just to sit and watch them. But not this morning. He buried his throbbing head in his hands.

"So, what's it all about?" Amy asked, as she found a semi-comfortable flat rock to sit on. A breeze from the creek drifted by, carrying grassy odors. His spirits lifted temporarily. He gave her the down-and-dirty version of what had happened yesterday and last night. He didn't spare himself, taking on a lot of the blame and responsibility.

"So you think you may have been a stupid butt-head. Anything else?"

Brad flopped down next to her. "I think that about covers it, thank you very much."

"And?"

"And what? What else is there? I feel like dirt. Why did I have to blurt that out to Justin? Now he thinks I really *am* going with him." *Could I toss out the training camp just like that?* "And I really like Crystal more than any girl I've ever known. But she can be pretty … insensitive." Amy thought that over, and he could tell she struggled with the word.

"What do you mean … in-sen-si-tive?"

Brad loved his sister so much, she was so easy to talk with, but sometimes he almost forgot she had some difficulties, including finding the right words to describe feelings. "She just plain doesn't care about anyone but Crystal. Her mom told me that she had a few problems, and that I might be able to help her, but …"

Amy just shook her head. Brad could almost hear Crystal's comments in his mind, things she had said over the past few months, always spoken with a thin smile on her lips. "We don't want Pat and Linda to come with us, do we? You don't have to see Justin after every period, do you? Let Juan hang out with his own friends." He rubbed his palms on his pants. "And sometimes she makes it seem like she wants to own me. He imitated her voice. "This is my boy friend, the runner, Brad." It wasn't until he beat Carlos in the first meet that she really even talked to him. He wondered, what if he had lost his races? Would she still want to be his girl? "Man, I don't belong to her or to anybody."

Amy's eyes drifted over Brad's head into her own quiet place. *Bad choice of words, Brad!* Amy would love to belong to somebody, almost anybody. "Amy, look, I'm sorry. I ...," but his voice trailed off into nothingness.

Amy unscrewed the top to her water bottle. The slight noise drew the attention of the deer. With necks raised high and ears twitching, they sniffed the air before going back to breakfast.

"They're beautiful," she said.

Brad nodded and continued. "I may not know exactly who or what I am, but I do know I'm not a guy that Crystal can show off like a letterman jacket. That's bogus! She has these weird ideas about us hanging out all summer together without Pat, and especially without Linda." But despite his tough words, there in his heart was Crystal, warm in his arms, kissing him with a sweet passion.

Life seemed much easier when he was fourteen.

He covered his face with his hand. "I don't think Crystal and me are gonna make it." He didn't know if his sister would understand how he felt. She touched his forehead and twined his straggly hair around her finger. That was enough to tell him she shared his pain.

He looked across the meadow, fighting back tears.

"Okay, okay. I get all this stuff about how you feel, Brad, but tell me, what does this have to do with whether or not you go with Justin?" She looked at him with that question written all over her face.

The two deer stopped eating and suddenly looked up, staring at Brad. Their ears flapped forward toward him like they were also waiting for his answer.

Sunday brunch on the patio with cinnamon French toast smothered in syrup is my favorite breakfast. I love pure maple syrup. It's one of the only sweets I'm allowed to have. This is the special kind Dad picks up from the Co-op when he has appointments in Ashland. It has no … I forget what the words are … but it has no artificial junk in it. Mom told me I deserved having this special treat for a lot of reasons. She said, "Justin, you have learned what it takes to be a good friend. She looks over at Dad and takes his hand. "We are extremely proud of you." I don't know what the difference is between being proud of someone or *extremely* proud of someone. Anyway, I am *extremely* happy to hear her say that. I laugh out loud at my joke.

"Now what's so funny?" Dad asks.

"I'm one funny dude, Dad, and I made myself laugh."

Mom says, "Finish your breakfast, funny man, then get yourself into the kitchen and load the dishwasher."

Brad tried to keep from staring at his dad's bulging eyes. His father blinked, swayed a moment and plopped into his easy chair. "You're … we … I …"

When he finally spoke, it was obvious how much effort it took for him to get control. "What do you mean, you may not go to the training camp?" His dad asked the question in a low, tense voice through scrunched teeth.

Brad had been pretty sure his news flash would go down bad, but he had no choice, he had to at least discuss it with his Dad. The timing was good, or so he thought. It was Monday evening after work, they had just finished a great meal and his dad was getting ready to watch the playoffs: The Blazers and the Knicks.

"Well?" he roared. "Answer me!" So much for self-control. They were not off to a very mellow start. Brad rocked from foot to foot while standing there. "Look, I said I was just thinking about it. Geezo, it's not like I said I was volunteering for the Marines."

His dad's hands strangled the rolled-up copy of today's *Mail Tribune*. "Don't get smart with me. What in the world put such a crazy thought in your brain to start with?" All control of his voice was gone.

"Sorry, Dad, but it's not so crazy. Ya see, Justin's going to be …" Brad spilled the story about Justin and the state Special Olympics, but he didn't mention anything about the whole Crystal episode. By this time his mom had heard his dad yelling and was standing at the door of the TV room. She listened silently.

"Don't get me wrong," his dad said, trying to sound reasonable. "What you did for Justin was dandy. But that's over now. You need to think about yourself." He got up and put his arm around Brad. "It's time for your career, your education. Hey, it's your life now. And you have to do what's best for Brad, right?"

Brad mumbled, "Right." But what he couldn't say was that was the whole point. He did have to do something for himself, not for the team, the coach—and not even for his dad.

His mom stepped into the room and stood directly in front of Brad. Her voice was as quiet as night. "I think you understand what Dad's saying." Without turning from Brad, she went on, "Fred, I know you love and trust Brad." Then she did the coolest thing: She looked right into Brad's eyes, into his brain and nodded the slightest bit. It was as if she knew exactly what he was thinking.

"Brad, your father and I are extremely proud of you and we know that you will do the right thing. You understand what I'm saying?"

His dad stepped closer to them. "That's just what I've been telling him. Do what's best for Brad. Absolutely!"

"Yeah, Dad. I will. Absolutely."

Chapter 31

The field made the high school tracks Brad had competed on seem lame by comparison. The college stadium held thirty thousand, easy. Over the years, the family had driven up to see Corvallis track meets and football games, but they always sat in the stands, never right down here on the grass. He stood alone in the center of the field before anyone else came out of the dressing rooms. He closed his eyes and the wind whispered, its voice like a distant, cheering crowd. One day they could be cheering for him. Of course, he had dreamed of becoming the idol that Prefontaine once was at U. of O. in Eugene; that was only natural.

When he opened his eyes again, they fell on the fluttering, orange pennants placed every ten yards around the perimeter of the football field. The words on them read "Special Olympics – Oregon State University."

Brad stored his dreams of idols and cheers. That was for another day. Suddenly the field erupted as hundreds of kids spilled out of the runway onto the track and turf. They scattered, running and laughing, happy just to be here. A familiar-looking boy wearing a raggedy sweatshirt and backward baseball cap jogged toward Brad. "I know you. I'm Donnie from Ashland. Remember me?" He flashed a big, toothy grin and extended his hand. Brad remembered Donnie all right. They shook hands and Brad promised to come help him right after he finished with Justin.

The summer sun climbed over the rim of Reser Stadium, shortening the shadows and heating the mid-July morning. Justin was out there somewhere with his friends, his other friends. Brad smiled to himself picturing Justin's face all lit up. That was a mental photograph Brad would never lose.

And there were other faces too that smiled after he had told them of his decision to come to Corvallis: Sara, Pat (although he was bummed out at first), Juan and, best of all, Amy. He'd never been able to deal with her problems before. He had just let them slide by. Now he felt he could grab hold of them and be who she needed him to be, her "big" brother, even though "technically" she was older.

And, of course, there was Crystal. After he told her, she seemed to look right through him for a long time; then she turned and walked away. They had talked to each other since then like nothing had gone down between them, but neither had spoken about dating any more. He missed her something fierce. When he woke some mornings, it was there, left over from a dream shadow in his memory. His phone would ring. It was her. "I'm sorry," she would say. "I was so stupid. I want you to take as much time as you need with Justin. And when you come back, Pat and Linda and all the guys, we'll have a totally excellent welcome-home party for you. Brad, I don't care if you never run again. I just love you … you … you."

"You, hey, you!" A deep voice interrupted his fantasy. A burley, coach-type rolled his body toward Brad. "Hey, you Lockwood?"

"Yeah, that's me. Am I supposed to be somewhere?"

The man pointed to the near sideline where a group of adults and kids were hanging out. "Go on over there and ask for Coach McKenzie. She's looking for ya."

Brad plunged into the crowd of kids. They joked and laughed, sipping on their slurpies and punching one another playfully on the shoulders, just like any group of kids. They all had challenges one way or the other, but they really weren't all that different from other kids. Just a few months ago Brad was freaked when he learned he had to work in a special education classroom. Now he was not uncomfortable at all to be with a whole bunch of them. It was a bummer that they got that label "disabled."

A slim lady in sweats blew the whistle hanging around her neck. She was in her thirties probably. Her hair was short and dark and she was wearing sunglasses. Her shirt had "Ariz. St." written across it. She called various groups of kids to her, sorted them out and then sent them to their places on the field. An adult went with each group. This was much more organized and professional than the meet in Ashland.

"Hi. Are you …?" The tag on her shirt read "McKenzie."

"Hi, Coach, I'm Brad Lockwood. I hear you're looking for me."

"Good to meet you, Brad. Have a seat while I get what's jokingly called brunch around here." She trotted over to an equipment table and poured herself a plastic cup of coffee and took a dry-looking bagel from a tray next to the coffee pot. Sitting down on the grass next to him, she sipped her drink and nibbled the bagel. "I love it here. It's after eleven o'clock and it's not a hundred degrees yet. This is the greatest."

She sipped again. "I'm sorry, want some?" She offered him a chunk of bagel. Brad shook his head, no. "You've been working with Justin at the meet, right?"

"Yeah."

"And spending some time with a girl who hangs onto him all the time; she's my daughter, Penny."

Brad pictured the quiet girl; she had one arm that hung sort of limp. "Oh yeah, she has dark hair and a great smile. She's cute and she looks like you."

She laughed. "Thanks." She told him that Penny had spoken to her about Justin and Brad. "And I hear from Justin's folks that you're about the best junior sprinter in Oregon. That so?"

"I'm pretty good. But I've got a way to go."

"That's what I'd like to talk to you about. I understand that you gave up the state invitational to come here."

She motioned to the field of kids running, jumping and throwing, their arms and legs in constant motion. "It must have taken something pretty strong inside to pull you away from that dream to come to this."

It had taken something strong all right. The morning after he and Amy had taken their bike ride up Wagner Creek, he had looked at himself in the bathroom mirror, only this time he was not looking for signs of a pimple. He was looking for a sign of who was really in there. He had been troubled over Amy's question: Did being hurt by Crystal have anything to do with Brad's decision to go to the Special Olympics meet with Justin? Brad would remember that moment for a long, long time.

He took in a full breath it seemed like for the first time in weeks, clearing his lungs and his head and shouted at his reflection, "You dummy, you total all-out moron!" *This isn't about Crystal! It's about me – me doing what's right – what's right for someone else, not for Brad. I was blind not to think past Crystal. If I want real friends I have to be a real friend to Pat, to Juan, to Sarah, and most of all, to Justin.* And then the image of a troubled girl came into his mind, a girl who needed someone to be honest with her, someone who could be her friend and help her. That girl was Crystal.

And now the sun was shining on a gazillion kids here at Oregon State's track stadium. He watched a small bug scale a tall blade of grass. Finally, he shrugged and pointed to the kids. "They're a pretty good payoff."

Coach McKenzie put her cup down. "You got it, Brad. It is a great pay-off. Listen up a minute: There are about a dozen coaches here, including a few with special needs kids of their own who came to compete." She named them, mostly head coaches at universities around the country. Brad had heard of a few of them. "I happen to be a track coach at Arizona State."

Suddenly her name clicked in his mind. Sure, he had seen her name and her picture in lots of track mags. "Yeah, yeah. I know who you are now." He was embarrassed at not recognizing her before. "It's a real pleasure to meet you." This lady was a great sprinter and was an even better coach.

"So here's the deal: a little payback time. If you'd like to spend the evenings and maybe stay over an extra day in Corvallis, some of us, myself included, would like to help you train. Think you could arrange that?"

He sat stone still, unsure if he should ask her to say it again. Could he have heard her right? Did she really say they wanted to …?

"Brad? Brad?"

His mouth worked, but his voice didn't. Finally, in a high, quivery voice, one he thought he had stopped using about three years ago, he was able to respond. "Thank … thank you. Yes, I do. I mean, I can."

Coach McKenzie got up without having had time to take more than a bite or two of her bagel. "See you at five right here." She was gone. After about ten minutes, or maybe it was an hour, he really didn't know which, Brad became aware of the smell drifting from some open bottles of rubbing alcohol and liniment. The pungent odor stung his nose and brought back images of his own track seasons. He already had a pretty good mental scrapbook of memories. And now there would be some new ones.

Over by the goal posts he noticed a familiar figure and face. Sarah was at the meet working as a peer counselor. When he told her what just had gone down, she would be blown away. Yeah, she would giggle that funny giggle and poke him in the ribs. "Way to go, Lockwood!" Then she would give him a big, sisterly hug. Well, maybe not exactly like Amy.

He studied her as she helped a few kids do some warm-ups. Odd, he realized, that he had never noticed her before. Not *really* noticed her. Suddenly it was the most important thing in the world for him to go see her. Up off the bench, he almost bumped into a couple of kids as he sprinted across the field.

It was cool that she was here, but not surprising. Seemed like she was always around when someone needed her. She waved at him, her dark hair making springy little curls over her forehead. "Hi," he heard her small voice sail across the distance between them. She was wearing her dad's Petaluma Marathon t-shirt and cut-offs.

"Hey! Guess what?" His breath came in short bursts, he was so excited. He told her about the private coaching, and sure enough, there was that giggle, the poke in his ribs and a hug.

No, this was not like Amy's hug. Not at all.

They stood back from one another. Rosy splotches colored her cheeks, her eyes, large pools of dark chocolate, focused on him. He didn't know exactly how the idea popped into his head, but he knew it would be super if she would go to the movies with him tonight. Yeah, that would be cool.

Way cool!

Chapter 32

The summer is over and my high school career starts tomorrow at 6:48 a.m. That's the time I have programmed on my clock radio. It's set to the oldies station, KEZI, 1310 on your dial. I am ready. My pack is filled with five spiral notebooks, three pencils, two pens, a package of Sharpies, my prescription bottle for the school office to keep, and in the morning I'll need to pack my lunch. It will be a fruit cup and ...

"Justin," Mom calls out from the dining room. Her voice just makes it through my ear pods into my head. "Did you turn off your I-pod yet and take care of your back pack?"

I shout back, "Dad already ask ... asked me about my pack, and he said I can I ... listen to music 'till 9:30."

Mom's words are muffled, covered by the high voice of Johnny Nash singing, *"It's gonna be a bright, bright, bright sun-shiny day."* I think they keep checking on me because they want to know how I'm feeling about my first day at high school tomorrow. They must remember how nervous I was on my first day at Pearblossom. That was on my fifteenth birthday, April 1st.

I'm only a little nervous about high school because Brad is going on the same school bus with me. He and my folks worked it out so I could ride with him.

I'm sort of glad and sort of sad that summer vacation is over. I had lots of fun going to Emigrant Lake every week to the water slides with Brad and Sarah, and sometimes Elena's Mom let her come with us. She drove us there and stayed to keep an eye on Elena, but I didn't mind. We splashed a lot of water at each other and played water soccer. Brad showed me and Elena how to do the backstroke. So I'm sad that it's over, especially since I won't get to see Elena every day at school; she has one more year at Pearblossom. We plan on trying to be together on some Saturdays. But I'm glad that I will be a high school freshman – starting tomorrow morning.

At 9:30 p.m. I turn off the music and leave on the little red night-light that is plugged in next to my nightstand. Mom will come in at 10:01 to do what she always does: She checks to see if my blanket is covering me and if my alarm is set. Then she will sit on the side of my bed, kiss my cheek and whisper, "Pleasant dreams, sweetheart. I love you." I pretend to be asleep, but in my mind, I say back, "I love you too, Mom." Smelling her sweet flowery perfume is a great way to end the day.

My shoes are lined up next to my bed and the window is open just right. Red shadows from the nightlight color the pictures in my brain as I feel myself drifting off to sleep. Just before I fall asleep, I remember the conversation I had with Brad. I asked him if he would still be my aide in high school this year. He touched my shoulder when he answered and looked at me right in the eyes. I didn't look away. "Justin, you won't need an aide any more – you have me as your friend.

In my near-sleep I hum the James Taylor song, "You've Got a Friend." It is on Carole King's best-selling 1971 album called "Tapestry." It was number one for fifteen straight weeks.

The words sing over and over in my mind:

"You just call out my name …
And you know wherever I am,
And I'll be there.
You've got a friend."

"Tapestry" was on … the … charts … for 302 weeks … and … and … and …

DATE DUE

APC

Autism Asperger Publishing Co.
P.O. Box 23173
Shawnee Mission, Kansas 66283-0173
www.asperger.net